Anna Blundy has worked in the news media since leaving Oxford in 1992, from doing the photocopying at ABC news in Moscow to being the Moscow bureau chief for *The Times*. She lives in Italy with her husband, Horatio, and children Lev and Hope.

'The author sees the details of life and places as through a microscope, picking out jewels for us to savour, and the Zanetti books are comic thrillers of great distinction'
Guardian

'Insider knowledge of the media industry has allowed Blundy to create a witty, outrageously outspoken, adrenalin-junkie anti-heroine whose adventures will have every girl wishing she could be Faith . . . even if it's only for a day!'
Lancashire Evening Post

ALSO BY ANNA BLUNDY

My Favourite Poison

ANNA BLUNDY

sphere

SPHERE

First published in Great Britain as a paperback original in 2008 by Sphere
Reprinted 2009

A CIP catalogue record for this book
is available from the British Library.

ISBN 978-0-7515-3856-4

Typeset in Caslon 540 by M Rules
Printed and bound in Great Britain by Clays Ltd, St Ives plc

Papers used by Sphere are natural, renewable and recyclable
products sourced from well-managed forests and certified
in accordance with the rules of the Forest Stewardship Council.

Mixed Sources
Product group from well-managed
forests and other controlled sources
www.fsc.org   Cert no. SGS-COC-004081
© 1996 Forest Stewardship Council

Sphere
An imprint of
Little, Brown Book Group
100 Victoria Embankment
London EC4Y 0DY

An Hachette UK Company
www.hachette.co.uk

www.littlebrown.co.uk

My Favourite Poison

Chapter One

Unexplained deaths weren't such a big deal in those days. Come to think of it, they're not such a big deal nowadays either. But back then Russians, who are bleak at the best of times, were in a shortage-of-everything-fuelled pit of despair and most of them felt that death was probably the easiest way out. You can imagine the shrugs of the old ladies, muttering under their cheap fur hats, their hands purple and swollen from the cleaning and the hauling of string bags, saying that she was probably drunk, she always was, that that boyfriend of hers was one of the bandits flogging black-market food aid and, anyway, hadn't she been into prostitution? None of this, as it turned out, was true.

The tests showed that she'd been as sober as a judge (not a Russian one). How they can tell this after a grizzly exhumation I have no idea. But they were pretty clear about it and who am I to be arguing? Especially now. And there was zero evidence that she had ever been desperate enough to go on the game. Then the teachers at her son's nursery said she'd been a doting mother who always turned up on time, was friendly with some of the other mothers and gave thoughtful, but not lavish, presents to the staff before the New Year holidays. When questioned (by self), the neighbours in her block who were unlucky enough still to be alive denied ever having seen strange men entering or leaving her apartment. They also denied, untruthfully, spreading rumours to the contrary. As far as they were aware, they now said, the little boy's father was the man who'd shared the flat with pretty Katiusha, though he was often away.

Katiusha, *kudryavaya*, with the blonde curly hair, who was found at the bottom of the stairs next to the mail boxes in a sea of her own blood. It was the *makalatura* collector, the waste-paper man, who found her and dropped his sack in horror. He was immediately arrested and roughed up at the police station. In typical Russian weirdness he was more pissed off about not getting his sack back than about being wrongfully arrested and brutalised. They kept the hessian sack as evidence. Though as evidence of what never quite became clear.

Her boyfriend was arrested too, obviously. Well, it always does turn out to be the husband or boyfriend. Like that woman they dragged out of Coniston Water thirty years after she'd disappeared and it took another eight years for them to actually pin it on her glaringly guilty murderer of a husband.

But actually the guy had not been around when she fell. There were no head wounds or blunt instrument wounds or any wounds at all really, apart from those inflicted by the fall itself. In the end, nothing seemed to suggest foul play (I love this use of 'foul'). Only the incredible amount of blood, seeping into the lift shaft according to the cleaner, pointed to something darker. Even her clothes, cut from the body by pathologists, were drenched. The coroner concluded that the most likely cause of death was a sudden brain haemorrhage (an *infarkt*) followed by a dramatic, and unusually violent, fall down the stairs. The bleeding remained unexplained but there were euphemistic references to 'women's affairs' which suggested that a miscarriage might have been precipitated by the accident.

The boyfriend must have taken the poor kid straight to a home because he was never seen again, apparently – left to grow up in care. The word 'care' here used in its loosest possible sense. In fact, in no sense that in any way relates to the generally accepted meaning of the word. Russian orphanages are not nice places. But you already know that. I was tempted, at the time, to try and find the boy, assuming his name hadn't been changed. But, instead, I allowed myself the fantasy that a childless couple from Kentucky had come over and adopted him and that he was, this minute, eating cookies and drinking milk at his kitchen table, getting ready to go out into the garden to kick a ball around with his dad before tucking into a delicious mom-made supper of cornbread and chicken wings or whatever it is they eat in Kentucky. Never mind that he was more likely to be sniffing glue in a Petersburg cellar and being pimped out by a vint addict.

Chapter Two

Weirdly, I met Alex in Cairo. Well, I say met. But back to that in a second. I'd been in Baghdad. Yup, they eventually let me go back even after embarrassing the whole newspaper and losing my mind the last time (minds are so tricky to find again). It's all different there now, anyway. You just kind of stay in the Green Zone eating Burger King take-out (no, really) and you end up feeling as though you're trapped in some kind of submarine with bleak fluorescent lighting and an air of doom emanating from the people who are supposed to be doing some good but in fact gave up years ago. They all have that look on their face like they're on the *Kursk* sinking to the bottom of the ocean and the captain has just told them there's limited oxygen and no way back to the surface.

Everyone who steps out onto the streets of Baghdad for more than eight seconds is absolutely terrified of all the different murderous and messianic cults who are waiting with baited breath for someone to kill and, apparently, the return of the Mahdi, last seen disappearing down a well in the year 939. One bloke and his gang in Sadr City seem to think that killing Sunni people with an electric drill is going to ensure

4

the Mahdi's swift return and them a place in heaven. Mad, you might think.

But then you get the journalists. Mostly they are the kind of idiots who, in the hope of seeming trendily pro-Arab and anti-American (i.e.: Israeli), write crap for the left-wing press and the radical (puh) new television networks about how the oil laws were just passed to stitch the whole thing up for the Brits and Americans and not leave any revenue for Iraq when, in fact, the opposite is true. But, because of the terrible publicity – mostly written by Rory Ungerer, who wears a string of leather tied round his neck (you know the type) – all the deals are now falling apart.

And then you get the ones who are just absolutely desperate to go out and get killed (Rory also falls into this category – for membership you must not only wear bits of string but you must also have your shirt open to the middle of the chest at all times). They come back looking slightly disappointed to be alive but very keen to tell you exactly *how* nearly they died, while cracking open a beer from the buzzing machine and leaving their flak jacket on – almost excusable just for insulation as the air conditioning inside the Green Zone means it's about minus 30 all the time. I spent my shivering nights longing to be touched and mesmerised by the helicopters that float down into the compound with their lights flashing like giant fish or UFOs.

I left Ben with Eden in Italy. Well, he is his dad, there's no denying it. Eden has graciously retired from the wars and writes a Tuscan life column for the *New Yorker* all about how he presses his own olive oil (a lie – last time I was there a total of nine olives hung on the tree and anyway you have to put them under running water for forty days and forty nights or something to make them remotely eligible for consumption), and how he shops in a real village where, everyone knows each other and everyone has time for a chat. (Also a lie. He buys in bulk from Esselunga near Lucca – unless it's Sunday, in which case the whole population of Tuscany goes to the hypermarket in Gallicano which is the only place, apart from church, that's open). I know I'm supposed to be devastated, being parted from my own flesh and blood for weeks on end, crying into my vodka every night and wondering if his tooth is being properly cleaned. But, to be honest, I would recommend amicable joint-custody to anyone considering getting their own life back and not being incorporated into some bloke's personality. Women who pretend that they enjoy every moment spent with a small person who can't speak or walk, needs to be dressed, fed, held most of the time and paid attention to all of the time, including all night long, is as much of a liar as Eden Jones with his truffle pig (he does not, in reality, have one). It is soul-destroying and desolate work that makes the mind and body atrophy (looking after children, not snuffling for truffles). Is it worth it? Yes. Are there moments of pure joy that I never imagined would be possible? Yes. Would I die for my son without a second thought? Yes. Would I like some time off to work and not have to worry about somebody else for a bit? Well, what can I tell you?

I mean, we did try, me and Eden. We lived in my dad's house in Sicily after he died last year. We even got married for the Lord's sake. But it was a joke. We couldn't do it. I got to the point where if I had to look at another lemon I was going to squeeze the juice into my eyes and scream until someone took me back to the real world where people fight over arid bits of crappy land and die for whatever madoid thing they believe in. And as for the family 'business', well, I was a psychopath to think it might suit me. The triplets, my half-brothers, were pretty quick to a) realise this and b) oust me in an affable and bloodless coup.

Anyway, Ben loves staying with his dad. They eat pizza and paddle in the river at the bottom of the mountain and Carolina from the village comes to the house to look after him when Eden's working and she brings her two basset hounds. Ben chases them round the house shouting, 'Dok! Dok!' So that's him amused all day. They grow up so slow . . .

So, there's me trapped in the Green Zone writing story after story about the daily casualties, though without actually seeing very many of them, when the student riots mercifully start in Cairo. There's an election coming up otherwise, obviously, none of the English press would give a toss. (Some bloke, El-Baz, is actually going to run, just to make it look real). Not that they give much of one in any case but enough of one, as it turned out, to send one raggy little correspondent over there. Now, luckily the paper thinks I know about Cairo because I used to go out with an Egyptian bloke who runs a Middle East think tank. Also, they are aware that the readers got Iraq-fatigue five years ago.

'Get your bony arse over there, Zanetti,' Tamsin, my editor, said. 'Claire's booked you into the Nile Hilton.'

My arse, for the record, is not bony. It's not my fault that Tamsin put on five stone after she came out of the closet.

'I prefer the Mena House,' I grumbled.

'Yeah. Tough Shit, Zanetti. Just really such incredibly tough shit.'

'Got it.'

'Good.'

I was lying really. I love the Nile Hilton. But if you mention a more expensive hotel that you prefer then the desk feel like they've got a bit of a bargain making you stay at the place they suggested in the first place and they don't make so much fuss about your expenses. They stopped paying for laundry, personal calls and mini-bar about ten years ago which is, as you will appreciate, nothing short of an outrage. Made us start flying slime class too. Or working class, as Eden calls it.

Complaining about the hotel they put you in is a good way round all this. It means they might overlook the regular emptying of the tins of macadamia nuts and the vodka miniatures, and write them off as 'entertainment'. This doesn't mean going to the cinema. It means wooing contacts. Which one tends, in an ideal world, not to do in one's bedroom with the help of a macadamia nut. Though it happens. Well, of course it does.

Pip Deakin, the BBC's Mr Hardman 'I Am Just Really Intrepid', who actually had a breakdown and is now much nicer (terrible but always true), got caught charging hotel porn to expenses. He had failed to realise that the films are named and itemised on the bill. Someone 'accidentally' put the foreign expenses email to him on global so that correspondents the world over got a copy of it. 'Please confirm that the items charged – *Lusty Busty Bitches* and *Greta's Gagging For It* – were relevant research items for your Zimbabwe trip, otherwise, unfortunately, the company will not be able to reimburse you for the $12 per film itemised on your hotel bill.' Sent a shiver of terror down spines in all four corners of the globe, let me tell you.

Anyway, Tamsin and, apparently, Claire, our foreign desk manager, do not know that the Mena House (Churchill's favourite hotel, incidentally) is miles out in the desert near the pyramids (the Giza ones, not Luxor) and would be a ridiculous place for a person to stay if they were hoping to cover any story in the city. Though in the end . . . well, more of that later.

*

I was so dazed by the flight, annoyed by the long hot queue for visas at the hole in the wall, plagued by the bank of moustachioed men who immediately hurled themselves at me shouting 'Taxi! Taxi! Only a hundred pounds!' and hassled by the crowds of suitcase-wielding people that I almost forgot how much I love arriving in Cairo at midnight.

Having finally passed through the hands of four different men (all of them taking a small cut of the fare, shoving scrumpled notes from fist to fist in the dark with a sharp whisper) on the long walk to a rusting taxi in a far off parking lot, I slumped into my seat and lit a cigarette, winding the window down with a metal knob whose plastic handle had fallen off decades ago. The driver flicked on the vast radio that occupied the entire seat next to him (those ones people used to carry, inexplicably, on their shoulders), fiddled with the bent aerial and pulled out onto the flyover with a screech of rubber and a thirty-second long lean on the horn. I considered asking him what he thought about the democracy demos. 'Do young Egyptians want and love democracy?' I might ask him. The classic piece – rehash Reuters and get a quote from your taxi driver. 'Young Cairene Mohammed Gaber insisted the country must change, saying, "If you take a left off Shehab Street you can miss the traffic at the lights."' You know the type of thing. I decided not to bother.

Teetering above the city on roads that darken every Cairo pavement and run past the fifth-floor windows of filthy colonial buildings, the washing hung out on the Parisien (they should be so lucky) balconies to catch the black pollution of the tumbling lorries that pass within an inch of the elaborate ironwork, we sped dangerously through the honking, flashing night traffic, past illuminated palaces surrounded by palm trees, dingy cinemas with badly painted posters pasted up outside, juice bars, chess cafés and narrow stinking alleys.

The heat and smells washed through the car, annihilating any trace of the Western world that still clung to me. And I smiled.

I know from experience that I stop missing Ben when the back wheels leave the ground. And that was already seven hours ago.

Which is how I got to be sitting on the lovely shisha terrace at the Nile Hilton smoking a lovely shisha. I pretend to myself that because it tastes of honey it is not the same as smoking a whole packet of fags in one go and is therefore not breaking my promise to Ben to stop being such a chain-smoking alcoholic. Not that he asked for this but it seemed the least I could do in my new role as mother to small child who smells like biscuits. Since I am not, technically, smoking I feel virtuous and allow myself to order a little tiny vodka off the nice waiter whose collarbone I would quite like to kiss if I am honest, which usually I am not.

The wizened shisha bloke in long skirts and a white cap comes hobbling over with a tongful of burning coals. I say 'Shukran' and he smiles revealing no teeth. Not a one. He offers me another lump of tobacco, which in the old days on the river boats would have been hash, but I say no, 'Khalas', and he shuffles off, apparently delighted.

Despite the new security at the hotel – a few metal detectors that go off every time someone walks through but which are basically unmanned – there is a peace about the Nile Hilton with its little patisserie, its funny swimming pool almost on the main road, and the noise of the honking screaming traffic on all sides. You can see the river through the pollution haze from pretty much everywhere: half a mile wide, pale muddy brown and lined with palm trees and a few floating restaurants with neon signs on top. The odd felluca bobs about, a barefoot bloke in hoisted-up robes keeping it mysteriously afloat by leaping from one side to the other over the terrified (or, perhaps, drunk) tourists.

Anyway, I have failed to find any rioting students, although I haven't looked that hard because I don't have to file until tomorrow night, and I have my cowboy boots up on the chair opposite and am relaxing into the sweet tobacco-smelling Cairene evening, the sky going that toxic red-ish orange and a crowd of glossy women taking their seats next to me, all holding glittery clutch bags, when suddenly . . .

This guy comes hurtling through the revolving doors shouting in Russian. He was scared and perhaps injured, but I couldn't quite see how. Everyone turns to him, alarmed, because, although we're all pretending to be completely safe and calm, the threat of terrorist attacks on tourist places is real (if minimal) and the slightest kind of upheaval makes everyone panic immediately. He looked behind him with a sharp twist of the neck and then, without any kind of warning, sort of dived at me, knocking me off my wicker chair and flat onto the tiles behind, him landing on top of me and then rolling, perhaps gallantly, off me before it got too awkward. I was winded and smacked my head hard on the floor. I wondered if I would be concussed, though it's hard to tell the difference between concussion and a couple of shishas and a vodka. A few people screamed.

Contrary to the expectations of everyone on the shisha terrace, nobody followed the man out of the revolving doors waving a gun, machete, knife or any other kind of weapon. He himself was not visibly armed. So, the women sat up straight again and the waiters came running in their white tuxedoes to help us, assured that nobody was about to kill them. Clearly this was a misunderstanding of some kind and the man was not Egyptian, after all (foreigners are assumed to be rich and essentially a bit stupid and helpless). I had spat a mouthful of vodka into my attacker's face (by accident, of course) and he was getting up, wiping it off with his shirt sleeve when a pair of waiters grabbed him under each arm, hoisting him to his feet.

'What the fuck is your problem?' I asked him, standing unaided. 'Christ.'

The waiters were hovering but had been more cautious about touching a woman, even though I was the one who had ended up underneath in the crush. Usually I am awarded honorary man status in cultures where women don't drink, smoke or opine. But not this time.

The man ran his hand over his forehead and looked at me. He had a big scar across his jaw, blue eyes like shards of Siberian ice and a wide high-cheekboned face. His blonde hair was shaved close to his head and he had the shoulders of someone who had not shirked his military service. He had a badly swollen eyelid and a bottom lip that was split and bleeding as though very recently punched. I asked him again what his problem was, in Russian this time, and then sat back down.

'Another vodka please, Yosri,' I smiled to the waiter and took a long puff on my shisha. The bustle of the terrace got going again and the Russian bloke pulled up a chair: crisis over.

'Sorry. Fuckers came into the flat in Mohandiseen. They've been following me the whole way. I don't think they dare sniff me down here though,' he said, looking round briefly and then smiling, relaxing, sniffing briefly like the dogs he was imagining. He was speaking Russian.

'Which fuckers exactly?' I wondered. After all, there are, as we all know, a huge number of people in the world in frenzied competition for the title.

'Ach. Some guys.' He shrugged, laughing now and touching his lip with his finger, looking down at it to see the drop of blood which he sucked off. 'I apologise extremely for jumping on you. I was trying to jump over you. To hide behind that stove,' he said in English, pointing to where the man with the heap of smouldering coal was standing. 'Not as fit as I used to be,' he said.

'Happens to us all,' I smiled. 'Want a vodka?'

This perked him up no end, though I have to say that Yosri looked a teeny trifle reluctant to serve my new friend, perhaps unimpressed by his style of entrance.

'Alex,' he said. 'Alex Lvovich Karamzin.' A strangely Western first name for such an exotic type. He was the right age for it though. It was cool in Russia in the 1980s to Westernise your name, and you were always meeting people who claimed to be called 'Alex', 'Mike', 'Eugene', and 'Serge'. Like as though anyone has ever been called Eugene or Serge (Yevgenii and Sergei). Still, he'd left his exotic surname alone.

'Karamzin? Like the poet?'

'Great-great-grandfather. Or great-great-great-great. Whatever.'

'Cool.'

'If you like that sort of thing.'

'Faith Cleopatra Zanetti.'

'Cleopatra. Wow.'

'Yeh. Especially here.'

I laughed and offered him a puff of shisha which he turned down for a disgusting Kosmos cigarette that immediately made the whole world smell of Moscow in 1985.

So we went to that place in Zamalek with the big brass tables, under the overpass, where all the foreigners and foreigner-groupies go. I smoked seven cigarettes and in about fifteen minutes drank a whole bottle of Lebanese Ksara Rose (my favourite wine in the world – I have been to the vineyard in the Bekka Valley and it is as close as it is possible to come to paradise: the smell of the earth, the view of the mountains, the rose petal taste of the wine . . . okay, enough). Anyway, I couldn't stomach the Egyptian stuff, though they insist it's good. But then the Georgians think theirs is nice too. There's no accounting for taste (or lack of).

I felt I'd earned it. It's true that I hadn't as such located any actually rioting students but that was because they'd gone home and stopped rioting before I got there. I had, however, phoned a girl called Jamila who was head of one of the students' unions and she assured me that she had been rioting furiously for democracy and, not only that, but she claimed to have been beaten by a policeman. She also claimed that she was going to give me an interview in the morning. So this, in my view, left me free to hang around with Alex who turned out to be quite good value. When I told him I'd gone off the rails a couple of years ago he froze and looked at me.

'Just for clarity,' he said, 'this is you on the rails, is it?' The phrase doesn't work in Russian and it made me laugh.

He was from a closed town where they make nuclear weapons out in the Urals. His mother and father were both physicists. Now, of course, the town doesn't make anything and isn't closed any more. Though I'm sure it will soon be up and running again under their new leader. Not that anybody has the remotest desire to go in and nobody has the money to get out. So all these eminent scientists are subsistence farming in what used to be their back gardens out in the Ural mountains, supplies from Moscow no longer arriving in the weekly lorry.

14

'But mostly they are just drinking. And shooting each other.'

'Right.' I nodded.

He'd been in Chechnya and when I said 'Me too' he choked on his mouthful of beer. I was going to tell him I'd been in Afghanistan as well but I didn't want him to keel over or anything. He told a funny story (well, funny in that Russian way – i.e. really really depressing) about going up into the hills to get drunk with some of his unit and most of them getting killed in an ambush on the way down. Hey, it was the way he told it. And then, in that very very Russian way, he suddenly went soulful and said how strange it was that his friends would never get old, not even as old as he was now.

'Doesn't matter age. Matters what is in your khart,' he said, in English again. It has been put better in its time, of course. 'Age shall not wither them . . .' and all that. But boys dying while their mothers are at home, hearts aching with pain and loss, well, it doesn't matter how you put it.

I nodded and thought about Ben. The only person who's ever really been anywhere near my heart, even if I am glad to be having a break.

'You are thinking about your child?' Alex said to me.

I had forgotten this about Russians.

'Yes.' I smiled as the waiter put down a huge pancake drenched in syrup and white cheese, some chicken legs, bread, green sauce and a bottle of wine.

'Me too,' he said, digging his fork right into the middle and pulling out a thick dripping mouthful that he had to lean over the table to catch.

'My son's with his dad in Italy,' I said. 'My husband, actually. But we're not . . . you know, any more . . . exactly.'

Alex laughed. 'I understand. My wife and I too. She's

15

Egyptian, in fact. Yes. I understand,' he said and held my gaze in that way that sends shivers down my spine. Well, it does.

To get past this and back onto safer territory (and before anyone thinks this is weird, I just want to say, in my defence, that there are an awful lot of people for whom the very concrete world of conflict and hard unearthable facts is far safer than an emotional conversation), I asked him again who he'd been running away from this afternoon. He was so ordinary, again in a very Russian way (i.e. really really weird), that I'd almost forgotten about being jumped on. It's funny because at the time, sitting there, I thought he'd answered the question but I suppose, in reality, he hadn't.

'It's a thing from Chechnya. And Dagestan, you know?' he mumbled, licking syrup off his fork and glancing up at a group of American students who had just walked in, bright sporty jackets and bouncing trainers. In fact, as it transpired, he wasn't lying, though the word 'thing' perhaps didn't quite cover it. And, the thing is, I DID know. Or, at least, I was arrogant enough to think I did. I'd written stories about all the shady stuff the Russian army was up to in those days. Brutal rather than shady, perhaps. And the Chechens too for that matter, though arguably (and, hell, there are plenty who'll argue) more justifiably. I rescued Don McCaughrean from under a car in Gronzny once. So perhaps I assumed that Alex had . . . what? I don't know now. Maybe that he'd run off with some equipment or deserted or something. Beaten up the wrong prisoner. Now, obviously, in retrospect (in which everything is obvious), they wouldn't follow him to Cairo for that. Not that alone, at any rate.

But the truth is, without intentionally sounding too arsy about it, that everyone who was in Chechnya, in whatever capacity, was changed by it. It was a pointless, nightmarish and brutal war that triggered off something not that dissimilar to a religious conversion in almost everyone who was there. And it also, as it was doing now, created an instant camaraderie: an instant feeling that anyone who had been there too was a friend, someone who really understood and had seen.

On the lighter side, I'd just left Baghdad, was on the rioting student case and, honestly, I didn't care THAT much about what this man's deal might be. It was just nice to meet someone I could talk to without having to pretend to be someone else. Most non-Russians find me too this or too that and I have to smile and nod and try to seem normal. 'Oh, fine, thank you. How are you?' Not, by any stretch of the imagination, my forte.

And it was here, of course it was, that Don McCaughrean of the aforementioned Grozny rescue (ungrateful bastard) found us. He was in Cairo doing a thing for a magazine about over-population, taking moody pictures of the City of the Dead where everyone lives in the tombs and they've opened little shops in them and stuff. It's bizarre. And those lovely shots you get of the rooftops, all of them inhabited, tents and washing lines and mosques on the dusky skyline all the way out to the pyramids. Well, I'm assuming that's the kind of thing he was shooting.

He shoved his way in through the ornate wooden doors, knocking over the reservations lectern and swearing. He had big sweat patches under his arms and his stomach was visible through the strain in his shirt where a button had popped off. He was carrying his camera bag over his shoulder and a tripod in the other hand. He stumbled towards our table, red and gleaming. I pulled at a coil of my mad blonde afro (I can't help it. Born like that) in preparation for a Don onslaught.

'Faith Za-fucking-netti!' he shouted, putting his tripod down and slapping me hard on the back. 'They told me I'd find you here. Fucking shit-hole rat-pit of a city, isn't it? Full of fucking A-rabs.'

'Don, this is Alex,' I said. 'Alex, this is my colleague, Don McCaughrean.'

Don shook hands with Alex vigorously and then started hitting himself all over with the palms of his hands, looking confused.

'Here, have one of mine, Don,' I said, holding out a packet of cigarettes to him. What can I say? I bought some at the hotel, excusing this action to myself with the trauma of my Alex assault. As long as something is rationally justifiable then it's okay, isn't it? Very male, I know, but it works for me. I think.

'Oh, ta, ta, yeah,' he said, taking one with fat fingers and pushing his face into the middle of the table to light it off our glass-globed candle. A droplet of sweat hit the brass tabletop.

He sat down hard and his chair creaked under the weight. Look, I'm the last person in the world who's a fan of Fat Humour in general. Falstaff, puh. But the man is fat. It's descriptive rather than judgmental, or a shot at some cheap jokes. I hope . . .

The waiter came up, dressed in a loose white shirt and one of those grotesque beards that is a thin line around the mouth and usually goes with sunglasses poised mid-forehead, and offered to take Don's bag.

'No thank you, sonny Jim,' he said. 'Just keep your hands off, okay?' Don does not like people interfering with his equipment. Some Freudian explanation for this, no doubt. 'You know they're all buggering each other up the arse, Egyptian boys, don't you?'

Alex ignored this comment. It is in some way related to

18

his camera bag. All those who wish to approach it are taken, in Don's booze- and sun-addled mind, to be homosexuals.

'Don. It's the twenty-first century. It's okay to be gay, you know. Just close the closet door behind you when you COME OUT!' I said. I couldn't help it.

Don lifted the middle finger of his right hand at me, swept his hands over his forehead to wipe it clean and put his elbows on the engraved brass table, blowing a stream of smoke into Alex's face. He looked at Alex through watery eyes, sloshing red wine from our bottle into a water glass and taking a huge swig. He wasn't rising.

'So, you've scored already have you, Eff Zed? You want to watch her mate, that's all I can say,' he told Alex. 'She'll fry your balls up with mushrooms for breakfast.'

'I shall bear this in mind,' Alex assured him.

'Shalo? Don?' I said.

'Yep?'

'Shut up.'

'Okay.'

'He's not always like this,' I explained to Alex. 'It's just sometimes he comes across like a total arsehole.'

Alex nodded.

'Well, basically he is a total arsehole.'

Alex laughed.

''Swrong with me?' Don wondered, burping.

'Nothing, Don.' I kissed his fat cheek. 'I love you just the way you are.'

'Slag,' he said, wiping off my kiss and picking a piece of chicken up off my plate, he dipped it idly in the melokhia and then stared at what he had done, incredulous. 'What in the name of fuck is that shit?' he shouted.

'Melokhia,' I told him.

'When it's at home?'

'Bright green semen. They serve it with everything. Blend of semen and snot.'

He winced and wiped the sauce off (I think it might be parsley-based, in fact) on his napkin, popping the leg into his mouth now and pulling the bare bone out with a flourish.

'So, what we doing?' he asked, speaking with his mouth full.

'Student riots,' I told him, picking Don's cigarette up out of the ashtray and smoking it myself. 'You know. Democracy.'

'Schmemocracy. Tediumsville,' he spluttered. 'Who gives an old man's bollock hair about that?'

Odd to be dismissive of democracy in front of a Russian, I thought. And Don lives in Russia too, where nobody could claim the ideal was flourishing – when you haven't got it you really notice. The place is getting scarier and scarier. But more of that later.

'The editor of the *Chronicle*?'

'Tosser.'

'Well, it got me out of Baghdad.'

'Baghdad?! Coolage. Did you see Rory Ungerer out there? Brilliant bloke.'

'Ugh, Don!'

'What? Wouldn't shag you?'

I raised a disdainful eyebrow. I am good at this.

He changed the subject. 'Hey! I shot some brilliant stuff in the City of the Dead today.'

'I can imagine,' I said.

'Amazing scene with this old sous seller and the kids buying this crap off him. Wouldn't touch the shit myself, obviously. Already got the runs.' He patted his enormous blancmange belly, leaving a greasy palm mark on the front of his shirt.

Sous is the liquorice drink that people sell from big brass samovar things that they carry around on their backs and pour into the glasses that hang off their belts.

Alex, who was looking seriously bored and irritated, was, I thought, about to get up and leave when Don pulled off his usual, though always staggering, social coup of suddenly being charming. He spoke to him in Russian.

'So, where are you from, mate?'

Alex raised his eyebrows in astonishment and looked over at me. I shrugged.

'Semforov 90,' he said, fixing Don with his eggshell eyes.

'Oh, yeah. Up there in the Urals.' Don nodded. 'Beautiful around there. Must be tough going now though. Not producing any more, are they?'

'No. It all stopped about ten years ago. Have you been there yourself?'

'Yeah, yeah. My wife's got a friend out there. Svyeta Aslamova. You probably know the family. The dad was a technical assistant or something?'

Alex laughed. A closed town is a closed town. 'Yes. I know them! I was at school with Sveyta. She moved to Moscow.'

'Right. My wife was at university with her. We live out in Peredelkino . . .'

Well, and off they went.

You see, Don met this beautiful young student in Baghdad about five years ago and Irochka seemed not to mind that he was fat, ugly and rude. She saw the beauty within (puh) and he moved to Russia to be with her. The product of this togetherness is Don's third child – Donchik, baby Don – who must be . . . well, he's at least a year older than Ben. Other people's children: not my area of expertise.

Now who the hell knows what came over the three of us but, after a few more drinks, we got into a rusty old Peugot

21

of a cab where they pump the exhaust back into the main body of the car, and, listening to the wailing local pop music and very very nearly killing a donkey that was weaving through the traffic with a load of oranges on its back and being insistently beaten by its hunched master, we drove over the Nile where we took it upon ourselves to get onto one of the touristy restaurant boats that have cocktails and belly dancers. We were pissed. And I love that tourist schlock. I'd be buying a little cartouche with my name on it before you knew it. Did you know that the word 'cartouche' for those things (you know – the lozenge-shaped deals with the pharoahs' names on?) was invented by Napoleon's soldiers who thought they looked like the cartridges on their guns? Well, now you do.

We sat out on deck and watched the traffic scream, honk and flash on the opposite embankment half a mile away across the murky water. The boat rocked almost imperceptibly but just enough to make you feel wobbly when you stood up. The air was warm, thick and sweet (partly because when the wind is right or, rather, wrong, you can smell the tanneries from over the other side of the dusty city) and the belly dancers immediately got Don crouched behind his camera, swearing about his light meters and wobbling around on deck, climbing up forbidden ladders to try and find his angle. He loves this kind of stuff. Colours. Movement. He would like to have been a fashion photographer if only it was a bit more dangerous. You know, if they shot them in Mogadishu or something.

Hey, they probably do for all I'm aware. Not my area.

'You are very beautiful, you know,' Alex whispered across at me (the cigarettes and coffee on his breath somehow sexy), ignoring the semi-naked voluptuous goddess shaking her breasts over his shoulder and leaning in close across

22

the stiff white tablecloth. Odd that eye make-up hasn't changed much in this area of the world for more than three thousand years.

Here we go, I thought.

'Alex. If you want to sleep with me, just ask. You don't need to give me all this crap.'

Well, honestly.

He smiled and touched my cheek with the back of his hand.

'Ah. And nervous. A lady who can't take a compliment. Women should glow when they are complimented, especially a very beautiful one,' he smiled, picking up his glass of beer, the dancer still wiggling behind him in pink chiffon and jangling all her brass discs. Why do foreign men think we want to hear this stuff? Why? Why?

Actually, that's not fair. English men think we want to hear this stuff too, they just don't know how to do it. Which is lucky, if you ask me.

'Right,' I said. 'And they should probably cook men supper every night, clean the loo, not get paid for all the drudgery they do and then shut up if they get raped too? I suppose compliments about being the "rock" of the family and a wonderful nurturer are somehow meant to be payment for a lifetime of picking egg off the floor with your fingernails? Are they? *Da? Nyet?*'

'Okay. Okay. Okay, Faith Zanetti!' he raised his hands in surrender.

I realised, I do realise, that I am not exactly dream date. But I can't stand all the crap. If you've got something to say, spit it out, huh?

And when the coloured lights on the fellucas had started blurring into each other in my drunken gaze I decided it was time to surrender too. That is, to go to bed. Alone.

'Time to go, Lardinio,' I shouted to Don, who was standing over by the guy doing the barbecue, and inexplicably pointing his camera directly at the flames.

'Bugger off,' he said back, without looking at me. 'I'll see you at the Hilton in the morning. I think that one with the green veil has got the hots for me. Those tits might even be real, eh?'

'Night then,' I said. 'But I doubt it.'

'Nice to meet you,' Alex added. 'Good guy,' he said to me quietly, again close enough for his breath to touch my cheek. Why is this erotic? I suppose it is a rehearsal for the moment when his breath might be on my cheek in a gasp of ecstasy. Well, that must be right, mustn't it?

'He is really. Yes.' I smiled, leaving two hundred pounds (no, Egyptian ones, for God's sake) on the table and moving over towards the gangplank.

The poor bloke who had to wear the fez (the main hazard of working in the tourist business) nodded graciously to us and said Goodbye, come again, and held his hand out for Alex's money. I stumbled slightly on the gangplank and held onto the rope at the side.

This, it turned out, was my mistake. I mean, among other things. The rope was only draped over the metal pole on the riverbank and it flailed away, slopping its end into the water below. I toppled over after it, my boots not holding the wooden planks under them. My suddenly very sober brain had time to fully register that we were about to be under water, possibly cold water. All in a fraction of a second I thought about how I'd get my boots and jeans off, was glad I wasn't wearing my leather jacket but had my money and room key in my back pocket, tried to remember if I was wearing pants, thought I should swim to the nearest felluca rather than to the walls of the riverbank. And I wondered whether the current was strong. Then I just shut my eyes and held my breath. And in the same instant I felt Alex's arms grab one of mine near the shoulder. A few of the people on deck who could see us started shouting, the belly dancing music stopped. It seemed for a second as though I was taking Alex down into the dark river with me because he fell to lying across the gangplank with the weight of me. I ended up dangling off him by one really really painful arm like a heroine in an Indiana Jones film, suspended over a ravine or something.

'Oh fuck fuck fuck!' I screamed.

'Give me the other hand,' Alex hissed.

'I can't.'

'Give me the hand,' he insisted. One can be quite insistent in these situations. And not many people have shoulders and backs as strong as his.

I twisted round and managed to raise my arm, every cell now fighting against what it had briefly thought was inevitable – a long swim into the middle of the Nile.

'Okay. I pull you up now.'

'Excellent.' I nodded. 'Yup. Do it.'

And he did. He hauled me up out of the black abyss, scraping half the skin off my stomach as I came over the edge of the walkway to scramble up and lie next to him, both of us draped ridiculously above the river between boat and bank.

I stood up and waved at the spectators.

'I'm fine. Yup. Fine. *Mabzut*. Superb. Just slipped.'

Alex stood up after me and waved as well. Somebody started clapping.

Standing safe on the concrete now I grinned at him.

'My hero,' I said, holding my hand out to shake his. He stepped up beside me but ignored my hand.

25

Some old bloke in robes asked us for money for having watched our car which he hadn't because we didn't have one but I gave him some anyway.

'So, Faith Zanetti. Would you like to sleep with me tonight?'

Ah! A pro.

'Did you push me off that bloody thing?' I laughed, scraping my hair back off my face to see him better.

'No. You fell. Bad rope. Too much to drink.'

'Hmm.'

'So? Would you like to?'

You see, I always find myself in the business of protecting people. I feel as if I'm forever dragging someone or other out of a burning building and into a helicopter or an armoured personnel carrier, pulling them out from under cars, hauling them through caves to salvation on a distant beach. Alex had bowled me over and picked me up twice. Literally. And he'd protected me from the Nile. A small thing. A slip, a little accident, but they say it's the little things that count. (Then again, 'they' say a lot of things. Like 'it's not rocket science', 'he's cooking with gas', 'think outside the box', and stuff. So, obviously, 'they' can't be trusted.) I had disappeared on my evasion-tactic thought train.

I laughed at myself. God, it was all such hard work, being me. Do you want to or not, Faith? Take your own advice. Spit it out.

'Yes. Thanks. That would be lovely. Why don't you come back to my room? We can get a cab on the bridge.'

'Good.' he nodded. And I hoped he wouldn't be one of those blokes who think oral sex is rude but expect you to be impressed if they've got a big willy.

The deal closed.

Chapter Three

My night with Alex was . . . nice. No, more than nice. Fun. But, being the first person I'd gone to bed with since deciding I couldn't be doing with being married to Eden (not that I told Alex this, obviously), it was more of a liberating thing for me than an earth-moving extravaganza of lust. Then again, he got champagne out of the mini-bar afterwards and we swigged it out of the bottle and then we sat up in bed and played 'catch the mini pretzels in your mouth'. But he refused to join me in singing the Soviet national anthem when I won 17–12. This, he thought, was beyond bad taste. Well, how was I supposed to know he had issues with the aftertaste of the Communist regime?

So when I woke up I felt, annoyingly, as if I had betrayed Ben as well as Eden (even though, really, the main reason I didn't want to stay married to Eden was because I caught him getting a blow-job from the girl who looks after the lemon grove outside my father and Annarita's house). So I phoned Brandeglio as soon as Alex got into the shower and told Ben I had seen a camel and would bring him a toy one back.

But then he said, 'Mummy where?' And tears just spilled out of my eyes.

'I'm here, baby. Coming to get you ever so soon, love. Can I talk to Daddy?'

He put the phone down on the terracotta floor and shouted, 'Dadaaaaaaaaaaaa!'

I heard Eden trot over.

'Don't be upset, Faith love. He's fine.'

'I'm not upset. I'm fine too. Just a momentary, you know. Love you both,' I said, and hung up. Well, it was true. Whatever the . . . complications.

Then, suddenly, just as I was hauling myself back into the appropriate personality for the occasion, the muezzins started singing from every mosque in the city, all the voices rising into the sky like a flock of birds. I went out onto the balcony in my robe to listen, awe-stricken somehow. The hangover, perhaps. But when I looked back I saw Alex, towel round his waist, bowing his head to the floor in prayer, facing . . . man alive! Could it be Mecca?

'Whoah!' I said, leaning in incredulously, not managing to take my fag out of my mouth before speaking. He looked up and smiled.

'I converted in Chechnya,' he said and carried on. Something rather moving about the prostration, humbling. Not as weird as it sounds, either. There were quite a lot of guilt-inspired conversions, both real and metaphorical. People would 'realise' that they were doing something terrible and would suddenly want to ally themselves to the people they had been so horrifically oppressing, in whatever way.

'Holy fuck,' I muttered, shaking my head and wandering over to where I'd dropped my jeans last night. Well, it didn't seem to have done Cat Stevens any harm. I considered saying this, but didn't fancy Alex's chances of having heard of Cat Stevens.

When he'd finished he got dressed and kissed me on the cheek. I was sitting, morose, in an armchair facing the Nile and checking my emails (just one from Tamsin entitled '500 words by 4' with no message underneath it – the cause of my aforementioned moroseness).

'I'm going to London in the next week or so,' he said. 'Got to pick my stuff up from here first. Give me a call sometime. I'm based in Earls Court,' he said, and scribbled his phone numbers down on a cream Nile Hilton envelope with the thin hotel pen.

'You live in Earls Court?'

'Sure. Whole Russian exile community in London. Didn't you know? Non doms? Abramovich? Yes?'

I raised my eyebrows. He laughed.

'I spend more time here, in Cairo, though,' he said. 'My business is here and in London so I rent a place there too. Backwards and forwards. Like a cucumber.'

I didn't even bother to ask what his business was or in what situations cucumbers went back and forth. In any case, I could vaguely guess at the business. What do any of those well-built Russians do? Every time I ever talk to the person I'm sitting next to on a plane he always does the same thing: security, risk assessment. This means that anyone who wants to do business in Russia or with Russians hires someone to tell them how dodgy the people they're getting involved with are. This always strikes me as funny. Hell, I could tell you that for free. And as for the risk assessment guys, why are they all so butch, ex-army, ex-security services? Because it's . . . that's right! REALLY risky.

'I see. Okay. Well, I'll . . . give you a call,' I said, and waved my hand at him. I probably thought that was the last

I'd see of him. I mean, being realistic. I didn't know at that point that none of this was going to be a matter of choice. I got in the shower and turned it up to its hottest setting. When an affair is over I need to stand still for a bit, let it wash away, enjoy letting go of it. I love that feeling.

So, Don was down in the marble and gold lobby in front of a big plate of assorted baklava pastries.

'Decent shag?'

'Not bad, thanks,' I said, shaking some water out of my curls onto his face.

'Hey, I was on that plane from Jakarta that went down a couple of months ago, you know,' he said, poking a honey pastry into his mouth.

'You were NOT!?' I said, surprised.

'Well, no. But I was in Sumatra doing the earthquake when it happened.'

'You're an idiot,' I said. ''Sgo.'

Don got up reluctantly.

'Bloody Nora,' he said, presumably complaining about the weight of his camera bag or his lack of an assistant or my unwillingness to so much as hold the tripod.

Whatever.

'Come on, gorgeous.' I smiled, leading the way out past reception and into the glare of the street.

Jamila lived in her parents' flat in Ma'adi. It's one of those areas with wide, densely packed and fuming roads and narrow pavements, shops selling garish clothes and sequinny bags and clean, overly-lit restaurants thronged with the *jeunesse dorée* who drink Coke and eat pizza. No melohkia for them, thanks, and who can blame them? Jamila's building was off the main road and we had to walk through a dusty courtyard with an ancient climbing frame in it to get there. Modern Egyptian architecture goes very heavy on the grey concrete slab. The boab looked us up and down suspiciously but lifted his robes to go barefoot up the wide, dark staircase to show us the right flat. He said a quick '*Saba khil kheer*' to Jamila before leaping back downstairs to his post, that is, the sack, basically, where he sleeps. She smiled at us. She wore a pale pink head-scarf, a black T-shirt that said 'Sure, Right, Fine, Whatever' on it in big gold letters, tight jeans and flip-flops. Her parents, apparently, were out. She smiled enthusiastically at us and invited us into the cool dark of their flat.

It was typically Egyptian in that way that you probably only recognise if you're not Egyptian. You know, it would be odd to say about someone's flat in London, 'It was typically English.' I have no idea what that might mean. Would it mean central heating, bad carpets, cigarette smoke and a big telly? Or would it mean stripped floors, a Queen Anne dining table and inherited china? Well, I'm not Egyptian, so I mean it was all gilt-backed chairs, plastic-covered sofas, the television on a soap with the sound off, rugs on the walls and a glass-fronted cabinet with family photos (that I now wish I'd looked a bit more closely at) and academic achievement certificates proudly displayed. A framed sura from the Quran on the wall in sworling black script on pale pink silk. 'Sweet Patience.'

She gestured to us to sit down which I did, creaking the thick plastic and making the shape of a bottom in it. Don stayed standing, breathing heavily and shifting his weight restlessly from foot to foot. He looked around, squinting, the obscenities buzzing round his brain almost audible. He was aware that he wasn't going to be able to shoot in the dark like this. Jamila went to the kitchen and came back out with a tray of lemonade for us. The tray had a picture of the Eiffel Tower on it and the lemonade was home-made with mint sprigs in it, the glasses dark blue with gold patterns round the top. Guests of honour.

The rioting, I should have mentioned, was not just about democracy. Or, at least, it was only indirectly about democracy. It was actually in protest at the death in custody of a university professor who had written anti-government articles. The police claimed she'd died of a heart attack but her daughter, who went to pick the body up, insisted she'd been tortured and beaten to death. Anyway, the daughter was herself Jamila's English teacher who was then arrested as well whilst actually giving a lecture on Trollope. Got it?

'What,' I asked her, 'do you hope to achieve by protesting?'

A pompous and banal sounding question, I suppose, but what I really meant was, Aren't you just pissing in the wind, complaining about police brutality in today's Egypt? I mean, what's the point? It's like Russia – after generations and generations of casual and brutal injustice, punctuated, in the end, by only a few years of relative sanity, people are used to it. And how odd, in a way, that in Europe we genuinely assume, for the most part, that if we're innocent we'll be found innocent. I mean, however terrible, miscarriages of justice are still a very big deal in England. And it matters, this stuff. I have to remind myself that it does, or be reminded, but it matters. If anything does. That, of course, is a rather wider question.

'We ask for the release of Karima El-Baz and for a proper investigation into her mother's death,' she said.

Ask away, I thought again. But I nodded sagely and she carried on.

'I'm sure you know that this country's human rights record is not impeccable. You only have to look at what Amnesty International says about us. They have started a letter-writing campaign on Karima's behalf, incidentally.'

Jamila then showed us a bruise on her arm which she said had been administered by a policeman's truncheon at the demo the day before. It probably had but it's my job to be sceptical and, frankly, she could easily have got it playing volleyball.

But you've got to love it, at least I do, when ordinary girls start trying to change the world. I was genuinely moved by this story, on grounds of sorority alone, and was proud of Jamila and her fervour. Envious of it also, of course. You can't fake the real desire to change the world, though most journalists try.

Then, just while I was getting all caught up in my sincerity and my glass of lemonade (the mint got stuck in my teeth), Don piped up. That is, he coughed phlegmily.

'Yeah, well I'd get a lighter shot up a nigger's arse, quite frankly. I'm going to have to shoot her outside. All right love?' he asked Jamila.

She looked at him open-mouthed. Her English was perfect but she'd never heard it spoken like that before. Did she smile? I wish I knew.

'Don't worry about him.' I smiled. 'He's a teddy bear really.'

Jamila stood up and checked her watch. 'Well, I'm meeting some friends for a further demonstration on Tahrir,' (yes, that's Liberation), 'Square in half an hour, so perhaps you could take your pictures there?' she offered, looking a bit less reverently now at her guests of honour, the very man who had been afforded the Eiffel Tower tray.

Don picked up a cube of pistachio nougat from a crystal bowl on the coffee table and squeezed it out of its cellophane packet into his mouth.

'Shuperb, shweetheart,' he spluttered.

Raising her eyebrows, Jamila took out her placard with a big black and white photograph of Karima on it (very beautiful and generally liberated-looking person, if a bit *Dallas*) from behind the sofa and we set off together in a ramshackle taxi. The traffic, as ever, was horrendous and, half-choked to death down the dust-clouded embankment, we only just made it in time for Jamila to get to the front with her banner and for Don to get the stuff we needed before the students' rage subsided. Not that this was going to be on the front page or anything. As my old editor (shot in Bethlehem in the murkiest of circumstances) never got sick of saying, 'Nobody reads foreign news.' I didn't tell Don this as he sometimes refuses to work entirely if he knows he's going to get cropped down to three centimetres square by 'some arse-wipe of a picture editor who doesn't know his arse from Ansell fucking Adams.'

I lit a cigarette and looked on, pulling my shades down over my eyes and breathing in the dust and fumes.

There were more girls in veils than I'd ever noticed in Egypt before but it was good to see them protesting at any rate. Maybe a hundred, a hundred and fifty people. I didn't even want to get started on a thought train about women's liberation. It always comes at the very bottom of the social upheaval pile. Can you imagine if men were never seen on the streets of some country or another, confined to their houses, not allowed to vote or to have any recourse whatsoever to the law, open to every type of abuse and, the Lord knows, suffering it. Well, there'd be an outcry. Wouldn't there? Oops. Got started.

They were already shouting slogans, the red insides of all those open mouths looking like any mammalian threat, when we pulled over next to the old bus station behind my hotel. But when Jamila arrived they seemed to move aside for her respectfully, murmuring hellos like a secret, and a boy with a new moustache and a maroon leather jacket handed her an old holiday camp megaphone and she began to lead the chanting, her voice loud and strong, her right hand raised. She was a natural. The traffic swirled around us and people carried on getting on and off buses, in and out of taxis and going into the two- and three-storey fast food places that dominate the square (which isn't remotely square but a kind of dusty grey expanse of nothingness with a vast Soviet building at one end that Krushchev sadistically gave Nasser as a present, and the pretty, low Arabesque thing that is the American University just next to it).

The police were standing around, thin-eyed, with intimidating moustaches and slightly incapacitating riot gear, but they didn't look worried and obviously weren't about to start charging or firing at anyone. For today the demonstration did stay peaceful (though don't imagine the secret police weren't watching from some fast-food window or another and taking down the name of every single person with 'views' about the government) and in the end Jamila and a couple of girl-friends decided to go to the cinema. '*Love Actually*. My friend adores Hugh Grant,' she said, waving her banner with a twinkle of her black eyes.

'Have fun,' I shouted.

I thought of those riots in Paris not long ago, when every correspondent in the world went running off for their French dictionary in the hope of being sent to cover them. I spent a couple of days in the suburbs interviewing disaffected rappers and eating a lot of couscous but I remember thinking how ironic it was that all these young people were protesting, rioting at not being considered French, when in fact there is just nothing more French than a bit of a riot. In demonstrating, they were demonstrating that they are entirely integrated, utterly assimilated into the native culture. Stand up for your rights and expect to be bloody heard.

In Egypt, though, you'd be lucky.

Back at the hotel, I phoned up some official types. Ministry of this, that and the other. Huge in Cairo – all very Soviet. There are a lot of old Egyptians who studied in Moscow or worked with Russians on the Aswan Dam and what have you and can still remember how to say *zdrastvuitye* – it means 'hello': just say 'does your arse fit you?' very quickly. Oh yes, they insisted, she died of a sudden heart attack and Karima El-Baz, the lunatic daughter, is being detained for her own safety and might need psychiatric treatment – and all that depressingly familiar stuff from before the end of communism, becoming all the rage yet again. I cracked open the macadamia nuts and filed by four o'clock London time. Not that this in any way satisfied Tamsin who was all like, 'We haven't got the budget to send you flying round the world and putting you up at the Ritz for five hundred measly words a day, Zanetti.'

'Tamsin, hello? Earth to foreign editor. You asked me to come. You asked for five hundred weasly words.'

'Measly.'

'Whatever.'

'Yeah, well, that was before Ed Theroux leapt on my back about budgets. Cut. Cut. Cut. Can you do a couple of features to justify the trip or something? Can you talk to Barbara?'

'Okey dokey. Put me right on through.'

God, it was irritating. Barbara is the editor of the featurey bollocks section. We're supposed to be pleased when we get to write the longer kind of pieces that someone does actually read ('My Near-death Experience at the Hands of the Taliban' type of thing) but in fact it's usually all padding and no substance and I just feel like I'm painting pictures instead of communicating facts. Which I hate and am crap at.

But, looking on the bright side (as I gather one is supposed to do), it was hardly hacking away at the sides of a salt mine with my ragged fingers and I could get it all done this evening.

So, I speak to Barbara and call her Babs just for fun (she wears a badge that says, 'It's my parents' fault') and I offer her a thing about the population and overcrowding stuff because I know Don's already got the art. She's not convinced.

'Hmm. We have a largely female readership for *C2*, Faith. I'm sure you're aware . . .'

The idea being that women aren't interested in news features per se. They say things like 'per se' a lot on features. Oh God. Okay, okay.

'The life of a belly dancer on the river boats?'

'Ooh. Now that DOES sound interesting.'

'Righty-ho.' I sighed and lit a cigarette and thought about Alex's shoulders and the taste of blood on his lip.

I switched the news on to distract myself. Which was how I heard about the arrests. Fifth item, after a thing about a global property market slow-down. 'Human rights groups have condemned the arrest of six student demonstrators in Cairo this afternoon. Four women and two men were taken into custody when police . . .'

I just had a feeling. She hadn't, of course, been going to the cinema. Stupid, Faith.

Chapter Four

I spent a boring, depressing and hot day sitting in a waiting room at the Sayyeda Zeinab police station in southern Cairo hoping to see Jamila. I was on a wooden bench, the fan didn't work and the thick yellowish paint was peeling dramatically off the walls. There was a laminated poster drawing-pinned up to one wall with what appeared to be a list of rules. The understanding was, I felt, that whoever you fancied yourself to be you were probably disobeying most of them and would surely be executed. Occasionally a woman would walk through crying, her mascara running. Occasionally a stray cat walked in and I hissed at it until it dashed back out into the white blaze of the day. Occasionally an officer in that rather sinister and surely hot black uniform appeared from the grey metal internal door, looked at me with a cross between lust and distate (easier to achieve than you might think), asked what I was doing there and then went again. It was actually the same bloke at least four times. The only upside was that not only are you allowed to smoke everywhere in Cairo, you are almost obliged to. Although I was the only person waiting, you could hardly see across to the opposite wall for smoke, a build-up that had probably been gathering for thirty years.

Eventually, my bloke with the thick waxy 'tache and the black get-up with beret told me that Jamila had been presented for prosecution at the Darb Al Ahmar office but would be back tomorrow. I told him I was press in the pathetic hope that this might make him think twice about pulling her fingernails out with pliers or whatever, though, in fact, he probably had nothing at all to do with her. That's the trouble with this kind of bureaucracy. It's completely impossible to get access to anyone directly involved which is, I suppose, the whole point of it. I produced a card out of the back pocket of my jeans with the logo of the Egyptian Organisation of Human Rights on it and tapped it meaningfully. Actually, they have managed to get a few prosecutions over torture in police cells, but most of their cases remain entirely unlooked at.

I couldn't even be bothered with vodka and shisha when I got back to the hotel. God knew where Don was. Or, that is, I hope He didn't know. He would have been shocked. I drank out of the mini-bar, phoned Ben, cried and crawled into bed, shattered and annoyed at a pointless day waiting for nothing and nobody. Police station waiting rooms not my all-time favourite venues.

I dreamt about a train. It was glamourous and Orient Expressy, full of well-dressed people chatting and drinking champagne, a handsome waiter with Brylcreemed hair wove up and down the restaurant car with a silver tray of glasses. It was the 1930s and he sat me down with some other travellers, obsequious, bowing. But then somebody realised. We realised that actually this was the Holocaust and we were being taken to be killed in a camp, to be stripped of all our glamour and clothes and dignity and shot in the back so that we would fall into a deep grave on top of other people, some not yet finally dead. Somebody tried to leave the carriage and the waiter stopped him, confirming what we already knew. We were prisoners. He was apologetic. Just doing his job. Following orders. The man next to me – good looking, a father, glasses, beige mac belted at the waist – started to cry and I held his head in my hands and woke up, heart pounding, breath short.

So, when Jamila called me, at about eight o' clock the next morning, it was basically a relief. Obviously my visiting-card heavy-handedness had worked. She was out already and wanted to meet!

But not as urgently as Al Jazeera International wanted to. Could I appear, the assistant producer asked as I lit a cigarette and took a can of Coke out of the mini-bar, in forty minutes. It would be live, she explained, from the Cairo bureau and they would send a car. Four seconds later Tamsin called me from London to tell me that they were about to phone me and that I must ('Seriously, Zanetti') do it. I drank my delicious breakfast beverage, got dressed and ran downstairs through the lobby (where they were getting ready for a huge wedding) to the car that was waiting for me on the road, the Al Jazeera logo on a big piece of card inside the windscreen.

You see, I probably wouldn't have seen Alex again if I hadn't happened to run into him so immediately after our first physical encounter. Ha! At least, I thought then that it had 'just happened' that I'd run into him, like you do. I didn't want a boyfriend. Really, I didn't. Ben's got loss built into his life already what with our comings and goings (more for his shrink – hey, someone is going to make a fortune) without my letting him get involved with yet another person he'd inevitably lose. I say I ran into Alex as though we were buying fags at the same newsagent. In fact, it was much funnier than that.

This show I was doing was their breakfast thing (bright background, bright jackets) with people (me) droning on about Russia. A journalist had just been pushed out of his apartment window to a concretey death, something that is becoming a bit of a pattern over there. So they needed people on to do a spot of droning and if it's Russia it's often me, though I've never done it from Cairo before. They send you into make-up first (they make up pundits and anyone with any kind of position but they don't make up ordinary members of the public which is why they always look so pale and crap on TV against the manicured hosts and other guests) where I learnt, after a terrible experience with what the 'artiste' called his 1960s Twiggy look, to ask them just to de-shine me if they think I need it. Nothing else. I don't wear make-up unless I am interviewing someone who I need to flirt with (mainly Russian or Arab dignitaries). In that situation I sometimes even put my one skirt on. And crippling shoes. Anyway, there I am in make-up and it's time for me to go on the set and the girl with the ponytail, flip-flops and clip board says, 'The other guest is already on set, so just sit to the right of Sabrina.'

I am rushed on while they show a clip of the apartment building and the blood on the pavement and I sit down and am miked up in a mad hurry and, distracted by Sabrina's yellow skirt suit, I only notice after she's actually asked me her first question that the other guest is Alex.

So Sabrina says, 'We've got Russia expert and former Moscow correspondent for the *Chronicle* Faith Zanetti here in the studio. Faith, is this – the third death of an openly anti-government journalist in under a year – now becoming

41

reminiscent of the Soviet, could we even say Stalinist, regime?'

And I'm like, 'Well, Sabrina . . . Oh! Hi!'

And she's turned towards me with a very strained and expectant smile, her whole head bright orange with stage make-up and she's obviously none too impressed that I've addressed the other guest who's off-camera.

So I carry on. 'Sorry. Well, I think it is beginning to look a little that way, though obviously we aren't yet dealing with the kind of scale of . . . blah blah blah.'

Well, you can imagine.

'Former Russian Army Captain Alexander Sorokin, would you agree with that?' Sabrina says, spinning deftly in her chair.

He did. Or he didn't. I can't remember and, anyway, who cares? He corrected her on his title though, but he was too polite to correct her on his name – I couldn't BELIEVE she'd got it wrong. The name she'd mistakenly used did, actually, ring a bell, but I had no reason to fish the memory out or wonder about it. I looked at him on the monitor and his chiselled face and Siberian summer-sky eyes were even better on telly than in real life. I stuck my tongue out at him while he was talking and he twinkled at me. Afterwards, while we were standing around waiting to be given wet wipes to get the make-up off, he said, 'I thought you were going to call me.'

'Did you?' I asked.

'I hoped you would.'

Sabrina interrupted us. 'Fantastic, Alexander. Thanks so much. Again!' she laughed. She kept her back to me. 'There's actually something I'd really like to chat to you about. Lunch perhaps?'

She put her card in his hand, her mike-lead trailing.

'That would be very kind,' he said, smiling politely. I grinned at him behind her great yellowness, rolling my eyes at her idiocy – like she can't even get a guest's name right. She swivelled round as though her swirly chair was still underneath her.

'Ah. Hope.'

'Faith.'

'Faith. Thanks to you too.'

We left together, refusing the purring Mercedes they'd offered us and walking out into the heat daze, right towards Zamalek. I hunched my leather jacket up onto one shoulder and Alex gave me one of his horrible cigarettes. I pushed a Nicorette out of the foil pack and put it in my mouth as well. Here's my theory: if you overdose on nicotine and make yourself feel sick it will be longer before you need another cigarette. They should put it in their ad campaign.

I inhaled.

'God, I used to smoke these during the shortages in the 1980s.'

'There were shortages in England too?' he asked, astonished.

'No! In Ryazan. I married a guy. A thousand years ago now,' I said, stepping off the pavement into an alley of cones round some roadworks that weren't being worked on. Too bloody hot. I didn't mention shooting my ex-husband dead in the Arctic tundra, but I didn't really feel he needed to know that about me. Might have put him off.

'You look too young to have been there then. I was doing military service when all that was happening. Picking cabbages. Ouside Omsk. You know Omsk? A lot of cabbages.'

'I'm 36,' I told him, pausing to digest this information myself. 'Christ! Don't know what I've been doing with my life. Though I HAVE been to Omsk. I did a piece about an old woman who wouldn't move out of her deserted building. Up and down to her flat on the twentieth floor every day, taking wood and God knows what. No lift. Nobody else on the whole estate. There are a hell of a lot of stubborn people in Russia,' I said, turning round to smile at him through the glare of light and the honking of a thousand car horns.

'I know most of them.' He nodded. Little did I know then that he was their revered leader.

We walked past the grease-smelling kebab shops – a red and yellow facade and the meat rotating in the window – and convenience stores selling piles of multi-coloured washing-up bowls, down the littered grey alleys of tea shops full of crouched men smoking and playing chess where, as a foreigner, you hardly ever go. Certain living, ordinary parts of a city fill me with a kind of horror that make me feel like the only creature alive in the world. A kind of existential angst I never got when, for example, I thought me, Don and Eden would never escape from that cellar in Srebrenica, the firefight outside so gruesome and so relentless. For example.

Alex gave a man with a radio a cigarette. I am always on the lookout for casual kindness. It is rarer than you might think and always a good sign.

'In the room the women come and go, talking of Michaelangelo,' Alex said when we passed a crowded shoe shop where women hustled for gold high heels. Cultured for some killer-army-colonel-turned-businessman. Was he a businessman? I realised I actually had no idea. And I liked it.

I raised my eyebrows.

'T. S. Eliot,' he said.

'Yes, I know.' I nodded.

'My father was professor of English,' he said.

'I thought he was a nuclear physicist.'

'And professor of English. And cellist.'

'Right,' I nodded. Russians.

Oddly, we seemed to end up, after a four cigarette walk, at Alex's flat in one of those concrete slab things that look seventies and institutional, just before the pretty bit of Zamalek starts. Well, I say oddly, but I have had too much therapy to believe that. I did 'need help' at the time – badly. (There is a fabulous old *New Yorker* cartoon of a boy standing by a rushing river where someone is drowning and shouting, 'Lassie! Get help!' In the next frame we see Lassie lying on the couch explaining some detail of his childhood to a shrink.) It all started with this breakdown I had in Baghdad which everyone attributed to some kind of battle-weary post-traumatic stress but was actually to do with having fallen in love. Pathetic really. Anyway, then the father I thought had died when I was little turned out to be living with his wife and sons in Sicily and it just really seemed about time to get myself looked at again. And anyone who's had any talking cure type-of-thing knows that the first lesson to be osmosed is that you are responsible for everything you do, say and think. Or, at least, that there is a reason for it and you can find it out and therefore make a more clearly conscious choice.

For example, you arrive late for your shrink session and they're all, 'Why do you think you were ten minutes late today?' And you're all, 'Umm. Because there was a lot of traffic. Why are you making so much fuss about it? It's only ten minutes!' And on and on about it they go until, sessions later, you realise that if you'd been promised a million pounds to be on time you'd have been on time, so what you are actually doing is prioritising. Deciding to stay in bed and cut it a bit fine, not allowing for traffic or whatever.

Okay. So, the upshot of this is that I knew we were going to Alex's flat and I wanted to go there because he is attractive and finds me attractive but I didn't want to openly acknowledge this to myself or, the Lord knows, to him. So there. Eden would be proud of me. Well, apart from the other man aspect of the enterprise. And the sex.

It was at that moment that Don called me (my phone sings 'Love Me Tender') to ask which pictures they'd used with the pieces yesterday. Why he can't check this himself I have no idea and where he was I also had no idea, though it sounded like a river boat bar if I'd had to guess. I gestured to Alex to go on up and I'd follow in a minute, standing under the portico where the boab sat smoking shisha with friends for a conversation that could get nasty. Alex unlocked his front door and pointed to the bell that had a 'K' on it. 'K for Karamzin.' He smiled and I pointed at my mobile phone and grimaced in mock agony.

'Don't dick me around Eff Zed. Just fucking tell me. What did they do?'

'Hi Don. Lovely to hear from you. Oh fine, fine. How are you? What's the weather like in Ma'adi? Bit grim here, as ever.'

'Zanetti.'

'Look, they used the student riot one with the Kentucky Fried thing behind it. It was big. Nice.'

'Page?'

'Seventeen.'

'Cunts.'

'Oh come on, McCaughrean. It was a quarter of a page just for the picture and it wasn't exactly a scoop or, like, breaking news. You know . . .'

'And the dancers?'

'Green veil on her fag break.'

46

'Excellent. God she's got nice tits,' he said with an odd smile in his voice (the reason for which would soon become apparent).

'And . . .'

'AND?! Woo hoo!'

'And the one with her pulling her jeans on with the girl behind her doing her eye make-up. Okay?'

'Yeah. Well. Not bad. So, I should be expecting a cheque for two pounds fifty then.'

'Don't hold your breath. Have you shot Jamila?'

Don laughed, wheezing and coughing as though he had been holding his breath for some years.

'Not yet. Big spread in *National Geographic* with the population shit next week,' he said, audibly lighting a fag.

'Excellent. I'll buy it. Listen, I'm actually at Alex's so I'd better go.' I was trying to hang up.

'Alex?! The Russian bloke from the boat? Why, Faith Zanetti, you old romantic! The same bloke twice? Warms the cockles of my balls.'

'Does it really, Donald?'

'Nope.'

'No, I suppose not.'

'Okay. By the way, Yeltsin's about to die. Rushed into Kremlin Hospital this morning with heart failure. They haven't announced yet. I'll give you a buzz.'

And so will everyone else, I thought. Poor old Boris Nikolaevich. Bet the obits that I don't write won't give him much credit for leaving the press free and insisting on democracy. Still, living fifteen years after a quintuple heart-bypass is impressive in itself.

'Sure,' I said and snapped my phone shut. The world wouldn't be right without Don McCaughrean and his scoops. He does this whole buffoon thing but he's got his ear to the ground. What does this mean? It means that every month or so he calls his friend in the Kremlin Hospital, a nurse he's cultivated, takes him out for lunch, buys him a few vodkas and says to call him if anyone well known comes in. Fine. Easy. But Don is doing this with a hundred or so contacts at a time, from duma deputies to minor mobsters. Everyone calls Don first. He gets to the war before it starts. A British soldier gave him a discreet bell just before all the trouble in Zimbabwe, told him he was on call to be posted there and that something must be up. Or must be about to be up. Most times it's someone who's in shipping. The arsenal has to get there before the troops somehow, right?

I press the 'K' button and stand there, the sun now really hammering down on the pavements. Nothing. I press it again, beginning to feel a bit irritated. I mean, what am I, on some kind of date, standing in the rain waiting for an answer? Well, I can't help it. Positions of powerlessness don't come easily to me. Or, rather, a zen state of acceptance, joy and inner confidence doesn't come easily to me when in positions of powerlessness. On about the tenth frenzied ring I was about to go home when an old man with a Yorkshire terrier on a thin red lead came out of the door. His back was hunched in the way that makes you immediately stand up straight and he wore a threadbare tweed jacket and smelt slightly of dead cat. Or it could have been dead dog. Moustache. Hair slicked back. Gauloise in his lips.

Don has a test for the standard of development of whatever country we are in. It is called the dead dog test. The test is how long it takes for a dead dog to be cleared from the street. I seem to remember that Sierra Leone failed miserably with never. It is not a bad economic trend barometer, in fact. What's the point in clearing away the one when the stench of all the others is overwhelming?

'I'm visiting Alex Karamzin in flat K,' I said, enjoying saying 'Karamzin', and the old man looked up at me rheumy-eyed and smiled, understanding English. He had once been handsome and, ludicrously, this made me want to cry. Really must double my dose.

I walked past him and into the hallway. It had been carpeted thirty years earlier and the greasy white plastic knob on the wall switched a very pale dim yellow light on for just long enough to be able to wade through the heap of junk mail and onto the bottom step. I walked up to flat K in the dark. A couple was rowing in flat F.

Anyway, the door to K was slightly open, a shaft of light coming out into the grimy corridor. So I pushed it and went inside. There were piles of video tapes (oddly retro) in the carpeted hall and there was no air conditioning. I faced a mirror that needed cleaning and went into the lounge. It smelt of stale smoke and looked like a furnished rental that he'd been renting for a long time. There were letters and a bottle of vodka on a smoked-glass coffee table that was surrounded by three old and not matching sofas (nobody who owns a place buys three sofas, especially when they live alone). Two dead plants stood on the window ledge and the fireplace was blocked in with chipboard. A Steinway baby grand, with sheet music and full ashtrays littered about on top of it, dominated the room. It was light in here, with very high ceilings and it must once have been nice – before 1973 some time.

'Alex?!' I shouted. 'Where the fuck are you?'

I heard a funny little sort of mewling in reply and looked for the animal that had made it. The animal was, of course, Alex himself. The 'they' of our first Cairo meeting appeared to have been back.

He was crouched behind the third, cream leather sofa by

49

the radiator, his hands bound behind his back with black gaffer tape, his feet out in front of him also taped together. He had another piece of tape over his mouth and a slash across his forehead that was bleeding horribly into his eyes, clogging in his eyebrows. It looked as though it had been made with a razor blade or a Stanley knife.

'Jesus,' I said, kneeling down to untape him. I did his mouth and he gasped in relief. He had inhaled some blood through his nose and was finding it hard to breathe. The wrists and feet were more difficult than you might imagine and I went into the kitchen to look for some scissors. Clearly, he never used the kitchen. There were a few more video tapes and discs actually on the flat electric hobs and the greasy light switch clicked uselessly. It looked as if he did his 'risk assessment' mostly using a camera. All the units were dark brown and dirty, but there were scissors in a drawer.

'What on earth happened to you?' I asked him as he got up and went into the bathroom. I stood outside the bathroom door looking at my boots and I repeated my question a few times in a variety of ways. Replacing 'earth' for 'fuck' and then 'hell'. He came out with a wet face and hair, a towel clamped to the wound on his head.

'They are trying to frighten me,' he said. Yup. Well, I could see that.

'Is it working?' I muttered, though I didn't think he was likely to appreciate the comment. It was working quite well on me. I mean, it's not as if I was on a story. I was trying to have a little affair. It wasn't going that brilliantly. But they never do, do they? Complicated people have complicated affairs. Is that right? I expect so.

'They want to stop me speaking out. But I am not afraid,' he explained.

'No?' Best to wait. Pretend not to be too interested. And, to be truthful, I wasn't THAT interested.

'You really don't know who I am, do you?' he asked, as though not in fact requiring an answer and certainly not looking as if he was about to tell me.

Noop, I thought. Not a clue, mate.

He lit a cigarette and sat down on the sofa he'd been dumped behind.

'But, Alex . . .' I began, sitting down too, leaning my elbows on my knees.

He was apparently lost in thought and I was feeling quite edgy. Not because I thought anyone was about to come back but because, well, he seemed so different somehow.

'Alex?'

He flickered back into life, took a long drag on his cigarette, unscrewed the half-empty (not half-full. Explains a lot. Or, rather, nothing) bottle of vodka that was sitting on the coffee table with his letters and took a swig. He looked tearful but angry too. Driven.

'Yes?'

'How did they get away? I was standing on the doorstep the whole entire time and I didn't see anyone.'

'They were waiting for me.' He nodded. 'Lucky you didn't come up with me.'

You said it.

'It wasn't an old man with a dog was it?'

Alex laughed and touched his head, which had stopped bleeding and was looking a bit less dramatic than before.

He gestured towards the bedroom and I got up to have a look. Big double bed in a mess, hideous built-in wardrobes, open window and – I leant out – a fire escape down into a shabby courtyard with a few dead plants in it. I went back to Alex.

51

'God. How many of them were there?'

'Two.'

'And what is it they don't want you to talk about, exactly?' Oh no. I was interrogating him. Bad habit. Bad. Bad. Bad. I never know what else to do in these situations. I support the 'the more you know the easier it is to deal with' school of thought, but there are many who veer the other way.

Alex sighed deeply and looked at me as if trying to find something out about me, his blue eyes suddenly as big as the sky. Fat chance. Nobody finds out about me by looking. I think being female probably helps with this. Expectations about femininity, about what 'women' are like, are pretty standard. Women are emotionally intelligent, gentle, bad at maths and with low spatial awareness. All that kind of sexist bollocks. When really, women can be as stupid, violent, numerate and able to park a car as the next idiot.

I was worried he was about to quote Dostoevsky or something, you know how they do. 'Pain and suffering are always unavoidable for a large intelligence and a deep heart.' Searingly insightful observations on which to base one's life, all lifted from the pages of *The Brothers Karamazov* or something. (FYI – it is pronounced 'karamaaazoff', not, as most English people seem to think, 'karamattssoff'.) I don't think so. Too Russian, all that inevitable suffering. I prefer Bob Dylan for life maxims. 'If something ain't right, it's wrong.' For example.

Anyway, as it turned out, he didn't quote anything.

'Faith Zanetti, I think I will tell you one day. You will write about it. But not yet.'

I had a bit of an inkling as to the kind of thing it might be without him bothering. Ex-services Russian with business contacts in Britain, the FSU and the Middle East. I mean, honestly. It was amazing he was still alive, really.

'Right,' I said.

He gave me a significant look.

You know how people do that with journalists? They always say things like, 'Better be careful what I say! You might put it in your column!' When a) they have never said anything remotely interesting in their whole entire lives and never will and b) I do not have a column. Once had a thing with a psychologist and everyone said to him, 'Ooh! I expect you can see right through me!' and things like that. In fact he spent his whole life in a lab cutting bits out of rats' brains and couldn't have had less insight into human beings.

So just as I was about leave, not keen to enter into whatever his secret deals might be at this point, to put it mildly, he went and sat down at the piano and started playing a Haydn prelude. Now I couldn't really imagine his 'story' surprising me much, but this certainly did.

He became calm and powerful, as though he had flicked his tail coat out over his stool and the auditorium had hushed and darkened. The vibrations of a grand piano from very close up are as beautiful and as soporific as the movement of a train. I shut my eyes and let them hum through me. He had hired a crane for two thousand Egyptian pounds just to haul the piano in the window, he told me. And then, when I had completely relaxed and was almost asleep, thinking about a *Magic Roundabout* lampshade my cousins used to have, Alex came across and touched my cheek and it made me want to sink into oblivion and somehow disappear into the incredible expanse of Russia, to listen to him playing Rachmaninov. He had big hands. You need big hands for Rachmaninov. I am told. Because that's what I thought about while we were having sex. The endless train journeys, the birch trees and villages and the sky that goes on forever.

53

Ridiculous, I know. But it's better than football scores or whatever men claim to think about during sex. Better? Well, maybe not. Just a variation.

The sun pounded on the window ledge and the woman upstairs paced the floor.

Chapter Five

I snuck back to the hotel around lunchtime (a delicious tin of macadamia nuts for me, thanks), slightly ashamed of myself and, a default reaction to any slight attachment to anyone else, missing Ben.

Al-Ahram, the English-language paper that got shoved under the door onto the beige carpet, had a headline about the Egyptian Museum and the new temperature-controlled display of mummies. I felt like a temperature-controlled mummy myself – it was freezing in my ice-tomb of an air-conditioned room.

Jamila had insisted on meeting in the City of the Dead where Don took those photos a couple of days earlier. So, she'd gone all cloak and dagger as well as freedom-frenzied, which seemed a bit exhausting. But, fair enough, the poor girl had just been in prison and probably didn't much want to go back there. Talking to a Western journalist so immediately wasn't the subtlest move. Still, there must be plenty of discreet places to meet in Cairo without going the whole hog with the crumbling tombs, little processions of people paying respects and those blokes who recite as much of the

Quran as you pay them to, nodding their heads and looking generally devout. I often think about them when you see the pictures of all those Madrassas, religious schools in Pakistan and all over the place, where they're accused of training terrorists. All they seem to do is learn to recite the Quran which must seriously restrict their career prospects – basically whittling it down to being a tomb reader. Lot of tombs, I guess.

The taxi pulled up on a side street next to a juice bar with its metal awning half-up, half-down. A couple of young men were drinking from big plastic cups of orange juice on the dusty pavement, a chessboard between them and the juice man leaning over to inspect the moves. Inside the older boys, decrepit men, were playing at tables, drinking coffee and smoking shisha. There were bags of rubbish in the road and a couple of dogs sniffing at them idly, as though obliged. We were near the tannery so the dogs could probably smell better things in the air. I know I could – it brought me close to gagging so I lit a cigarette. Ah, that's better.

A group of raggedy girls ran up to me in rubbery flip-flops and ancient summer dresses, screeching and laughing and wanting me to take a picture of them on my phone (very sophisticated miming, involving pickpocketing my phone, handing it back to me and then organising themselves in a smiling group). I took the picture and then they sold me a packet of tissues and followed me, delighted and laughing, saying, 'Hello! Hello! Welcome!' A woman in a black headscarf leant out of a window behind a string of washing and shouted at them, but she was smiling too. I waved and the girls all screamed with glee again. They were still with me when I found Jamila on the arranged street corner next to the Kodak shop (the grimy Kodak hole in the wall, that is). Someone was doing kebabs on a stand outside and they smelt great. I was about to buy one but Jamila stopped me.

'Disease,' she said and shooed the girls on with a short hissing speech. I was going off her a bit.

Though it was hotter than it had been last time I saw her, she was wearing a shiny long-sleeved blouse buttoned up to the collar and a floor-length blue nylon skirt instead of jeans. The whole look a lot more Islamic, though I was in no position to have an opinion really. I mean, wear what you like. I was in raggy old jeans, a white T-shirt, cowboy boots and reflector shades and I don't think I was winning any awards for style either.

We seemed to go through an archway in a sand-coloured disintegrating wall and were then immediately surrounded by the tombs. These aren't gravestones. These are huge memorial vaults with a little garden (puh) outside and then a huge capacious and cool inside with the tomb perhaps in it or perhaps underneath it. The idea is that the garden is kept shady and well-planted so that the family can come for the day and spread a picnic out and drink mint tea. There are festival days when you are supposed to be doing that and it's chaos in here then. Balloons and candyfloss, music and garlands of light, food stalls and a lot of muggings. But normally nobody much comes (unless you're Om Khalsoum – a singer whose tomb is always covered in flowers with at least four chanters outside it at any one time as well as groups of fans sitting crying in the dust) and the toothless bloke you pay to guard your family's tomb has moved HIS whole entire family in to live there. So most of these tombs have actually become family homes with chickens squawking around in the garden bit, dirty children (so thin compared to our dumplings at home) pootling about hassling the tourists and women hunched over little fires or sweeping the yard. Strange and beautiful. But that's often the trouble with romance abroad – lovely but you wouldn't actually want to live in one of these. Clearly.

'They released me,' Jamila said, walking quickly as though she was going somewhere. This seemed unlikely.

'Yes. I've been calling but nobody would tell me anything. I waited in the station all day yesterday.'

There were a lot of things I wanted to ask her but I was waiting for her to tell me.

'I heard they've released Karima too,' she said. 'She's in a psychiatric hospital in town but she's free to discharge herself, *al hum dil'Allah*. I am going to visit her, maybe take her home, tonight. But it seems strange, don't you think?' she wondered, flashing a glance back at me as we walked.

'Well, I suppose if the Western press is interested and what with the election . . . They probably want to seem reasonable for a bit until afterwards.' I guessed. I mean, let's face it, the *Chronicle* wouldn't be running this if there weren't elections coming up. Basically, the British line is that Egypt is essentially friendly. The country wants to remain secular in an increasingly crazed religious environment, it tolerates Israel and is largely peaceful and a tourist destination for thousands of Brits a year. We are not about to rock the boat, and anyone who tried would have MI6 giving them a bit of a calm sort of a talking to. BUT, the broadsheets don't want to look too wishy washy in their coverage and feel that they at least ought to point out that human rights abuses in Egypt pretty much abound and that the election is likely to be on the dubious side (what with nobody else being allowed to run and all that). So here I am. But make no mistake about it, there will be a big pro-Egypt op-ed piece in the comment pages on the day my Jamila piece goes in. An op-ed basically dictated by the Foreign Office. I mean, we all love democracy, we do. But don't let's disappear up our own arses about it or anything.

Jamila looked incredibly nervous. Prison gives people an edge. You always see it. She had that horrible shaky thing that recently-released people have, even when it's only been a day or two. As though their freedom is an illusion, they are being followed and might be right back inside in a second. Which here, and in a lot of other places, is a perfectly rational concern.

'I know,' she said. 'I know. But it was so sudden. They wanted the name and address of everyone at my demonstrations. They had photographs. And then – pouf! Bye bye. Go home. We don't mind any more.'

I agreed with her but I agreed with myself too. They would probably pick her up again in a couple of weeks, unless . . .

'You should vote for the President and write a piece for your student newspaper about how great he is and how your experience has changed you,' I said, just thinking aloud really as she shot ahead of me, throwing up the dust with her soft shoes. I was pretty much surrounded by children all the way, laughing and grinning and wanting to touch my hair. I stamped my cigarette out in the sand and noticed that she had stopped walking and was staring at me, her whole face pink with rage and incomprehension.

'I thought you were a journalist! I thought you were on the side of truth!'

She meant it too. Oops. I mean, fair point.

'I am! I am!' I said, playing for time, waiting for an argument of the utmost sincerity to lurch into my booze-addled brain. 'I just thought you might want to be left alone for a bit . . . to . . .'

A man in blue swimming-pool shoes, shiny cheap trousers and a T-shirt offered me meat in a pitta bread wrapped up in foil from some kind of thermossy bag he was carrying on his shoulder. He was smoking a cigarette without moving it from his mouth. His teeth were all dark dark brown. I took it and gave him ten pounds. Jamila was too angry to comment. Let me get ripped off with amoebas into the bargain seemed to be her view.

'Faith. I wanted to have a serious conversation with you. I wanted to learn about democratic institutions, about how to change my country, what to do next. I did not expect to meet with this level of cynicism. I want to show you something,' she said, spinning round the edge of a very ornate iron tomb-gate and going back, I thought, though I couldn't be at all sure, the way we'd come.

My kebab was actually quite good and I followed Jamila meekly, trying to shoo the children away without being mean, feeling slightly ashamed but also slightly defensive. It was just because she was so young. I wouldn't want Ben to risk himself for a principle. I would, if this ever cropped up, try to move him somewhere where he wouldn't need the principles, where his idealistic views were standard enough not to bother commenting on unless you were a real zealot. Perhaps I should try and get Jamila a job on the *Chronicle* in London? No, she's too high-minded. Page after page of first-person pieces by smiling women who realise they should just stay home with the kids and obey their husband, long articles about face creams, exfoliation and being too fat or too thin, debate about plastic surgery – in a NEWSPAPER. It would just depress her. And that's never mind the rabid anti-immigration drivel, the insidious quiet serpent of anti-semitism (well, maybe that wouldn't bother her so much) and the endless coverage of the royal family.

So, these are the things I was thinking as we wove our way back through the labyrinthine City of the Dead, the golden stone and sand going white in the sunlight. I hardly noticed where we were when she picked up her skirt and tripped softly up the steps to the Ibn Talun mosque. My thoughts until now had been loud, loud enough to drown out the noise of the traffic and the crowds of people, the honking horns and tinny music coming out of everywhere.

But suddenly the air around me was absolutely silent and still and the sound of my boots on the cool stone offensively loud. My brain shushed itself and spoke in a whisper, watching Jamila negotiate a price with the black-swathed old man sitting on the floor by the entrance, who was guarding a heap of felt slippers and pieces of black material for putting on the heads of infidel ladies. He smiled a couple of teeth and gestured at me, clearly demanding an awful lot more money if that blonde frizzy person was coming in too. Stupidly, I handed him a couple of crumpled notes and Jamila looked cross but he looked delighted. Never mind the headdress, *habibti*.

We put our slippers on and walked into the wide, dark cloister. The cloister, high-ceilinged and broad enough for a grand procession, is a square around the central courtyard which, here, is open air, shimmering in the heat. Once, the whole population of Cairo could gather here to pray and it was built to accommodate them all. Now you'd be lucky to cram the population of the Nile Hilton in. And the astonishing thing is how empty and how far away from modern Cairo it seems here, so timeless and mute. I would maybe have asked Jamila what the hell we were doing here (I wasn't in Egypt to see the bloody sights) but I was so completely awestricken by the beauty and peace of it all that I didn't have any questions for the minute.

We crept round, absorbing the silence, our shoes shuffling on the marble and the row of lamps, dangling low from the vaulted ceiling, swung in the slight breeze, making them look eerie, as though pushed by ghosts. I wished I could have shown Ben, but banished the thought as quickly as it came. Missing people is useless and painful – I had spent my whole life learning that.

Jamila led me up a winding staircase through a gate towards the back of the mosque and I realised we were climbing the muezzin's tower. And it was there, in the cold stone corridor, reaching for the heavens that, alone and in absolute quiet, Jamila turned to face me and took her clothes off, dropping them all defiantly to the floor.

Eyes as wide as saucers I coughed and took a deep breath, all ready with my rather well-worn speech about how I have a boyfriend and am not really ready for a relationship. The most famous lesbian in the business once came up to my room at the Mille Collines in Kigali, pissed as anything, and let her robe drop from her shoulders. I was so stunned that she'd put my hand on her right breast before I could start explaining that, attractive though she was blah blah blah. In fact I was in there with Eden, one of our first nights together, wild and passionate and extremely heterosexual. Those were the days . . . Okay! Matter in hand.

'Umm, Jamila.'

But, of course, of course, I was being stupid. She wasn't making a pass at me. And if she had wanted to this would hardly have been the location for it. Though she was so utterly beautiful that if I was to take anybody up on this kind of offer it might have been her. But that wasn't it at all. She was showing me something that the gloom had momentarily stopped me from seeing. My eyes adjusted quickly. She had been horrifically tortured, leaving just hands, feet, face and neck free of injury. A lot of the wounds (electric cable lashes?) were still open, seeping. The bruises covered basically her whole body though they'd concentrated, hadn't they, on her breasts. Punishment for being female an added extra. Cigarette burns? It looked like it.

I put my hand over my mouth and shook my head, tears stinging my eyes. But I didn't cry. I owed her that. Who was I to be crying when my body was all intact?

'Oh God. Jamila. You need to be in hospital, love. We should get this seen to—'

Jamila laughed. Not a real laugh. More a sort of sound denoting absurd naivety in the laughed at.

She started to put her clothes back on.

'But they let you out,' I whispered.

'Yes, Faith. They released me. And they have released Karima too. They will wait to see how we vote, if we write articles in praise of the regime that showed us how to behave in future,' she hissed, spitting at the floor in front of my feet, her face streaming with the tears that she must have worked so hard, been so brave, to keep in the whole time that they were doing this.

Dressed again, but dishevelled, she collapsed onto the narrow step, her face in her hands. I sat down next to her, the pair of us blocking the ancient coiling corridor, and put my arm round her shoulders. She flinched with pain and I took it away again, holding her hand instead. I kissed her knuckles and gripped tighter.

'Jamila, listen. I'm sorry. I didn't mean you should compromise your values. You are a shining light, a fire of goodness. Justice. I meant it as a mother. I'm a mother, you see. It sparks off these instincts, motherhood, just to keep vulnerable people safe. It's what we do. I'm sorry, I truly am. I wasn't trying to make you stop fighting. I was just doing what any mother would do, saying what we say.'

She sobbed into her hands.

'Nothing's going to change,' she said. 'Nothing is ever going to change.'

I wanted a cigarette but it didn't seem like the moment.

'Sweetheart. Nothing's going to change today. Or tomorrow. But there are enough of you. You'll keep going. These nasty regimes . . . they don't last forever. Something snaps in the end. You keep putting a chisel into the chink and eventually, eventually the whole thing comes tumbling down. You know that really, or you wouldn't be fighting now.'

And she looked up at me with such big black sad eyes, so hopeful, checking that I meant what I said, that I was sincere, that I smiled and, for a brief moment, I almost believed myself.

'Come on. Let's go,' I said. 'Don't we have to pick Karima up?'

And now she was following me. The person perceived to have the answers always out in front. The person with the questions struggling to keep up. Though she was now obviously a lot chirpier. Almost oddly so – a bounce in her step that hadn't been there before. There was a moment, looking for a cab on one of those streets with shops behind half-closed corrugated iron blinds, vaguely food-related smells coming out of them, when a black Mercedes sped round a narrow corner and seemed to be coming straight for us. I pushed Jamila into a stinking doorway and leapt in after her, frightening a semi-naked toddler on a plastic trike. The car scraped a wing against the wall and roared off. An accident. Probably. Or not. There are a lot of traffic accidents in Cairo. I didn't want to get paranoid. We both of us kept our thoughts on this to ourselves.

Back in a chugging smoke-filled taxi, Jamila made a few calls on her mobile phone, her face lighting up when a friend answered, turning to a glower for her explanation, the politics, then softening for the agreement of the arrangement and a goodbye. Hey, my Arabic's crap so I have to look at the other stuff. She had a little beaded tag on her phone with a Japanese pig thing dangling off it. Girlish and sweet, not the sort of possession a torture victim would have. When she'd finished, she snapped the phone back into her blue leather bag (worn with the strap across her chest in the least alluring way possible) and said something to the driver.

'I'm going home. Sabah's going to get Karima. I need to sleep,' she said.

'I'll need pictures of you, Jamila,' I told her, drawing deeply on my cigarette.

A row was going on in front of us: a crash, the men crowding round, smoking, shouting. It was hot, the tall palm trees providing zero shade and just looking dusty really. The dust seemed to come not only from the desert sand and the pollution, but to crumble away from all the grey concrete buildings too.

She nodded. This was not a small thing for her as a woman. But she knew what she had to do.

And speaking of pictures, there he was, the bastard, right in the lobby of the Nile Hilton just by the entrance to the Belgian pub (no, really). God, I was pleased to see him.

'Don! Don!' I squealed, the metal detector wailing behind me, nobody paying it the remotest bit of attention (it's my belt, always does it). I jumped up and kissed him.

'Where've you been? I've got so much to—'

'Hey, steady on. I'm a married man you know, Eff Zed. This python's out of bounds!' he said, feeling for his fags.

'In your dreams, McCaughrean. Listen,' I said, not knowing whether to tell him about Alex's weirdness or Jamila first. I went with the easier subject. 'You know Jamila who got arrested?'

''Course. Babealicious.'

'Yeah. Well. Tortured babe in police cell. They just turfed her out today. The first thing she did was call me. Brave really. Very brave. Anyway, you need to get some shots. It's nasty.'

Don looked upset.

'Cunts,' he said.

'The world over.' I nodded, and we went into the bar where, as it turned out, the belly dancer from the river boat was sitting in front of her Coke and Don's pint of bitter. He'd obviously been out to the loo or something.

'Oh. Hi,' I said, putting my hand out. 'I'm Faith.'

'Dahlia,' she smiled. She was wearing a lot of make-up. Like, a lot. And a very tight green top and jeans. She looked nice and I was immediately pissed off with Don for dicking her around – my instant assumption. When her phone chimed, a funny little belly dancing tune, she apologised and stepped outside into the brighter and even more air-conditioned bit of the hotel to take the call.

'Don! What the FUCK are you playing at?!' I asked him.

Don shrugged his shoulders and took a huge slurp of his pint, wiping his mouth afterwards.

'They're real, you know. Totally fucking one hundred per cent bona fide God-given tit.'

This, he seemed to feel, entirely explained his obvious infidelity in Cairo, thousands of miles away from his wife and son. His second wife and third son.

'Yeah, but Don . . .'

Don coughed. 'Eff Zed. If you're about to spin me some

66

sanctimonious drivel about fidelity in marriage and conjugal duty then you'd better check your fucking credentials first because unless you're Mother fucking Theresa you haven't got a leg to stand on. I like her, okay? And there aren't many people who are willing to put up with this rolling around on top of them if you know what I mean,' he said, patting his blancmange belly and making it wobble on purpose.

'Oh. I see,' I said. Irina wouldn't sleep with him any more. Well, they wouldn't be the first couple it's happened to. I held my hands up, palms out. 'Hey. Who am I to judge?'

'Who indeed,' Don agreed. 'Anyway, I'm doing a whole thing for the *Mail on Sunday* mag about her. She's famous here.'

'What's she doing dancing the river boats then?'

'Ah ha! Well, she was covering for a mate. Anyone could see she's a cut above.'

'Right, Don.' I laughed. Someone had put Cher on the juke box. 'If I Could Turn Back Time'. It was like being in Benidorm in here.

'Hold up a second, Donski. Didn't we just do that very piece for *C2*?'

'And?'

'Oh, nothing.'

Dahlia came back with a wiggle and a smirk.

'What were you saying?' I asked Don, trying to change the subject.

'Whatever he's saying, don't listen to it, my darling!' Dahlia gurgled, plumping herself back down next to Don and biting his ear lobe. No, I swear. I was there. She bit it. I could see that talking about Alex was going to have to wait for Don's hard-on to subside.

'Have you got to work?' Don looked at her pleadingly, both of them disappearing into a bleary-eyed, wet-lipped private world of flesh and emotion as though I wasn't there at all.

'I cancelled them for you, big boy.' She laughed, squeezing his leg and letting the tip of her long red nail brush the denim by his groin as she drew her hand away.

So, maybe he wasn't being an idiot at any rate then. Knew her game full well. Just lonely and taking what he could get.

Chapter Six

Much though I would have liked to wallow in Don McCaughrean's love life I was, in the way of these things, about to find myself back in London

'Guess who?' Tamsin said. I could hear her sucking on her nicotine-replacement thing. Well, I sneer. But I will probably end up with the same dummy myself.

'Good evening, Tamsin,' I said.

'Yeltsin's dead,' she hissed. Whoah. She's as sharp as a tack. 'Do you want to do the obit or the op-ed? Duffy's champing at the bit for the op-ed because he knows Berezovsky, but it smacks of bias to Sam. What do you think?'

Think? Think! I never do anything of the kind.

'Umm. I'll do the opinion. You can use the obituary I did five years ago for the front, can't you? It's on file.'

'Yes. I KNOW, Zanetti, thank you very much. But it needs something at the top about the timing – you know, the father of Russian democracy dies along with democracy itself as his successor, once the loyal servant of his bear-like master . . .'

'Yup. Yup. Got it. Okay. Please stop. If you could write you wouldn't be editing.'

She laughed. 'Oh. And Cairo. McCaughrean still hasn't wired the torture pix – has he actually taken them? – and News Overview want to do a spread on it for Saturday. You know, empowered Egyptian women. Look where it gets them. That type of crap. You need to be here. We can get you on the flight in two hours. Can you make it?'

'Don't be ridiculous. There must be something interesting happening somewhere in the world? Surely. Anyway,' I quipped, 'I fancy some holiday.'

'Apparently there isn't. Anyway, it's coming out of the Overview budget. Holiday?' Now she was almost beside herself with laughter. The very concept of time off just bewilderingly, side-splittingly funny.

'But . . .'

'But I'm hanging up now, Zanetti. Go and have a doughnut.'

I phoned Eden immediately and tried to churn the relevant bits of my brain into emotional action. I would be holding my boy in a few hours.

In the end I waited for Ben and Eden at Heathrow, sitting in the Costa Coffee with my third double espresso, rapping my fingers on the table and checking the arrivals sign every four seconds like a maniac, even though I knew what time they were supposed to be landing and had already asked twice if the plane was going to be delayed.

'No, madam.'

'All right. All right. Keep your hair on. Only asking.'

I was focused and nearly light-hearted, could already smell my little boy's fat tummy and feel his soft doughyness under my fingers.

When they finally came round the corner I was leaning over as far as I could so that they wouldn't be visible for more than a millionth of a second before I saw them. Ben was asleep on Eden's shoulder and I ran round the crowds to snatch my son out of his arms and press my face against his hot red cheek. Eden put his bag down on the floor and I squeezed Ben so tight that he woke up.

'Mama,' he said, droopy-eyed and still dreaming.

'Hi, baby,' I whispered. 'Hello, little man.'

He reached his arms round my neck and smiled.

'Nightmare of a flight. Bloke over the aisle throwing up all the way.'

'Oh God,' I said, kissing Eden on the cheek over Ben's head. He smells of the sea does Eden Jones. I shut my eyes and didn't let myself wonder what had happened or what we were playing at.

There's a line from a film when a wife leaves her husband saying, 'I don't want to be married any more.' And he says to his friend, 'Like it's the institution or something!'

But in our case, I think perhaps it is the institution.

'Listen,' Eden said, running his fingers through his hair (Eden has very tanned forearms, the hairs bleached in the sun) and then bending down and getting Ben's little Thomas the Tank Engine suitcase out of his own big brown one. 'I've got to run. My flight's in forty-five minutes and Christ knows how you get over to Terminal 3 from here.'

'Oh! Where are you going? There's a train, I think. You going straight back?'

'No. Khartoum. Then on to Darfour. Big *New Yorker* thing.'

'Fantastic.'

'Have you ever BEEN to Khartoum?'

'Fair point. But how are the people of East Coast America going to manage without your insightfulissimo informazione?'

71

'I wrote two in advance, baby!' he said, punching the air in mock triumph.

So he kissed Ben on the top of the head and held his little hand for a bit before disappearing, loping into the crowds with his bag slung over his shoulder, leaving us standing there, paralysed for a second by sudden loss, people moving around us, announcements being made, our stuff at our feet. It flickered unpleasantly through my mind that perhaps Eden feels like this when I leave, too. I shook the thought out of my brain but still it took me a second to heave my armour on, having leant, as I always do, on Eden for the minutes that he was there. There are not many people I can do that with. Shut my eyes. Well, one actually and he was on his way to Terminal 3.

'Come on then, boy. Let's get you home. Kristy said she'd cleaned the flat and left us eggs for tea,' I told him, marching off with the bags towards the relative home of the taxi stand, with its comforting chugging line of beetly black cabs, their orange lights so oddly English, their contours so reassuring. Kristy is the babysitter. One day Ben can tell his shrink how I abandoned him for my job and left him to drag himself up in the cruel cruel world.

Look: partly, I know I'd go insane (more insane) and take it out on him if I couldn't work. And, partly, I've seen children who have a hard life. He is not one of them. Anyway, as far as I know they don't do twelve-step programmes for war correspondents. And the alcoholics' one doesn't seem to have quite cut it either. Though I only actually got to step three: We make a decision to turn our will and our lives over to the care of God as we understood him. What the hell has THAT got to do with a gin martini up with a twist?

Kristy has 'Serendipity' tattooed on to her shoulder and she eats three Flakes a day.

72

'Kisty,' Ben murmured and I cuddled him all the way home.

I kept him in bed with me all night, occasionally reaching over to stroke his hot cheek and to smell his breath, and, in the morning, I got a mini cab that smelt of Magic Tree into Canary Wharf to face Tamsin. Everyone looked pale and overweight, especially Dave on Home News who looks as if he died years ago.

'All right, Eff Zed,' he croaked without looking up from the glow of his screen.

'Looking as foxy as ever, Dave,' I said, walking past, hoping that some part of him might believe me. The whole paper was in a Yeltsin frenzy, mostly looking for the pictures of when he was embarrassingly drunk, as if that was his legacy. Even the flooding up north was being knocked off the front, and you know how much the British papers enjoy a flood. I had been put, essentially, in charge of Boris Nikolaevich coverage, and I can't deny that I enjoyed the power rush. Pathetic really, but status anxiety is a common feature of motherhood. Here was my life back at last. When we'd put the paper to bed the editor brought a case of champagne out for the newsroom (which, with Sam Fischer, is really saying something) and, not having eaten all day, we were all pissed immediately.

So, basically, Kristy already had her duffle coat on and her rucksack on her back when I ran into the flat at eight-thirty. She hates it when I'm late.

Ben was sitting on the floor with two handfuls of banana, laughing.

I got him to sleep in his cot, singing a sad Russian song about a coachman dying on the steppe (most Russian songs are on this theme). A drunk couple was arguing in the street outside: she was crying, shouting, he was telling her to be quiet, shouting even louder. But Ben fell asleep half-smiling, curly head on his pillow.

I was just considering resigning from the paper altogether and taking him off to run a mother-and-son coffee stall on the beach in Negril when the doorbell rang. I padded off to the intercom in pants and a T-shirt, picked up the receiver and heard a very familiar voice, all jaunty and sunny morningish, though it was now officially late evening.

'Khai! Can I come in?'

'Who is this?' I said, joking. I know, I know. Freud. Did he live for nothing? Nothing is 'only' a joke. Though I'd thought he was a few time zones away I knew perfectly well who it was.

Alex was crestfallen and I immediately felt bad.

'Umm. It's me. Alex.' I could hear the noise of the street, people coming out of and going into restaurants, the traffic and the church bells from up the hill. Hadn't I said goodbye in Cairo yesterday? And I'd sure as hell meant it. I do not liked being stalked to my door. I do not find it charming and impulsive. I find it pushy and oppressive. And how did he find out where my front door even was?

'Sorry. I recognised your voice. I was . . . joking. Well. Yes. Okay. Come up,' I told him and buzzed him in. I didn't want him to come up. I didn't want Ben to meet some bloke I'd slept with twice. And I didn't want Alex to see me in my other personality. But I was hardly going to turn him away since he'd come over and all.

I opened the door to the flat which I'd painted blue after Ben was born. It has a brass lion's-head knocker on it too. Ludicrous but somehow pleasing. So Alex came bounding up the stairs carrying a vast bunch of pink, red, and white roses and a bottle of Pshenichnaya vodka.

'Khai! Khai!' he said, coming in and not seeming to notice

74

my near nudity. I went away and put on a grey silk kimono that Eden once pulled out of a suitcase for me with a flourish. Da daaaa! In the old life.

I pulled the curtain to the bedroom across and came into the sitting room, blinking. Alex was peering at my stuff, his whole body taut with energy. He must have been a scary soldier.

'What happened to this?' he asked, picking up a mobile phone that is bent almost in half and slightly burnt-looking.

'It saved my life so I kept it. Shrapnel,' I said. He nodded.

'And this. Israeli, no?'

'Yes! Well noticed. He gave it to me as a souvenir after, well, whatever.'

It was a gun holster. There was a photo of me getting my award off Norman Tebbit (what can I say?) and some empty shell casings, that kind of stuff.

'Ben's asleep. My son,' I said, glancing back towards the bedroom.

'Ah. Right,' he whispered, looking sheepish and apologetic.

'So. Um. This is a surprise,' I added, getting shot glasses shaped like geese (from the Stalin-era Goose factory) and twisting to look at him. A machete from El Salvador hung on the doorframe just above his head. A sword of Damacles, I thought.

'Not good? Sorry. I just, well, I wanted to see you. Do you think I should be an English man and wait a week before I call you? I hear they do this.'

I laughed.

'No. No. I don't think you should be like that! It's just . . . I don't normally . . . And daytime. It just a feels a bit . . . I'm not looking for a boyfriend, Alex.'

'Ah. Yes. Yes. Understand. Understood, I mean.' He was

jittery. He was always jittery, except when he played the piano. His eyes were grey tonight. Strange.

'I've just put an issue to bed about Yeltsin.' I sighed. 'May he rest in peace.' I smiled.

Alex raised his eyebrows, staggered.

'You wrote that he tore Russia apart with brute alcoholism, wrecked the economy and impoverished his people so much that they elected an autocrat to replace him? He did nothing to clean up The Service. Nothing. I warned them . . .'

'Uh. Something like that.' I smiled.

Actually, I'd said he launched democracy and a free market on an admittedly unsuspecting people and that his reputation was damaged only because he refused to consider any kind of censorship (in stark contrast to his murkier successor). And that his only real mistake was to be tolerant of the old KGB people instead of wiping them out as ruthlessly as he wiped out the Communist party and its misguided principles. And now they're back, and Yeltsin's honesty and politics have been diluted by a new tyranny. Blah blah blah. I was sad, if the truth be known (which I try not to allow). I'd met him a few times, showing my Kremlin pass at the gates, awe-stricken at being able to enter (that's what growing up with the iron curtain and the apparent certainty of imminent nuclear holocaust does to you), amazed by the sheer size and enthusiasm of the bloke. I should have put in that thing he said about a man living like a burning flame or whatever it was.

It was only at this point, slapping myself awake with a blink, that I noticed the big gym bag Alex had brought up the stairs with him. In a flash of panic I blushed and gasped in the sudden overwhelming fear that he thought he was going to move in. Toothbrush. Shaving foam. That type of caper. No! Help!

Unfortunately he clocked all this and gave the bag a gentle kick on his way over to put the roses on the table and open the bottle. All my cups and plates and stuff are on shelves above this table and the opposite wall is all books. The shelves were put up by Patrice, an alcoholic friend of mine, so I think they will probably all fall down one day soon.

'A little present for – Ben? Did you say Ben? What is this short for?'

'Well. Benjamin. But we never use it. Little? That doesn't look like a little present.'

Alex was about to comment when Ben himself came toddling out from behind the curtain in his nappy, dragging Mallowy bear, who smells of sick if you ask me. When did he learn to climb out of his cot at night? I smiled at his audacity.

He froze when he saw Alex (Ben, not Mallowy – who continued to dangle), tried to stop dead in his tracks but in fact toppled over backwards to sitting, still staring.

I went over to pick him up.

'Hey, baby. What are you doing awake? This is Alex. He is from Russia. I used to live in Russia when you were in my tummy,' I explained. Ben laughed and Alex waved.

'Come. Come and see,' he said to Ben, so I put him down and let him pootle over to Alex and his big black bag. I love the creases on the back of his knees.

'You want to do the zip?' Alex asked him, showing him where to pull it. I smiled and took a sip of my vodka, raising my glass to Alex in acknowledgment of the toasts we should be making.

'Boris Nikolaevich!' I said and Alex scowled.

'They're sending me back to Cairo,' I said, only admitting it to myself as I said it out loud to him. God, what was I going to do with Ben? Eden was in sodding Darfour. In a flash of maternal madness I had considered taking him with me. But Eden would kill me. Whatever you do, as a woman with a child, you must never mention that you have a child at work. Men can bring in pictures of their babies and show them to everyone as proof that they are secretly nice and caring and everyone gives them extra moral highground points. Women must pretend that the child doesn't exist. It makes people panic and think you are going to want to go part-time.

I was going to have to get Kristy to move in for a bit. Not ideal, but then what is? And, let's face it, she's probably better at it than I am. She seems genuinely not to be bored in the sandpit, she appears to positively enjoy chatting to the other mothers and carers at the drop-in at the community centre (an activity that represents to me the very fiery abyss of hell itself), and as for clapping along and singing 'Wind The Bobbin Up' down at the library's singing and story time, why it is her very life's breath.

I kissed Ben's peachy cheek and sighed.

'The elections. You know. Build up. I don't know why the paper's interested. It's normally all "Why Is Childhood Disappearing?" at the weekend. Or "What Has Happened to the British Countryside?"'

'What has happened to the British countryside?'

'I don't bloody know. Never been there.'

Ben pulled the zip back and shouted, awe stricken, 'Train! Train!'

The present was a bag full of Brio train set pieces, all the wooden track and stations and stuff and millions of little trains and carriages and people, a bit battered but perfect.

Alex took a few pieces of pine track out and ran a small red train along it backwards and forwards. Then he held the train out to Ben who took it and ran it along in the same way, beaming his head off.

78

'God, Alex, that's amazing, thank you so much!' I said. 'It's fantastic. He loves trains. Well that's something for the babysitter to do with him while I'm away.'

In fact I was pissed off. It was an intrusive kind of present. Was he trying to ingratiate himself by being nice to my son? Or was I just being mean? Maybe he had it in his flat for some reason and wanted to get rid of it. A Russian would never admit that, of course. If you give something to a Russian and say you don't want it any more, they will be incredibly insulted. It's only a gift if it's something you DO want. Same with food. An English person would say, 'Oh, have some more. I'll only have to throw it away otherwise.' A Russian would hear, 'The dog's scraps are all that's good enough for you.' You have to say instead, 'I have been cooking for four days especially for you. Please humour me by trying some.' Well, you get the picture.

Together, while I leant my not bony arse against the table and drank my coffee from my 'I Love Intercourse' mug (Intercourse is a town in Pennsylvania. No, I swear), they built a track that ran around the entire room. Maybe I was just irritated that Alex was keeping Ben up at night. Or that he was proving to be a bona fide nice guy. And a very handsome one, I realised I had been avoiding knowing. I am such a sucker for cute. He reminded me of those Soviet posters of square-faced earnest-eyed muscular peasants scything down the wheat or whatever it is, especially when he plays the piano and all the tension disappears from his face.

He seemed to know what I was thinking.

'So. You are not looking for a boyfriend.'

I laughed and shuffled back to actually sit on the table, swinging my bare feet. 'No. It was a fling. Is a fling.'

'A fling?'

'A not serious relationship. Just for fun.'

'Fun,' he said, bemused.

'Yes! It's what we have in the decadent West,' I explained, doing a little upper body dance move in my kimono to demonstrate, shaking my hair.

'Ah. Fun. Excellent.' He beamed. 'Your hair looks like fire round the edges, in the light like that. Not English hair.'

'Not very. No.'

I have a relative from the Italian bit of Switzerland. Perhaps it is an area of the world where they are famed for their blonde afros. I've never looked into it.

I don't suppose they do a strong line in fun up in Semforov 90. Or, actually, they probably do – some kind of backlash. There is definitely a phenomenon, a bit like Don's dead dog test but the opposite, whereby people in the worst places seem the happiest and most fun-loving. You always hear it, don't you? Travellers coming back from Africa or some Central American war-torn hell hole and saying what marvellous, welcoming, hilarious and smiley people they met.

Ben muttered 'fun' to himself and carried on pushing the little trains.

And somehow Alex stayed after Ben had gone back to sleep (made difficult by Alex's 'fun' bedtime impressions of bears and wolves). He made a weird Russian stir fry (you can take the boy out of Semforov 90, but you can't take Semforov 90 out of the boy) and later, much later, he played the piano on my back under the duvet and I was supposed to guess what piece he was playing.

'Umm . . . "Always A Woman to Me"?'

Hysterical laughter.

'Faith Cleopatrovna! *Nyet!* It was Shostakovich, Festive Overture. *Dura!*'

'*Sam durak*,' I said. 'I am Faith Karlovna. Cleopatra is just another name.' It was a pathetic effort to claim some ground back. He wasn't having any of it.

'Okay. Try this!'

He played again.

'The William Tell Overture!' I tried.

This time he laughed so much he cried.

'It was Chopin!' he spluttered, wiping tears from his cheeks.

'Oh.'

And so on.

When Ben woke me up shouting 'Shoaf! Shoaf!' (in reference to the army horses trotting up the hill in threes to be exercised) Alex had gone, leaving a note on the table telling me to meet him at The Ritz before my flight, at midday. I sighed and I kissed my son on the nose and leapt up to look at the parade with him, weighed down with sadness because I knew I was going away again today. And he didn't yet. Strange how quietly a heart can break.

To be honest, I probably wouldn't have seen Alex again, spent the night with him again, if he hadn't forced me to. It was getting too serious too fast and I wasn't interested in anything that might have the end result of his asking me if I'd seen his wallet and genuinely expecting me to produce it for him from whatever hiding place he'd found for it. Isn't that what relationships with the opposite sex eventually are? The person with the vagina ends up being the answer to 'Is there any toothpaste?', 'Have we got pistachio nuts?' and 'Where's my wallet?' Never mind 'What's for dinner?', 'Are my shirts ready?' and 'Are the children grown up yet?' if we're getting really old fashioned (though, of course, entirely contemporary for most women in the world). No ta.

Also, I was slightly dreading having to hear about what psychotic mafioso from Novocherkassk was after him and why – I knew that's what our meeting was going to be about. But, let's face it, scoops were thin on the ground. I was basically spending most of my time either in Cairo police stations, sitting in taxis in a traffic jam on a bridge in the astonishing heat, or smoking shishas on the terrace of the Nile Hilton. None of which occupations was really justifying leaving my son behind again with some killer nanny whose whole diet consisted of Cadbury's Flakes. I might as well see if Alex's story was something publishable. It wouldn't be though. They always name names and have zero proof and rich Russians are wildly litigious. I would avoid sexual relations. Must not have sex with handsome Russian man. No. No. No.

I hugged the breath out of Ben and left Kristy in the doorway, holding him while he tried to pull her earrings out, running down to my cab in the kind of chaotic rush that might distract from the sadness.

'Bye, baby!' I shouted back up, as though it was the most normal thing in the world to be flying away again, the words 'chronic separation anxiety' flying round my head as a portent of my boy's future emotional state. Never mind my own, for God's sake.

I do love The Ritz. My boots sank into the deep carpet and a footman in a top hat bowed his head as I swept through the revolving doors. Inside, amid the frenzy of pink and gold décor, a pianist in tails was playing 'Fly Me To The Moon'. A table of middle-aged women were drinking champagne, laughing and picking tiny but elaborate cakes off a heavy silver stand on their white-clothed table. A handsome elderly businessman sat on a gold chaise longue drinking tea out of a deep turquoise cup and the carefully constructed mood of elegant and timeless serenity swept over me.

'Hiya, gorgeous,' I said, slumping down across a low table from Alex who sat, nervously, on the edge of a delicate arm chair scanning the room.

I leant over and kissed him on the cheek three times in Russo/Arab fashion. Don once told a young journalist who'd gone to meet Boris Yeltsin that the protocol was to hug him and kiss him three times. Apparently Yeltsin took it in his stride. It was not, incidentally, the protocol. Nuh uh.

Though it was with Arafat in his day. He had wet lips and smelt of a thousand aftershaves.

'It's goat, Eff Zed,' Don insisted. It wasn't.

'The net is closing around me,' Alex sighed, not seeming to notice our surroundings.

'It is?' I said, and I picked the tiny drinks menu up.

'Can I get you anything, madam?' The waiter bowed.

'I'd love a vodka. Neat,' I said. His face registered no surprise.

'Of course, madam,' he replied, backing away.

'Faith. This is serious. Switch your tape recorder on,' Alex said, keeping his eyes down, resolved to tell me everything.

I choked on my smile. Tape recorder? I don't walk around like an intrepid investigative reporter in a film. You know, scribbling in my note pad. Little arrows pointing to the top of the page where I have written 'CIA? White House!?' Yup, I have discovered that the octopus tentacles of what seemed like a simple robbery and accidental death actually lead all the way to the top.

'Alex. I didn't bring a tape recorder. I have a good memory,' I said. It's true.

Okay. Okay. I was being an arsehole. I borrowed a biro off the waiter ('Let me just fetch one' he said, and came back

83

with it laid out on a starched napkin on a silver tray – a Bic biro) and I wrote on the back and front of three old travel schedule print-outs, a torn apart cigarette packet, my boarding card and, eventually, the bill.

Alex talked. And talked. And talked. My eyes widened. And widened. And widened.

Chapter Seven

Alex's unit was stationed in a makeshift barracks just outside of town. It was 1999 but they weren't partying. They had put up the grey tents themselves, arriving at eight o'clock in the evening just as the blood-red sun was seeping down behind the mountains, inhospitable mountains silhouetted like craggy looming monsters ready to suck the town whole into their dark throats and bellies as soon as all light was extinguished from the world. Alex hammered huge rusty tent-pegs into dusty barren earth and Misha 'The Owl' stirred plov in an aluminium pot over the gas burner. The URPO commander had got drunk at a brothel in town and was lying on a cot snoring loudly, occasionally whispering 'Nadya! Nadyenka!' Nadyezhda was his wife, raped and murdered by Shumayev, a Chechen warlord whose village had been razed to the ground under the commander's orders two years earlier. The embers glowed for a week, they said. Not that he'd been a nice guy before that, obviously. Shumayev had bided his time before his special trip to Krasnoyarsk. He threw Nadya's naked and twisted body out of his black BMW onto the pavement outside the commander's apartment with a note stapled to the hand. 'To the man who raped my home-land. Thank you.' The commander, who had been on compassionate leave, begged to be posted back to Chechnya. His wish was the authorities' command. Finally, someone who had seen the Chechen terrorists for the scumbags they are, was the thinking. It was very common. To let people settle personal vendettas. They were unlikely to have crises of conscience, you see.

In fact, as I dimly remembered from the Al Jazeera thing we were on together, Alex wasn't in the army, he'd corrected her, though he did go to a military academy. He was trans-ferred, for single-minded devotion rather than brilliance, to counter-terrorism, trying to break up organised crime gangs. Dangerous stuff. Serious stuff. I mean, would you want to find the former Soviet Union's illegal arms, drugs and women dealers and give them the sort of ticking off they might understand? No, you wouldn't. This was the kind of work that requires a man to be brave and blinkered. He was serving his country and, apparently, serving it well. He ended up a senior player in a division of the FSB (which used to be called the KGB after it wasn't called the NKVD any more, but, interestingly, Russians now find themselves accidentally saying KGB again. Same old same old) and to a large extent it's a hit squad. Tough guys with tough-guy rules of their own.

Tonight the commander was in no fit state. Alex, the quiet guy, effectively took over: receiving the orders from Moscow, setting up camp, boosting his men's morale with beer and food, talking about girls. Or trying to. That night, as he hammered, he could smell the fat from the pieces of lamb frying, was irritated by the noise of the spoon in the pot, longed to press a woman's body against him, his wife's or somebody else's. Sometimes it stops mattering. He sipped watery beer from his tin mug and got on with the job, ignoring the rumbling of his stomach and the pounding in his skull. He knew what they were here for and he was looking forward to it, proud of his role in keeping his country safe, just like his dad had done, though in a different way.

When the order came through his men were asleep or unconscious, their wiry blankets not much protection against the night cold. Two of them, The Owl and Danilenko, he had been at the Academy with. In the days when he still played the piano, Danilenko had still played the violin. But they had done things together that might make the blood of weaker men curdle. When these *gady* are kidnapping Russian children somebody has to show them who's boss. It's just that sometimes it's quite hard to know exactly who IS boss, if you know what I mean. But it's a question of . . . well . . . honour, dignity. All those things.

Later, I looked back at my notes from that evening and was stunned to find that I'd actually written down those words. Those very words, before anything had even happened.

The other boys in his unit were younger. Alex tried not to think about their mothers, how they would weep for their shivering sons in a hostile land. Denisov, for example, was only seventeen. Shouldn't really be here if you asked him. They don't normally take recruits. Too volatile. Alex himself had almost wept after Denisov's hazing. Deny rumours of initiation if civilians ask. They don't understand. And Alex, he knew not to interfere. Survive and you would become a man – one of the team. Die, desert, disintegrate in the head and you weren't fit for the job. It's as simple as that.

He woke the boys up and they loaded the boxes with the sacks of hexogen in them onto the back of the truck, a civilian truck that a farmer had delivered with a nod. He'd been well paid, Alex knew. And perhaps he would be killed later.

They worked like that, though Alex had chosen not to notice it at the time. Civilian clothes, of course. Turn the headlights off at a distance, keep quiet, don't speak Russian. Don't speak at all. He was doing it for the commander. In a couple of hours' time Shumayev would be shredded flesh spattered about in the rubble of his apartment. And good riddance.

Did it seem odd now? Was this the kind of thing they were often asked to do? Of course. It's what they were trained for. Not like this usually. They usually needed to get information as well. Bring them in. For a chat. Well, you know. And it was Denisov's turn. He would have enjoyed laying into someone else. He deserved it. Earning his wings. Spurs. Whatever.

I understood. It made my toes clench in my boots.

Well, perhaps it seemed odd and perhaps it didn't, Alex reflected. He was a different person before Allah had shown him the way, before his enlightenment. He knew this sounded trite perhaps, to the non-believer, but it was what it was. There is no denying the truth when it is laid before you, he said. He had been trained not to think, not to ask. It is important to remember that KGB meant something different in Russia to what it means in the West. In Russia, mothers and fathers were proud when their sons joined the KGB. They showed off to their friends, had people over for vodka and zakuski with every promotion.

And don't forget he had had a Soviet childhood. He had been raised to believe that there were wolves at his country's door, that the army – the *spetz sluzhby*, the special services – were what kept Russia safe. The children watching Cheburashka in their pyjamas and night dresses, drinking sweet tea with their mothers before being tucked in to a sweet lullaby. They wouldn't be able to do that without Alex standing vigilant at the country's door. He had believed that. He had believed a lot of things.

So, they lifted the explosives into the trucks, two men to each box, the wooden crates creaking as they hit the floor of the vehicle. Denisov had to be shouted at for smoking, exhaling dragon's breath in the night air.

'Do you want to blow yourself up, idiot!' Alex had shouted.

The others laughed.

'Do you want a blow job, idiot?'

Alex did not want to wonder if they had raped him. It was not impossible. Though when he was that age it had been a beating, nothing sexual. A euphemistic word for it: beating. But it was a long time ago. And it had made him the man he was. After the army hospital. Out in Astrakhan it was. A long time ago now.

They drove through the dark, along potholed dirt roads into town and then down potholed tarmac roads, ignoring the traffic signals that flashed for no one, the shops dark and shut, stalls cleared away, the brooding mountains waiting silently in the night. When they'd found the building in the maze of grim concrete high-rises, the same from Moscow to Magadan, he told the guys to get the explosives out and then go back to base. He would do the rest, him and Denisov. He could tell from the way Denisov stood up straighter that he was pleased, honoured. Well, it was his turn. They kicked open the door to the cellar – it had already been unlocked by the advance team, whoever they were. Deniability was important. Anonymity key. The less you know the better. It took twenty minutes, sweating into the wool of their balaclavas, the sweat freezing in the night air, to get all the boxes into the cellar. Didn't he realise that the whole building would go up? That there was no way such an enormous amount of firepower was going to be isolated to the one apartment above that particular corner of the cellar? Well, didn't he? Surely that would be more of a grenade-through-the-bedroom-window job, an approach popular country-wide?

It honestly wasn't a concern. The operation had been planned by others and he and Denisov were there to carry it out. The target was Shumayev. What else did he need to know? Was I imagining some other world in which he, Alex, could have thought, 'Ooh. This seems a bit on the excessive side. Perhaps civilians will be hurt.' And then he could have phoned his bosses in Moscow and expressed his concerns. And they would be sympathetic, a little taken aback. 'Oh. Well, we'll look into it. You might be right. Perhaps better hold off until we've made absolutely sure . . .'

This was a fantasy world. Not somewhere Alex had ever been. Not quite yet, at any rate.

He tipped petrol over the boxes, just to be on the safe side (ha!) sloshing it randomly in the dark. He hated the smell. He positioned the fuse and dragged it out of the metal doors. Denisov lit it and they ran, straight up the main road, their boots pounding, their throats constricting. They must have run for more than five minutes, fit men running as fast as they could. But even so they were flattened, winded, by the force of the explosion, the burning air pouring into their mouths, their cheeks pressed to the road.

'*Pizdyets*,' Denisov shouted, staggering to his feet along with Alex, continuing to run as the sky flashed orange and smoke billowed into the atmosphere.

And it was then. It was then Alex realised that something was not right. Not before, but now. His mind started whirring with the inconsistencies. Why weren't they bringing Shumayev in for questioning? Why had they blown up the whole godforgotten building? Why did he feel so alone?

And that's when, seemingly out of nowhere, a car skidded round a corner, four policeman leapt out shouting in a language he didn't know but could understand perfectly. It wasn't hard to guess what they were yelling and he wasn't about to get himself arrested. He already knew, in a flash, that he would be left to rot, his existence denied, the operation passed off as a rogue revenge thing plotted by a unit run by a damaged madman. THAT's why they'd put the commander back on the job. Of course it was. And what had Shumayev really done? I mean, what that anybody but the commander would care about? Stopped paying them for overlooking the drugs business? Threatened to grass about the brothels to a foreign journalist? Who knew. So Alex stopped in his tracks and began to raise his hands above his head. Then, as quick as he'd been trained, he pulled out his weapon and shot all four of them in the legs before diving into the grass at the side of the road, rolling as far as he could, crawling in filth. He'd seen Denisov go down. The guy on the right, the last to get out of the car, had pumped a round straight into Denisov's head as his knee caps exploded.

It was nearly dawn when he got back to the camp, muddied and wild-eyed, half expecting them all to have left in the night. The commander, in full uniform – smart, sober – on the phone, looked surprised. Too surprised. Had he really been so drunk the night before? Alex swallowed the knowledge that crept from his stomach to his brain like a worm. But the pair composed themselves quickly and the commander spoke as though he spoke the truth. As though nothing untoward had happened.

'Some cunts blew up an apartment block in town last night. Chechen terrorist scum. Shumayev and his men were seen leaving. 328 dead. A lot of kids. *Spets sluzhby* got straight to the scene, as you know. Well done with that.'

At this point he actually looked Alex in the eye.

'Big firefight. One of ours killed. Poor Denisov. So today we round up the bastard perpetrators, get a confession. Five of them. Must have been at least five of them. Get confessions and, er, head back to Moscow.'

Alex was finding it difficult to breathe.

'Shumayev?' he managed.

'Who?' the commander wanted to know.

Perhaps the words hadn't come out.

'Is Shumayev dead?' he asked.

'He will be by this afternoon, *golubchik*. I'd let you do it but I think the pleasure's going to be all mine.'

Now, it's not nice. Certainly not. But it happens, of course. The people who spot it are dismissed as conspiracy theorists. The people who prove it are shot in the stairwell to their apartments, their books published posthumously, their reputation besmirched from on high. What does not happen, however, what does not happen is this; the people involved in special operations themselves do not start complaining publicly. They do not go to their superiors and voice their worries about internal corruption. They do not name names. And they do not, not ever, talk to the press about it. These, the above, were Alex's mistakes.

'You fucking what?' I asked, looking up. 'You went and moaned about having to blow up a block of flats full of kids? To whom?'

Alex laughed. Though it wasn't the kind of laugh I've ever heard before. It didn't denote amusement, or joy, or anything.

'I know how it sounds, Faith. I'm not an idiot. But I used to be. I believed in the service. I thought the directors would be shocked. I thought it was an organised crime vendetta. I thought the commander had got in too deep. And he did round up the Chechens. He killed Shumayev with a pair of shears. And by the time he did it, it was a fucking mercy, Faith. It was only later, when they invaded again, invaded Chechnya, using the explosion, my explosion, as an excuse that I realised what a moron I'd been.'

My vodka glass was empty. I hadn't noticed it coming and I hadn't noticed myself drink it. The women and the businessman were gone and had been replaced by other groups of people, dressed to come to The Ritz in cashmere and diamonds, polished leather and silk.

'But you COMPLAINED? What did they say?'

I stared at Alex. He looked so different when he was talking like this. A whole other personality, the FSB guy, I suppose.

He did his awful laugh again. 'At first they said they'd look into it. My wife was pleased. Said it was a victory for justice.'

'The Egyptian woman?'

'Eman? No. First wife. A Russian. She died.'

'I see. I'm sorry.'

'Then they charged me with brutality. Put me in the Butyrka—'

'I've been there! I met Jesus there! Seriously, there was this guy, a prisoner, who . . .'

I looked at Alex and I shut up. It is a truly horrible prison. As opposed to what? The nice ones? Well, almost.

'Sorry,' I said.

The charges involved an arrest years ago, a video of Alex punching a tied-up terror suspect in the face. He could have got ten years. Technically.

'But we'd always been separate from the law. The case was absurd. I can tell you now that there hasn't been anyone taken into custody in the Former Soviet Union in the past

93

hundred years who hasn't been punched. I mean, that was the least of it. It's standard.'

I took a deep breath, sat up, puffed my cheeks out, composed myself and exhaled.

'Right,' I said.

'Look. I know now. I've been shown. Islam has shown me what it is to be kind. To be gentle. But all I mean is . . . the case was absurd. Everyone knew it. They were trying to discredit me before the piece came out.'

'The journalist?'

'A good woman. A true woman.'

'A dead woman?'

'Yes.'

Okay, so it wasn't a subtle or a sensitive question. The pianist had stopped playing.

'Alex. If this is true, why are you still alive?'

'Because I defected. Like the ballet dancers used to do. You know? And I have a panic button to the police in my flat in London. And in Cairo too, though, of course, I didn't have time to get to it when I needed it. And because they've, the Russians, the government, they have successfully labelled me as a lunatic. They thought they didn't need to. But now . . .'

I put my pen down and leant my elbows on the table.

'You're Alexander Sorokin?!'

'I was.' He nodded.

'Holy shit.'

I remembered the case. Who didn't? It was so Cold War. This guy charging into the embassy and sitting on the floor in the hallway, refusing to leave. It was a big scandal taking him, too. The Brits were saying publicly that he might be subject to torture and stuff if he went back to Russia. In the end nobody wanted to get all acrimonious so the Russians took a kind of 'Have the nutter if you want him' stance. But I didn't remember him being this cute on the TV. Didn't he have a huge beard? I think so.

'But if they want to kill you now why don't they kill you? No offence, but it wouldn't be hard. Why would they tie you up and cut you a tiny bit? That's hardly even a threat. It's weird.'

Alex sighed and, Russianly, drank the rest of his whisky in one gulp, breathing in deeply afterwards.

'Faith. They are going to kill me. The VKR [the Vneshnaya Kontr-Razvedka – Foreign Counter Intelligence] boys. They dust steering wheels with poison! They spray aerosols that give a man an immediate heart attack! They are toying with me like a cat with a mouse. But nobody believes me. Because they don't hurt me, because they disappear, because I can be dismissed as unstable.'

To be honest, I could see where they were coming from on that score.

'I can't get help. I must just wait. I left my wife, Eman, so that . . .' And he even bothered at this point, after everything he'd said, to glance nervously round the Palm Court and lower his whisper. 'So that they might leave her alone. I made it real. Told her I didn't love her. Got drunk. Slapped her. Walked out. One day she will know. Maybe. Maybe you will tell her.'

'Jesus,' I said. And I meant it. I was beginning to wonder if he might not be telling the fucking truth. Seriously. 'And Cairo?'

'I thought I could hide there. At first. I'm British. Have a passport in my new name. I felt safe there. Settled down. Business is good. A lot of Egyptians investing in Russia. And I work with a Russian with a lot investments here. I help. But now . . .'

'Now?'

'Faith, they are going to kill me. We can be sure of that. I won't be the first. So please. Please tell my story when they do. I will give you everything. Papers, tapes. Everything. The world might believe you.'

Hardly, I thought. I work for the *Chronicle*. It's not what it used to be. But it rides on its old reputation and maybe this time it would live up to it.

'Alex, Sasha – whoever you are – they're not going to kill you. Let's not let them. We'll think of something.'

Clutching at straws, well, sure. But it would have been even weirder, I think, to say, 'Oh, okay then.'

Alex shook his head and smiled at my naivety, as though faintly amused. He said he had more meetings the next day in Cairo. He was flying Egypt Air. The Russians were in town with security questions and answers and he seemed almost pleased.

'Danilenko's over to set some stuff up.'

'Danilenko from the operation?' I asked amazed, I suppose, that he was real.

'*Da*. Good guy. Solid guy. Demobilised now but still sniffing around for them, I reckon. Wants me to come in on a big oil thing with a double cut. The British oil people pay us to dish dirt on the Georgians and the Georgians pay us to say they're good guys. Get it?'

Well, I kind of got it. I believe we call it due diligence, one part of it at any rate. But back in the real world my taxi to the airport was waiting.

Chapter Eight

On the plane I think I started to realise what these Rachmaninov-playing hands had done. He had touched me gently, but that's not how he touched everyone. I imagined his flayed knuckles, the muscles twitching in his jaw. All that. Did he not hear the screams? Did he go into a deaf and blind zone that enabled him to do the job? Or did he like the screams, the power? He seemed so incapable of cruelty in this new personality, the Alex personality. But, I suppose, people do have a catalogue of personalities to choose from and it's just that I hadn't known that one. Though I don't suppose that any of the people who did know it (the living ones, I mean) would be forgetting him any time soon.

I wasn't sure. About any of it. I felt like a snake not quite believing him. But don't get me wrong, I have heard the apartment-block story before and always assumed it was true. But it was different, obviously, talking to the man who physically did it. I had no doubt that someone had. But surely, if he'd subsequently objected, in public, and it was true, he'd already be dead. That was the weird thing. I'd never heard of this cat and mouse thing before. Not very KGB, now or then. I couldn't quite buy it and it cast doubt on the rest, frankly: a certifiable lunatic or an ex-killer turned whistle-blower who's at the top of a KGB hit list? Hmm.

The man sitting next to me had Tourettes and told me that every night before he went to sleep he had to check behind the cupboard for an Italian chef wearing a motorbike helmet. Fifteen times. Drinking, he said, relieved his symptoms.

'Mine too,' I said, and we laughed and drank vodka miniatures all the way to Cairo.

On the way in through the hot dark, I called Don. He unstuck himself from Dahlia with enormous and, let's face it, understandable reluctance.

'Do you remember the Alexander Sorokin thing?' I asked, gesturing at the driver to turn the radio down.

'What? Where are you?'

'Here. Just coming in from the airport. Do you?'

'Do I what? I thought you were doing Yeltsin in London,' he burbled, confused.

'I was. Now I'm back. Elections, you know? Politics, Don? We cover it?'

'Speak for yourself.'

'Don. Wake up. Alexander Sorokin?'

'Defector? Sure. He lives here, you know. He's all wrapped up with whatsisname. Why?'

Trust Don to be lying in a hotel room pissed with a hooker and knowing more about my stuff than I did. How did he do it?

'Wrapped up with whom, Donald? I mean, apart from me.' I leant forward and got a light off the taxi driver.

'With you? How so, oh fair nymph? Fuck, I can't remember the guy's name. You know. Oligarch. Built all those hotels down at Sharm Al Sheikh.'

'Shit! Of course! Ismaelevich! The scrap metal bloke.'

'That's it. Ismaelevich.' (He pronounced it better than me.) 'Got a house on Bishops Avenue too. Next to Top Rack Mansion. The Russians have being trying to nick him for years but he doesn't stand a chance. All they've got against him is he's Jewish.'

'Well, that pretty much wraps it up in Russia.'

'Yeah. True. He's a sleazeball too though. That privatisation . . .'

'It wasn't illegal.'

'Nothing was illegal then.'

We were getting off the subject. The city swung into sight.

'Anyway, Don. Listen to me. Remember Alex?'

'Fuck me, Zanetti. You're asking me to remember a lot of bloody peeps here. This is the guy you fucked here and then fucked in London?'

'Don, my love, it's your turn of phrase. Yes. That's him. So, it turns out he IS Alexander Sorokin.'

'No way! Serious? That's HUGE! Doesn't look a shit like him though . . . oh, well, maybe. He was all beardy-weirdy when he defected, wasn't he? Could be.'

'He is. I'm telling you. Blew up an apartment block in deepest wherever and then started telling everyone.'

Don burped very loudly. 'He's a nutter though, isn't he? Last I read he was on about the president having sex with sheep or something.'

'Where did you read this?'

'Oh, someone's anti-Kremlin blog thing. Shame really. Because most of it's true, but he pretty much besmirches the name of everyone trying to save democracy in Russia because he's so mad. Alex is Sorokin?' He seemed to be digesting the information. 'Really? He seemed so nice.'

'"Besmirches the name"?!'

'Sorry.' He burped again. 'Translating from the Russian.'

A blog. Of course. Why does McCaughrean know EVERYTHING at the same time as appearing to do NOTHING?

'So what about Ismaelevich?'

'Oh, well, you know, he does this whole anti-government campaign because really he wants to go back to Russia and be president. Being a multi-billionaire with seven hotels full of Russians on the Egyptian coast isn't good enough for him.'

'President?! That's insane. They hate him over there.'

'He is deluded. Not a fucking clue. And Sorokin's in his pocket, basically. Ismaelevich wants an FSB stooge in his camp. Paid to keep coming up with secret-service scandals, keep his ear to the ground with the Russians in London. But seriously . . .'

'Seriously?'

'Well, you know . . .'

'I do not know, Don.'

'Well, you never leave the *spetz sluzhby*, right? It's like the CIA. "I never got the job." Sure you did. But you'll never leave it.'

'God.' I sighed as we hurtled past that white palace that they light up sort of pink at night. 'Did you take the torture shots?'

'Tomorrow,' he whispered.

'Okay. Listen, I'll see you tomorrow. Are you still at the Hilton?'

'*Al hum dil'Allah*,' he said and I heard Dahlia laugh.

*

Talking to Don about Alex made all his intrigue seem, well, more human, perhaps. I spent the night awake, drinking espresso brought up by the pretty after-hours room service boy who smiles like he's about to kiss you, and reading about Alexander Sorokin and Abram Ismaelevich on the Internet. It's so fucking cold inside that you have to open the balcony doors to let some heat in. There were lots of fellucas gleaming on the water and I could hear the music from the river boats on the other side above the screaming grind of the traffic.

So, basically, I was clipping my toe nails at dawn and I'd switched to an Egyptian TV channel in exasperation at the total crapness of the international ones, with all the distracting headlines running along the bottom of the screen all flagged as 'BREAKING NEWS' and yet almost none of them even mildly newsworthy. A weird amount of lipstick worn from Washington to Kuala Lumpa and that terrible terrible intonation started by CNN and copied lilt-for-maddening-lilt by Al Jazeera International, though even audible at the BBC and Sky. Punch a word a line is the rule. A line being as many words as you can say before you take a natural breath. It's about three. But the trouble is that the punched words are very very random. Like in that sentence they might have punched 'trouble' and then 'are'. Oh, and up at the full stop, of course. Why? Why?

Egyptian television seems to have the same problem as Russian television which is an obsession with gore and a surreal amount of access to crime scenes. So the camera is close in on the horrifically bloodied body of a young woman apparently at the bottom of some stairs, letter boxes visible when the camera wobbles showing you that she's clearly in her apartment block. At a glance I'd say a colonial building because there was a pretty wooden banister and a iron-wrought lift

101

going up the central staircase. But you can see we're in Cairo, somehow. The layer of dust, perhaps. Her clothes. She was lying in front of the lift. The cameraman seemed keen to emphasise her slightly open mouth. Because, of course, in a porn-free society this is all the porn they can get. Oh God, please let it not be true what I just thought.

The young reporter was holding a fat microphone and talking into it and I probably wouldn't have paid this any attention at all. I had had a cold shower and was dragging my wet hair back into a ponytail and not looking forward to dragging Don away from his sweetheart, all sticky and sated, to come and take pictures of Jamila. I had thought of ways to cover her up in one place while exposing her in another, of trying to relax her. Then I needed to get in to see Karima El-Baz too, though I didn't imagine that would be too tricky since Jamila was clearly her right-hand revolutionary. 'Blah blah blah, Alexander Sorokin, blah blah blah,' was what I heard. I wanted to be unsure, to convince myself that that's not what the reporter had said, standing in front of this bloodied corpse. But it was what he'd said. People slow down to pronounce names in a foreign language. They try hard to articulate, to get it right, to be clear. He had said Alexander Sorokin. That would be the same Alexander Sorokin with whom I'd had vodka at The Ritz yesterday. Oh holy fuck, was I going to have be an alibi? It flashed across my mind that this woman might be the Egyptian wife he'd left as convincingly as he could. What had he said? He said he'd hit her, hadn't he? Got drunk and hit her. The Russian definition of a good husband is, 'He doesn't drink and he doesn't beat me.' So he'd known what to do. Very very bad move in my view. I mean, assuming that a) this was her and b) he hadn't killed her. Well, he certainly hadn't killed her last night. He was in bloody London. They must have security cameras at

The Ritz. But was anyone going to believe me? Did he come and go with normal passports? I had not the remotest tiniest little bit of desire to be interviewed by the Egyptian police. No thanks. I intended to get out of the country to my baby long before anyone linked me to Alex. And I knew better than to call him at this point. My policy was this – not mention this to anyone and to hope nothing happens before I leave for London . . . this afternoon! Could I? Suddenly I felt incredibly sick and ran into the bathroom to kneel down on the tiles and vomit. Sodding kebab. Ugh.

Don was irritatingly perky as we set off in the blazing heat for Jamila's flat.

'Can we get her out on the balcony, do you think? Have you got the denials from the police? What about Karima? Are we seeing her?'

The taxi driver had a long black beard and kept pulling at it and then shouting out of the window at whoever had just cut him up, which was everybody.

'Don, I don't know, okay? I don't know if she's got a balcony, yes I've got all the police denials – called everyone just now – and Jamila's going to have to organise the rest if she's up to it.'

The flat seemed different this time. The boab didn't run up in front of us, just kind of nodded disdainfully from his outdoor card table under the cheese plant where he sat with his cronies and his cat. And inside things were less orderly, fuzzy round the edges though not exactly untidy: a picture askew, perhaps, a film of dust, an old newspaper still on the coffee table. There was no sign of the parents again. I was beginning to wonder if they'd been here since last time. Or, right in the back of my mind, if they even existed. Jamila had opened the door nervously, in her headscarf but this

103

time eschewing the Western look entirely and wearing all-covering long droopy clothes. She actually didn't look great at all, imprisonment and torture notwithstanding. Her skin had gone waxy.

I hugged her and explained that Don would do a bit at a time and she didn't have to get completely undressed.

'I don't mind,' she said, and immediately took every stitch of clothing off apart from the pink headscarf, standing in front of the sofa, naked and defiant. She obviously thought of herself as evidence against a brutal regime, rather than a woman without her clothes on. Don didn't dare ask her to move anywhere else, but he just sort of went all professional (like they do in a bright flash when lurching from a natural hippy birth with incense and a jacuzzi to an emergency cae-sarian with shouting, cutting and blood matches), switching as many lights on as he could, opening heavy curtains, swear-ing under his breath. Jamila stood perfectly still, most of the lashes healed now but the bruising, if anything, worse. I didn't want to notice that her pubes were ginger.

'Jesus,' Don whispered, walking round the back of her.

This time there was no minted lemonade and no sweets. I just sat on the plastic-covered sofa and played with my cig-arette packet. The silent television was on and I shivered when the item played – the body as lurid, the reporter as slick. Neither Don nor Jamila even looked up to where the television blared on its bracket. Why would they?

'We can go and see Karima now?' Jamila asked, pulling her clothes on, embarrassed now that the reason for her nudity had expired. 'If it's convenient for you.'

She adjusted her headscarf and grabbed her bag, all action, less vulnerability, keys jangling, motion. She went down the dark stairs in front of us and put herself in charge of grabbing a taxi, shouting '*Assalaamu alaikum*' to the boab and forcing his tableful of friends to reply along with him, '*walaikum assalaam*.' She sat in the front, gave the address in Zamalek and talked on the phone all the way, though it can't have been especially anti-government talk because the driver didn't take his ear off the radio, occasionally bringing his finger into play too, jabbing angrily at the crackling voices.

'Actually, Jamila,' I said, pulling my shades on as the sun hit me. 'Give me the address and we'll meet you there. There's something else I just need to do first, quickly.' My initial plan regarding Alex's dead ex was already falling to pieces.

'Eh?' Don wondered.

'Just want to check out the dead woman's place. Before anyone links me with Alex and starts looking. You know?'

'Sorry. Have I missed something?'

'Yeah. The news. Alex's wife found dead at the bottom of her stairs. He left her a couple of weeks ago. Claims he did.'

'Whoah, baby!'

'Seriously. It was on the news. Something something Alexander Sorokin, and all this grim footage of the woman.'

'So it could be anyone?'

'Could be. But it isn't. But, anyway, he's in London.'

'Okay then. Dead bodies here we come. Fuck, where's my light meter?' Don immediately on to the finer points of the job.

'They'll have moved her. But, anyway . . .'

Jamila told me where the Karima El-Baz residence was and we hopped into another groaning cab.

Don was taking up a lot of the back seat. He'd found his light meter, seemed not to have any questions about Sorokin, and his mind had drifted elsewhere.

'Nah,' he said, cracking his knuckles.

'Nah what?' I asked.

'Dunno.' He shook his head. We were both drenched in sweat already and it wasn't noon. 'Just don't like it.'

'Well, who does, Donski? Who does?'

'Yeah, but . . . Do you remember those corpses under the football stadium in Baghdad?'

Now what was he on about? Maybe it was me who'd missed something.

'The torture victims out of that cellar thing?'

'Yeah.'

We were on a bridge in eight lanes of solid unmoving traffic. One often is in Cairo.

'I didn't look, actually. Didn't even look at your pictures. But I remember the deal. Why?'

'Dunno.' He shut his eyes and shook his head again. This whole time he'd been whispering.

So I said, loudly, 'DON! What are you trying to say?!'

'I just think . . .' Don pondered, as a child tapped forlornly on the window. Don wound it down with great perspiring effort and gave him some money. He skipped away barefoot through the cars. 'I just don't think . . . Okay. Zanetti, look.' He was hissing in my ear now, his saliva wetting my cheek. 'Here's the skinny. Check it out. She wasn't tortured. I've been thinking and thinking and racking my brains and I don't know what it is or why. But I've seen and shot a lot of torture victims. That's not one.'

I sighed. Clearly the heat had finally boiled his brain into porridge. 'Don, you're insane. She was in police custody and came out looking like that. What the fuck do you THINK happened to her?'

'Zanetti you stupid slag, I'm telling you, I don't know. Maybe she got a mate to do it in there. Maybe she rushed home and did it herself. Maybe she and her fella are into really nasty fucking sex. I don't know. But it just doesn't look right.'

Now the really bloody irritating thing was that I couldn't argue with him. This is the kind of stuff Don knows about. He has to look at the injuries through his lenses, whereas I just kind of talk to the person. I have no idea in what way torture injuries differ from other sorts but it's the sort of horrific stuff that Don does, annoyingly, tend to know about.

He had his eyes shut again, the lids puffy, shiny and grey, threaded with red veins, and the traffic had started to move a little. They flashed open. He had it.

'Nothing electrical. It's all electrical these days. You know?'

'I didn't. Thanks.'

'Seriously.'

'I didn't think you were joking.'

It was not hard to find the scene of the crime. I mean, some contact of Don's knew the area in any case, texts coming through constantly on his phone. It was right in the centre near the Greek Club and that famous patisserie that's supposed to make you feel all part of a more elegant age but doesn't really. And Café Riche.

I love Café Riche. You feel like part of a real Cairene institution. There are big black-and-white photographs all over the walls of the luminaries who have eaten there, including Naguib Mahfouz whose photo (consisting largely of those huge 1950s black-rimmed glasses worn, in fact, by most of the depicted luminaries) takes pride of place in the middle of the back wall. On the menu you have the choice between ordering one, two or three hard-boiled eggs as a starter. They do quail and chips; that fantastic lentil soup that is basically the same across the whole of the Middle East, India and

Pakistan; melokhia with everything; and a wine list that they try to hand to women without a wince of disapproval. Some of them occasionally succeed too. The waiters wear floor-length white and blue robes and silly hats and the tiled floor gleams with grease. Now, obviously, this is probably about as Egyptian an institution as Roules is an English one. It's in one of the grand colonial buildings with balconies and shutters grimed grey by the traffic and heat and you'd probably be hard pushed to find an ordinary Cairene who'd heard of it. Still, I love it.

The police had cordoned off pretty much everything and we ended up giving out about two hundred quid in bribes to get up close to the building. Egyptian pounds, but even so . . .

It was strange walking up these streets, past Estoril – a hole-in-the-wall restaurant that inexplicably sneaks into guide books (some historical feature, I imagine) – with no traffic anywhere. The thing that most characterises this city is the appalling traffic and, without it, I found myself looking up at the buildings and into the shops and hearing the noises that would once have dominated Cairo – people talking, shutters opening and closing, dogs barking, the odd hoof clopping and the creak of all the make-shift go-carts that people haul stuff around on.

When we got to Eman Sorokina's building, number sixteen, next to the film-posters shop, they were just removing the body. Hordes of black-clad policeman were shouting in an effort to seem more important than everybody else, to move non-existant crowds out of the way and to shoo off imaginary photographers. Well, I suppose one of them wasn't imaginary but he didn't have his camera out. Yet. We stood back a bit, generally ignored by the uniforms, apart from the odd glance at my hair which always turns into a glance down at my tits and then, on the realisation that there's not much doing in that direction, back up to my hair again.

'How we gonna get in?' I asked Don, stepping back against a shop into the shade. A bloke shuffled past, pushing his face into mine and saying, '*Bakshish, bakshish.*' He wasn't even pretending to be about to do anything for the cash. I didn't give him any – I'd just paid a fortune to get this far.

'You could pretend to be Russian. Flash your press card?'

'Don't be stupid.' I sighed, lighting a cigarette and flicking the match across the pavement.

In the end I flashed my Canary Wharf coffee machine card, shouted the first few lines of an Akhmatova poem in Russian and Don shoved a hundred quid into the hand of an acned junior at the grand entrance way and another hundred into the boab's. The boab was standing inside, apprehensively shifting from bare foot to bare foot on the cold black and white tiles. This is where being a boab slightly falls to pieces on you – murders and stuff. The whole job, really, is security guard-slash-caretaker and if one of your residents gets iced you're going to have some explaining to do. Who you saw coming and going, who was seen falling down the stairs in a river of blood – all that kind of caper. He looked very nervous, clutching at his gelabaya, and happy to be tipped rather than arrested. They are always first in for a grilling. Partly rightly, because any crime perpetrator would normally need to bribe him to get in at all.

For the moment, all the focus was on the outside of the building, getting the body to autopsy without anyone tampering with it, disposing of it or generally paying anybody to do anything weird to it. Much easier said than done in these places, where murder is actually pretty rare. We wouldn't be hounded out before getting a proper look, I thought.

We stood by the lift looking at the grisly scene in front of us.

'Oh bollocks,' Don moaned, before running into a corner by the basement to throw up on some dusty tiles in the dark. How is it that he always forgets that he doesn't like the smell of blood? I mean, it's not as if it doesn't crop up a fair amount. In this case there was so much of the stuff that it was genuinely quite difficult to step around it. It was sprayed all over the walls near the bottom of the staircase as though she had maybe been thrown down and bashed against the steps a lot on the way. Is that possible? I don't know. I walked up to see how it might have been. It's the kind of thing where forensics or someone would have to build Eman-sized dummies and chuck them downstairs a hundred times. I couldn't imagine the Cairo policeforce budget running to that, frankly.

'Can you remember which way she was lying?' I asked Don from the top of the first flight, looking down. He wiped his mouth with the back of his hand.

'Dodgy yoghurt for breakfast,' he said. 'What?'

'Right, Don. Can you? Remember how she was?'

'Didn't see the coverage, mate. Soz.' He started to drag his weight and his cameras up to meet me.

'No, doesn't matter. I'm just wondering if you can do that much damage to yourself just falling.'

'Leave it out,' Don snorted. 'Who are you trying to protect? I fall downstairs pissed most nights. Twisted my ankle once.'

It seemed a reasonable enough point. I sighed and we climbed on, past those grand Parisian doors and up round the iron-wrought lift-shaft. It was almost cold in here.

Another police junior stood outside the open door to the flat. He was actually picking his nose when we rounded the corner. This might have been almost endearing if he hadn't eaten it.

'Um, *salaamu alaikum*,' Don wheezed. The boy raised his eyebrows.

'Oh, Don. Don't bother with a charm offensive,' I said, pushing past him and giving the boy another hundred pound note.

'Two minutes,' I said. 'Two minutes,' and I raised my finger to my lips.

Don said a few words to the boy and shouted over to me. 'Killed four days ago. Probably couldn't show the pictures until the police had done Christ knows what.'

Right. So I counted backwards, factoring in time differences and flights and all my confusion about what bloody day it ever is and concluded . . . yes. It was the day I met him. When he jumped on me. Four days ago. Alibi central. That's me.

'You're going to be a bloody alibi too, you know!' I screamed at Don. Okay, now I know it wasn't the brightest move, going to the scene of a crime I might end up being accused of. And it's not like I was inconspicuous or anything, but my perhaps lunatic sense of justice was getting the better of me. I didn't do it and I doubted Alex had either. I couldn't help wanting to have a look, you know? Ach. You probably don't.

'Nice.' Don nodded.

It was. She'd done it up in a kind of souk style with white upholstered sofas, white muslin curtains, shining terracotta floors and big brass pots with funny things in them – one was full of white pebbles, another was overflowing with ribbons of red silk. Oh, you get the picture. Tasteful, elegant, moneyed. Her wedding photo was on the low cherry-wood coffee table. Yup. This was indeed, as I had known in the pit of the

111

thing you know in, Eman Sorokina's flat. It looked as though they'd done it in Russia in some horrible house of weddings, but very smiley faces on the bride and groom. Annoyingly, my stomach twitched in slight jealousy. I had been strict with him about this being only a fling, but it was more than clear that I was only a fling to him too. Perhaps taking his mind off the fragrant Eman. Oh, shut up, Faith.

Don poked about in the kitchen.

'Mmm. Try this!' he shouted. I found him leaning over the stove by the window tasting something from a Le Creuset casserole.

'You are insane,' I commented and walked back into the living room. One bedroom, big white mosquito nets strung from a hook on the ceiling, French windows out onto a roof terrace, potted palms, a lemon tree, a gazebo with a blue mosaic table and chairs, a candelabra in the middle. Most people rented their roofs out to families who set up a whole life on them, you can see them in Don's National Geographic piece, a whole city above the city.

I supposed the Egyptians had already taken anything documentary, anything that could be 'evidence', and I didn't think it worth looking. Well, no struggle, no fighting anyone in the apartment, and no blood anywhere. So this had all happened on the staircase. This I didn't like. Or, rather, I did like from the point of view of protecting Alex. You see, it's very KGB, the staircase. Practically everyone who'd wanted an investigation into how the Russian government had handled Beslan (the school massacre), *Nord-Ost* (the theatre massacre) and Pervomaiskaya (the village massacre) had been murdered in their stairwell. Some suffered all kinds of hideous skin disintegration conditions before finally giving out (like the ones that the Ukrainian President Yushchenko had. He, unusually, pissed them off by surviving) but others were just shot or had mysterious heart attacks at the age of thirty-six. That old bloke who defected from the KGB years ago says there are loads more of these killings now even than there were under Communism. Then, at least, you had to put the paperwork through.

But there was something else bothering me.

I sat down on the sofa and a smell of attar of roses floated up at me. Recently changed and ironed cushion covers! God, I wish I had someone doing all that kind of crap for me in London. Perhaps it was, after all, time to take another posting. The perks of living somewhere second- or third-world really do know no bounds. Ugh. What was it? I thought of Ben and how he had held the little wooden trains, stared at them with such unadulterated joy. There was a connection. I leapt up. That was it! When we first met I'd said I was thinking about my son and he'd said he was too. But no child lived in this flat, nor ever had done.

'He said he had kids!' I told Don, who was looking in the fridge. 'Oh. For God's sake. Stop it.'

He ignored my telling off. 'So what?' Don wanted to know. He shook a carton of yoghurt.

'Well, he hasn't. Look! No kids!'

Don shut the fridge and shrugged. He smelt of beer. 'Zanetti, my favourite virtue.'

'Grace.'

'Grace. Not everyone has children in wedlock. Not everyone only does wedlock the once. Kids have this way of springing the fuck up the world over when you least expect it. Anyway, he was trying to get into your knickers, wasn't he? Don't get me wrong, Eff Zed but, given the brutal murder of his wife, I don't reckon you're barking up the tree what needs barking up. You know?'

Yeah. I know. But . . .

I gave up. 'Hmm. 'Spose,' I said, sighing. 'Okay. Yallah. Let's go. Can you get a couple of shots of the spatters on the walls on the way down?'

'Not without a tripod.'

'Use a flash.'

'Yeah, and why don't you write your pieces with a log of shit and a scroll of fucking papyrus?'

'Don.'

'All right. All right. Fuck.'

Nobody even seemed to notice us leave.

Chapter Nine

Now Karima El-Baz was something else. We had pulled up outside the beautiful Le Bon building on Zamalek island – the posh gardeny bit of the city where foreigners and rich people live, where the embassies are. Lush well-tended vegetation outside each building and smart guards in sentry boxes out on the wide pavements. People here spend most of their lives at the Gezirah Sporting Club (which mostly involves drinking cocktails) and they actually do things like walk their pet dogs – a luxury that would seem utterly surreal in any other area of the city. It's Knightsbridge, basically, but much lovelier because of the palms and the bougainvillea and, well, obviously the Nile. Omar Sharif lives in this particular building. A lot of Cairo is an imitation of Paris but the Le Bon building really could be in Paris.

'Whoah,' Don and I said in unison as we walked in. Jamila was waiting outside, but was too focused on her mission to notice or care about our reaction to the décor.

It was cool inside, but not the unpleasant icy blast of air conditioning. It was the lovely refreshing cool of permanent shade, marble floors and a nearby fountain that I could hear but not see. The place was gleaming clean, black and white tiles and iron banisters, vases of lilies on four different ornate tables in the foyer. You could smell the money. We walked up the kind of staircase that officers and their fiancées sweep down before gliding into the ballroom.

Jamila knocked with a small clenched fist on a glistening, newly-painted black apartment door, a Venetian-brass lion roaring from its centre.

'Chin up, McCaughrean,' I muttered.

'Only one thing I'll get up for you, Zanetti,' he murmered back.

A Sudanese maid in a silly black and white uniform opened the door and ushered us into a reception area that was even cooler. Temperature-wise. She held out a silver plate and stood there with her eyes down for ages. It was me, eventually, who realised what it was that she wanted.

'Your card, gorgeous,' I told Don, whisking mine out from my wallet and slapping it, at last, down on the tray. 'Seriously. I know about this posh shit.' The *Chronicle* card is lovely, all embossed and creamy, perfect for a silver salver.

Don, to his enormous credit, did manage to wrench his from his sweaty back pocket and, while it was one of those embarrassing unendorsed freelance things, it was double-sided Latin and Cyrillic, which you can't say isn't cute.

The maid rushed off, leaving the three of us shifting our weight and raising our eyebrows at each other occasionally, hands deferentially clasped behind our backs. And, about five minutes later, this goddess swept into view. She had thick, glossy black hair blow-dried into whipped egg-white texture and she was wearing a pink cashmere polo-neck and black trousers above a pair of pointed high heels as delicate as birds' bones. She rushed forwards smiling and smelling of lily of the valley. She was made-up and bejewelled, sure, but in the kind of way that makes you think someone looks wonderful rather than forcing you to notice why.

She kissed Jamila three times and hugged her gently. 'Darling, I'm so sorry,' she told her in English. 'It's all my fault. Totally my fault.' This woman was American. It was the way she'd said 'totally'. 'Was it awful?'

'*Aiwa,*' Jamila mumbled. Yes.

Then Karima directed her glitter at us. She held out a firm hand, the diamonds in her watch catching the light from the balcony behind her. The flat was full of flowers, cascading from pots and vases on every surface.

'You must be, let me see,' and she looked down at the cards she held in her left hand. She guessed right.

'Faith!' She shook my hand rigorously. 'Great to meet you. And Don! Excellent!'

So look. This is a woman whose mother was recently murdered by the police. I don't THINK so!

'I am so glad you're all on board,' she said, turning swiftly on her lovely heels and leading us across sparkling marble to yet another room full of huge vases of long-stemmed roses and Louis XIV furniture. This is a lie. I don't know what the furniture was. I know it was old, very well looked after and French. And included two chaises longues and a couple of fragile writing tables. Don sat down unapologetically on one of the chaises and it creaked beneath him. Karima winced but was too polite to say anything. She was also too polite not to pour out three glasses of Crystal champagne from the bottle in the silver bucket, the ice crunching as she removed it. She had that air of doing this for the first time, just to show off to the guests. Normally a servant would do it. Don's glass fizzed over and she laughed.

'Uh oh!'

117

Not only did she not give Jamila champagne but she didn't give her anything else either.

'So, you are Karima El-Baz?' I asked, thinking it best to check, after all.

She shook her fabulous hair and raised her glass. '*Kappa kappa gamma!*' she said, and took a sip.

Don came into his own here. He watches a lot of teen movies with young breasts in them.

'Ah. A sorority girl,' he said, excited in an utterly pathetic manner.

'Berkley, 1994. You?'

Don laughed so much his champagne went down the wrong way. 'Um . . . Sheffield Grammar, 1976?'

Karima didn't get it but laughed anyway, not wanting to seem foolish.

'Um, Karima. You were released from the psychiatric unit yesterday, after a week in police custody,' I began, wishing I had proper notes instead of this napkin from off the tin of nuts at the hotel.

'Oh, they're always sweet to me because of Daddy. You mustn't worry about that!' She kind of snorted in an extremely odd way, arranging herself with one foot tucked under her arse on the chaise longue next to Don. 'I get a private room and Samira brings me food from home!'

Jamila and I were perched on the other sofa, Jamila with her head down, staring forlornly at her shoes.

Right. Daddy.

'Daddy?'

'He's the Interior Minister. Desperate to change things but too scared to do the dirty work for himself. Typical Daddy!'

She had put 'dirty work' in the terrible double-fingered inverted commas so favoured by the annoying. 'Mom, though, was very driven. You knew she was dying, right? She'd had MS for fifteen years. They had this pact. He'd have her arrested, she'd take her stuff, whatever it was – cyanide, I think, VERY Eva Braun – and then he'd claim they killed her. Big scandal before the elections and the world taking notice. That was the plan anyhow. How do you think it's going?'

She looked at her pearly pink nails. Come to think of it, it was amazing that she could raise her hand with that rock on it.

'Um. I'd say oddly,' I admitted. 'And how do feel about your recent bereavement? You seem very . . . together.'

Psychotic, I meant.

'Hope—'

'Faith.'

'Faith. I don't know if you've lost a parent.'

'I have.'

'Well, Mom and I have spent a year saying goodbye. We were ready. She had deteriorated beyond what she could bear. You know? It was a brave thing she did for Egypt. I was impressed.'

'Uh huh.'

Don coughed.

'Oh! I'm sorry!' Karima laughed, rushing over with more champagne. 'I promised Samira I'd do it myself. BIG mistake!'

Jamila, who suddenly looked dirty and small, badly dressed, thin, pale-skinned and hunched, had not moved at all. Had not dared twitch. It didn't take a genius to see that she was in thrall to this woman. Her English teacher. The psychoanalytical transference was plainly in evidence, my lesbian fears not as far off the mark as I'd thought. She was in love.

'So you're a Trollope fan?' I choked out.

'Don't you worship him?!' Karima exclaimed. I was beginning to be able to imagine her lectures now.

'I've only read *The Warden*,' I told her.

'I hear it's crap,' Don added, ever so quietly. But Karima wasn't interested.

'So. It's great you came. Daddy's going to stand in September and the president thinks it's just a nominal, you know, to make him look more democratic. But Daddy thinks – well, we hope – he can win. What do you think?'

To be honest, I was so staggered by this whole thing, and the realisation that Don was right about Jamila's injuries, whatever the real cause, that I couldn't quite focus on the Yosri El-Baz election campaign. I was feeling queasy again.

'Who is this guy?' I hissed to Don through clenched teeth. Yosri El-Baz. Win? Umm . . .

'Well . . .' I began.

'Oh. It's in the bag,' Don shouted, raising his glass. 'In the bag!'

We all – well, we three – stood and chinked glasses with the Nile rolling by behind us and I started to realise what kind of thing had happened to Jamila. I had no idea, however, how much she knew about what had happened to her. She'd been set up but was she in on it? Had she thought it was the police who were torturing her? Had she agreed to this? Was I supposed to write a piece now about Yosri El-Baz, the potential usurper? I mean, not that I didn't feel one coming on but it wasn't necessarily the one Karima wanted me to write.

And then Alex called me on my mobile.

Chapter Ten

'*Eto ya*,' he said, as if I need telling.

'I know it's you, Alex,' I told him. I'd been expecting him to call. He'd been edgy before, he must be terrified now. Once he got picked up for killing his wife, they wouldn't let him go before his ninety-third birthday.

I left Don chatting to the seriously weird Karima and moved back into the hall.

'Faith, I'm in a lot of trouble,' he said. Just the effort involved in breathing sounded troublesome.

'Yes. I know. I saw the news.'

'I didn't do it, Faith. They are trying to discredit me before they kill me,' he gasped.

'I know you didn't do it,' I said. Well, I did. Didn't I? Yes. Yes. I knew.

'Are you saying you think they're going to kill you soon? I mean, sooner rather than later?' He was sucking me into his crazed way of thinking. But he certainly sounded condemned. Although, no, that's not right. The condemned go very resigned. I was doing a series of pieces about death row in America once and I ended up going to three executions.

When the final appeal is over (and fucking hell it is cruel how this gets dragged out to the last second) they go sort of calm. It's only the body that has a last little fight when the needle is inserted. But Alex was frenzied. And frenzy means hope, doesn't it?

'I think they already have killed me, Faith. I really loved her, you know.'

'Look. Let's say I believe you, and the FSB, URPO, *osobysty* or whoever, have killed your wife in order to discredit you. Isn't that enough? Once you have been written off as a murderer and are languishing in an Egyptian prison with only a falafel for company for the rest of your life, what does it matter what you say about Russia?'

He did that laugh again. I was not a fan of that laugh.

'You don't get it, do you? They don't work like that. They don't HAVE to kill me. Faith, they WANT to kill me. I betrayed the brotherhood. They want to teach me, and everyone else, a lesson. And then you will write your piece about me, finally in a reputable newspaper, and everyone would have believed my personal testimony, how they blew their own people up as an excuse for a stupid war. But now they won't believe. Now I am a murderer. A madman.'

I wasn't liking the sound of how integral I was to this whole thing. How did this happen? I was writing a story about a belly dancer and having a bit of a fling last time I looked. Now I am supposed to uphold democracy all over the known bloody world.

'We have to clear my name before I die if the world is ever going to take notice.'

Wow. What a sentence. I sighed deeply and kicked the leg of a delicate side table as gently as I could, half-hoping it would collapse and shatter the vase across the floor, spill the water, scatter the flowers.

'We?' For God's sake. He was paranoid and he had every right to be – grown up in the Soviet Union, worked for the *spetz sluzhby*, indubitably involved in the murkiest kind of crap under the banner of 'risk assessment' or whatever the hell he was calling it. But were the FSB seriously going to go to this much trouble to wipe out this rather meek defector pianist bloke who thinks the President gives it to sheep up the wrong 'un?

'You have to help me, Faith. Throw your phone away after this call. Destroy it. I'm destroying this one. Come and meet me at Abram's safe house. I am not well. Not well at all.'

No, I could hear that.

'You must be joking, Alex. I'm going back to London tonight. I'm not getting into this. Who's Abram?'

'You're not getting into this? You are a suspect, Faith. You will be. Killed my wife in a jealous rage. Maybe we plotted it together?'

'Are you threatening me?' Bastard. Though I had known immediately that this was true, of course. I'm not an idiot. Well, I am but not that kind of idiot.

'I am trying to get you to think clearly. If you prove this, and I can give you evidence, if you prove this it's a huge story! Think of your headlines, Faith. Come to Ismaelevich's. Quickly, Faith!'

I wished he would stop using my name. Oh, man alive. I was going to have to go to Abram Ismaelevich's safe house, wasn't I?

'I always thought they would kill him first,' he said, seeming almost to be chatting now. 'An accident maybe. Unfortunate fall from a balcony . . . I was going to kill him once. That's how I got to know him. The order came. They suggested poison but left it to our discretion. The new law. N 153-F3. We fought for it. I fought for it personally.'

At this point anything sounded as true as anything else.

This is the law, a revival of an old Soviet law, that says you can kill your country's enemies even if they're abroad. One imagines Mossad is free to do this too. Soviet laws came in four categories – published, unpublished, secret and top secret. And that's just the laws – never mind the punishments.

'I felt it would free us to do our job more effectively. Protect Russia more effectively. But, of course it just meant a free for all. No checks, no accountability. There is a spray, melts the insides . . . *shouf*!'

'Is there?' I asked, unable to believe that we were having this conversation, now, at this point.

'There is. Developed in the Kamera. You know? Off the ring road? Been doing it since the 1920s. Chemical stuff. Going nuclear now! Maybe. Maybe.'

'I'm not familiar with it, Alex. I'm not actually personally in the KGB.'

'Me neither!' he spat. 'I came and told him about it. The plot. And that was that.'

Chapter Eleven

Alex made me memorise the address and directions and repeat them back. I had to promise to destroy my phone, which I did, though I was none too happy about it because then Kristy couldn't call me and there were lovely photos of Ben on it, not least the one with the spaghetti. Taking a deep breath, I walked out through the gauze curtains and onto the wide sweeping balcony, throwing my mobile, with an enormous lob, out across the narrow road and into the river. Bye bye, phone.

Don, Karima and Jamila looked up at me when I went back into the room and, possibly overstepping the boundaries of the bizzaroid protocol, swilled the rest of my champagne down in one without taking a seat.

'Is everything okay?' Karima asked with a big bleached smile. I'm not trying to pretend that she really was this blank, this characterless, this cheerful about her mother's death and the huge compromises she must have been making for her father's political career. But what I am saying is that she was used to not showing anything, not so much as a flicker. And it was deeply off-putting. Though perhaps not if you were male. I expect male types can't get enough of this kind of thing. Keep you guessing. Never know where you stand. Yuk.

'Um. Not brilliant, actually. I'm going to have to cut this short. I'll leave you in Don's capable hands. Don, a word?'

I gestured him out of the room and I heard Karima start talking firmly to Jamila in Arabic, instructions to a slave. A tone she seemed to be used to.

'I've got a bit of an Alex issue. I'm still going to try and fly out tonight, so can you do a basic interview with Karima for me? Just get her to say that crap again, on the record, you know? Her mum committed suicide for her father's cause and that she had her own arrest staged? The lengths people have to go to in the name of political opposition? Even torture? That kind of shit.'

'Do you think the CIA's paying them? The Al-Bazs? I thought we all liked this regime?'

'Yeah. Dunno. They can't have come up with it all by themselves. Maybe this other guy, this Daddy, is promising to help with Iran. Who knows. I'll call someone in London when I get back.' Oh, but who? Who? My best SIS contact had been killed in Baghdad in that explosion in the Green Zone. He would tell me anything if I talked him through my blow-job technique. Just talked him through it. God I missed him. Had an enormous collection of bow ties. His funeral was surreal. His wife hadn't known what he did for a living and was very freaked out by the huge and scary-looking turn out.

Don grinned at me. He could do with a bleach himself. 'See what I told you about the torture!'

I picked a petal off a rose and crushed it between my fingers.

'Are you PLEASED with yourself? But someone bloody did it to her! It still must have hurt, Don! And for all we know she thought it was the police. It's not at all clear to me that she knows Mrs El-Baz's death was suicide or that Karima staged her own arrest. Ask her, can you? She looks like she's in a fucking coma.'

'She's a bloody self-harmer. Most young women are. Yeah, yeah. And I'll take a few pictures as well, shall I? I want fifty per cent of this month's wages, Zanetti. Astrofuckingnomical I bet they are too.'

'Compared to your fee, Don?! You're joking. They had to sack the Westminster lobby guy to have you on this.'

The maid walked past us and seemed to sniff in distaste. People this badly dressed obviously didn't come round for champagne that often.

'What's Alex's deal, then? Did he do it?'

'No. But he's done a lot of things. Don't ask.'

It's like what barristers say when you ask them if their client is guilty: 'They're definitely guilty of something.'

But then I had a thought. There isn't anybody in the world more trustworthy than Don McCaughrean. I mean, in some ways. I whispered the address in his ear.

'Just in case. I haven't got a mobile,' I said. Don wobbled backwards and raised his eyebrows. 'If you don't hear from me for a day or two. Okay?'

'Is this a Zanetti-in-too-deep thing?'

'I would say so.' I nodded, sighing. 'I would say so.'

I stomped towards the door and the maid ran after me to open it for me and shut it again behind me. The champagne and then the blinding wall of light and heat made me feel sick again. Should have waited until the kebab thing had passed before drinking , I thought, leaning over a potted fern and retching, to the absolute disgust of the better class of boab who was hosing down the lawn barefoot. I mean, that's how ritzy this place was – a lawn.

Chapter Twelve

I tried to keep in the shade on my walk to the main road and then I stood with my hand over my forehead waiting for a car to stop – one that was not officially a taxi. The taxis cursed me when I waved them on and groups of chatting women looked at me strangely. I thought an ordinary car would be harder to trace. I mean, I was conspicuous beyond belief. Tall, thin, green-eyed Western woman with masses of frizzy blonde hair dressed like a man. Just ask anyone.

The guy insisted on actually seeing the money with his own eyes before agreeing to drive me out of Cairo, craning round with his fag in his mouth, a photo of his granddaughter on the dashboard. He talked to himself all the way and I assumed he was praying, but he could just as easily have been reciting the lyrics to 'Hit Me Baby One More Time' in translation. He leant on the horn pretty permanently, stopping only to get another fag out or to wave both (that's both) hands out of the window at drivers who offended him. I never know how they choose when to get pissed off with other drivers. I mean, everyone is driving so fast, so dangerously, so aggressively that it seems extremely random to suddenly single one out for abuse.

We went over a series of narrow, disintegrating and very high-up flyovers, onto a huge motorway with those big green signs in swirling Arabic and boxy English overhead, visible clouds of dust and fumes, a boy in yellow shorts selling watermelons from a heap twice as high as himself at the side of the road and the odd dead donkey. Out on the left the pyramids came into view, at first mounds in the sky, maybe low cloud, then the definition sharpening and eventually, surprisingly, shaping themselves into neat triangles standing alone in the desert, the only interruption to the horizon. So familiar and at the same time so utterly alien.

We had swerved off, beeping at a snake on the road (seriously – now that showed his little reptilian arse) and suddenly we were on a sandy track alongside a stream that was lined with thin palms. Men and boys were bathing in the water with their horses, climbing on their backs, splashing the beasts and each other, screaming out at me when they saw the flash of blonde hair in the back of the car.

It is extremely unclear to me whether the men who harass women in Arab countries (albeit largely in non-violent and purely verbal fashion) genuinely believe that wearing a T-shirt means that you actually expose your genitalia when someone shouts 'Fucky' at you. Is it some statistical thing like dying under anaesthetic? One in a million Western women really does have sex on the street with someone who has come up and hissed 'bitch' in her ear and therefore it's always worth a go? Or do they just feel obliged to say something because you look different? But why is it something about sex? No doubt they are sex-starved to the point of absolute insanity, but even so. A touch baffling.

I had a piercing headache now and hardly registered the

beauty of this house when we approached it: an old stone monastery, perhaps, only a herd of goats and a naked boy with a stick on the drive up to it, hiding his eyes from the tornado of sand we created with the car. And then this – a low higgledy-piggledy series of buildings, fountains and flowers in the courtyards, rugs on the mosaic floors and intricate wooden carvings on the windows, designed for the women to see out.

'*Dobro pozhalovat!*' boomed Abram Ismaelevich, striding out to open the taxi door for me. I had not realised he would be here himself. He was thinner than he looked on television, younger, more vital. There is something of the drunken slob about him on camera, but I could see that he was super fit and probably never touched the stuff. Perhaps they like to go in close to make him seem unattractive ergo evil. He is the fourth richest man in the world.

In order to demonstrate this, he reached into the pocket of his white linen trousers and gave the driver enough money to buy a lot of land and build himself a house, even though I'd already paid him our agreed fee. He then leant into the window and said something in Arabic. I assume it was, 'If you ever mention you were here or lead anyone to my door I will have your children decapitated.' The driver clearly thought this was a fair deal, even grabbing Ismaelevich's head with both arms, pulling it further into the car and kissing his newly-shaven cheeks three times, tears bursting from his bloodshot eyes. Money can buy you love.

'Nice to meet you,' I said, shaking his hand as the car disappeared into the olive groves of the drive. 'I've heard a lot about you.'

He threw his head back and laughed. 'Lies!'

Abram Ismaelevich looked me up and down as though trying to decide something. Odd beyond weird to meet like

130

this. When I was the *Chronicle* correspondent in Moscow I must have put in a call a day to his people trying to get an interview. Even Don never got to Ismaelevich.

He reached out and took my hand, not to shake it but to hold it, leading me into the cool inner courtyard.

'My monastery!' he said. 'Coptic. They used to make wine here but I can't get the vines to grow. No green fingers.'

He had short gingery hair, thick but greying, orange eyes and eyebrows, freckly skin, broad shoulders, muscular fore-arms, a slightly waddling gait, tennis player's arse. What made this stocky little guy from Siberia look so obviously rich? His clean shave? His crisp shirt? Lemony smell? I honestly think it was the look on his face.

I had glimpsed the courtyard through the open doors even from the car, but it was just spectacular inside. There was a simple stone fountain with a bird-table type effort in the middle of it. The inside walls were a dark, cool, mildewy green. Two women in headscarves, long skirts and cream blouses were bringing food out onto a very low table, on wide brass plates. White cheese with pistachio nuts, wet green grapes, grilled sardines, lamb in cinnamon and pine nuts, baklava dripping with honey. Some of the floor's mosaic had been damaged but that only made all its intricate, coloured pictures of animals, birds and fishes all the more beautiful. Where there were gaps there were Persian rugs. The shade in the courtyard was complete and the walls were covered in sweet-smelling honeysuckle and bunches of purple wisteria. Wherever the thugs with machine guns were, and there was no question that they were somewhere, they were discreetly hidden. Ismaelevich was flaunting his taste and culture, not his money.

Alex was sitting on a low wooden chair, holding with both hands a blue-and-gold glass of mint tea with the mint sprigs poking out of it. He seemed to have lost a stone since I last saw him really not that long ago, his skin was pale green and his striking bone structure was now looking more like the blokes in that famous shot of the Yugoslav prisoner-of-war camp.

'Shit, Alex! What happened to you? I mean, I know what's happened. You must be devastated but, Alex, you really look ill, love.'

I knelt down on the floor in front of him and had my hands on his sharp knees, looking into his face.

'They have poisoned me. The bastards got me,' he said, smiling weakly. 'But I am taking manganese. I'll get it out.'

This is a stomach pump on the cheap.

Ismaelevich snorted, taking a seat and reaching for some cheese. 'Well, that'll kill you if nothing else does! They don't have the phrase "gyppy tummy" in Russian. He's been drinking the water,' he said, entirely unconcerned. 'But what we do need to be worried about – ah, thank you, *shukran*, *shukran*,' he said, taking a glass of tea from one of the girls, 'is this murder. Pushed down the stairs, it was claimed. But nobody seen running away. And too much blood for a simple fall. Unusual, don't you think?'

He looked at me, genuinely interested in my point of view. Ah, that charisma thing. Very attractive.

'I don't know anything about it. I don't understand Arabic,' I said. 'But, unusual, sure. It could win the Really Really Unusual award.'

As Abram laughed Alex's whole body convulsed and he leant forward with his mouth open, grey with pain. He gripped his stomach.

'Nothing left,' he groaned. 'Don't worry.'

It was almost touching that he thought I might be worried about seeing some vomit. In the circumstances. Almost.

Abram rolled his eyes as though Alex was always playing up like this, but I wasn't so sure. I was ill from that bloody kebab but it was nothing like what was happening to Alex.

'She was found yesterday afternoon. All they can say is that there was a lot of blood, some type of haemorrhage, but she wasn't beaten, cut or shot. Just pushed. I don't know how they can tell this. I do know that we need to get Sashenka here – sorry – Alex here, out of the country. Egypt is not the place for innocent until proven guilty. Nor Russia!' He laughed as though he'd said something funny.

'She loved,' Alex began to say, coughing, righting himself, sitting up with tears wetting his sunken cheeks. 'She loved baroque music.'

'What?' I asked.

'Corelli. Handel.'

Righty-ho. As soon as the doubt had registered itself in my skull, he went and said something so bizarrely unmurderous that I wondered at myself. I put my hand on his arm again. A big brown bird was sitting on a wisteria branch looking at us: an oligarch richer than God, a dishevelled female journalist missing her son, a KGB hit man who did look to me like someone who really had been poisoned. In the golden light, in this ancient monastery, the pyramids standing not far away in the desert, we must have been beautiful, I thought.

Abram was very attached to his phone and he paced around on it talking loudly in a lot of different languages. It was hard to remain unimpressed. You know, like when you try not to look at the bloke in the red Maserati because you don't want to be one of the saddos who is impressed by this crap. But then you look and feel really impressed and then ashamed, disgusted with yourself? No? Well, it's just me then. Anyway, I was having that same issue in the dust-orange Egyptian sunset

133

at this minute. I was going to have to haul some armour on, and I was facing the fact that I wouldn't be back with my Ben tonight though it made my stomach tighten all the way round to my back like a steel corset.

'So, was it Danilenko who poisoned you? Where were you? What did you eat?' I said without the required zeal. I could see myself rooting through some hotel bins in a few hours' time, and I couldn't claim to be looking forward to it.

Alex's eyes widened. 'Danilenko! No! Danilenko is a good guy. No way. Not Danilenko. How many violinists you know murder people?'

'How many ex-KGB blokes did you eat and drink with yesterday?'

Alex seemed to be mulling this over. Jesus Christ. 'Danilenko had a guy with him. Said he was in Chechnya too but I never saw him. Sasha.'

'Sasha?' Well that narrows it down then. Seal the fucking sea ports and airports, we're looking for a Russian bloke called Sasha. Please. I have only met a handful of Russians of either gender who were NOT called Sasha, and two of them were in this courtyard. Oh no. Hold up. One of them is called Sasha – it's the diminutive of Alexander.

'And then I had a drink with Pyetya who was on the organised crime beat with me back in the mid 90s, but now he's tracking Wahabists. This is what he says. With him I took a glass of water at La Bottega.'

'A glass of water?'

'And a vodka.'

'And a vodka?'

'And those little zakuski.'

I was sitting cross-legged in front of him and I put my head in my hands. 'And with the other spooks?'

Alex's lips tightened as though he wasn't keen on the way

I was talking about his friends. His friends who, if you asked me, had tipped a fucking truck-load of arsenic into his hummus.

'Also Bottega. I took a table. With them I ate. And drank. Danilenko was here! It was a reunion!' He was indignant, as though I was accusing him of getting poisoned on purpose.

'And did anything in particular taste odd, taste wrong?'

'Faith. It was La Bottega.'

Good point.

It's an expensive foreigner-trap with slightly lewd water-coloury murals on the walls, starched napkins, obsequious service and vile food. I would say don't go there (Faith Zanetti – tour guide to the world's biggest shit holes: Kigali, Baghdad. You know what, though? Some crapola channel would probably buy it. If they haven't already) but if you're in Cairo and foreign you will probably end up there. They serve alcohol at any rate.

'So, Alex. If you're right, and by the look of you I'm veering your way I have to admit, it could have been anybody. It could have been one of these Sashas, but it could have been anyone else who had a couple of pounds to slip to a waiter. It's like trying to find an honest man in the *spets sluzhby*.'

'Hey!'

'Present company excepted.'

Do I sound unsympathetic? I know, I know. But I was shocked by how he looked and I had shut myself down to anything apart from getting back to Ben. I regretted ever having anything to do with Alex and, had I had any idea what he was really involved in, I certainly wouldn't have had anything to do with him. And now the oligarch.

Ismaelevich was shouting in Russian currently. 'Take it to the printers and get some banners made up. They need to hit the streets before tonight if it's going to make any impact

135

at all. Where the fuck is El-Baz anyway? Is someone looking after him?'

He had that 'must I deal with fools' tone on and was plainly at a loss as to understand why this stuff hadn't got done without him having to ask. You know, like rich women who show the cleaner the dust under the china figurines. He snapped his phone shut and smiled broadly at me.

'I'm backing El-Baz but you can't imagine, Faith, how extremely difficult it is to get a man elected in this country. Seriously.'

Clever, I thought. He wasn't going to come across the shady powerbroker with me. He was going-to seem to come completely clean, admit his interest, explain the complications. Clever. Very good policy. He was famous for his PR. Well, and his unknowable wealth. The Russians called it 'robbery'. Usually in the same sentence as 'Jew'.

'I was at Karima El-Baz's place just now, actually,' I said, smiling back just as openly. Alex had started shivering worryingly. It was thirty degrees in the shade. But while I was beginning to believe him about being poisoned, it didn't occur to me at all, not consciously, that he might not recover.

'Flowers, right?'

'Yes,' I nodded.

'Christ. The woman puts in invoices that cover most of my budget for cut *zayobenniye* flowers!' This seemed unlikely. 'That's politics for you,' he sighed, toying with the idea of sitting, but clearly not very good at it.

'Why El-Baz?' I wondered, trying to look all as though the giddy world of politics was way above my pretty little head. Though things were getting a lot clearer to me one way and another.

'The current leader's trying to nationalise my hotels, Faith. Bastard communist at heart. These pan-Arabists, you

136

know? Just like Russia. I was lucky. Put all my money in Switzerland from the beginning. A Jew knows when there's a pogrom coming. The other idiots believed the lies. Kept the money Russian. Trickle down. Trickle down, my *zhopa*! Look at Khordokovsky.'

I'd rather not, I thought. The Yukos guy. He was the one they really made an example of. Got him on all kinds of tax evasion crap, stole all his assets back for the state. It's hard not to sympathise with the Russians who made nothing out of privatisation when all the Yeltsin cronies made so much. But it wasn't illegal, there were arrangements, they weren't actually supposed to be paying tax if they kept everything in Russia. Oh blah blah blah. Anyway, Khordokovsky, one of the world's richest men until recently, is now doing nine years in Siberia. Not fun. Most of his colleagues are dead. But nobody seems to mind any more. Oil. Gas. Oil.

'Right,' I said.

Ismaelevich was talking to himself now. 'Yosri El-Baz is a good guy. Quiet. Peaceful. Just got to keep his dick in his pants. People here, especially women, aren't going to vote for some stud.'

'And he finds this difficult, I expect?' I wondered, innocently. But it's incredible though, isn't it? How hard people find this. You'd think that you'd just say to yourself, 'Right. I'm going to be President of America for between four and eight years. During that time I'll be sure to have sex only with my wife. Just in case I get caught, because that would be catastrophic to my career and even, conceivably, the country.' But ooooh no. I mean, it's okay in France, where they seem to take for granted that the desire for power and adulation is going to translate into a desire for sex. Goes with the territory. Oddly, in the rest of the world people are always surprised. It happens less in Russia. They're all too pissed.

'I am afraid he is sorely tried by the effort,' Ismaelevich admitted, disappointed. This was a man who was obviously constantly disappointed by others' lack of the intelligence, energy, dynamism and drive that came naturally to him. He was clenching and unclenching his fist around a smooth metal object. It was a bullet.

At this point a slim, efficient-looking young man emerged from an archway in a white short-sleeved shirt tucked into smart navy-blue trousers with a belt. He nodded at Ismaelevich.

'Ready to go?' he asked in Russian.

'Yep. Alex? Got the passport?' Ismaelevich barked at Alex, annoyed at his slothfulness, apparently. Alex, who really did seem to be fading by the minute, nodded, his sharp blue eyes sinking into his skull. Where was the man who had kissed my toes yesterday?

'The passport', I assumed, didn't have any name on it that we'd recognise.

'Okay. Off you go. Better have him taken to hospital in London. Get him checked out,' he told the man, who was now helping Alex out of his seat.

I stood up and hugged him. He smelt terrible. Sour. Strange.

'Get well, okay?' I said, patting him in a horrible acknowledgment of the end of our sexual relationship. Just like that. A little pat instead of a squeeze and it's all over.

He looked at me, trying to bore his gaze into my soul. A last chance, little did I know, to persuade me, to beg me.

'Faith. You must clear my name. You must. We can do this. We can bring this *svoloch* to justice,' he whispered, pressing his bunch of keys into my fist.

I would have followed Alex to the helicopter but Ismaelevich raised his hand in an indication that I should stay put and I wasn't about to be difficult on this issue. As I once saw Trisha Goddard say on her morning talk show, don't sweat the small stuff. I love this advice for its ominousness. The suggestion being that there is going to be big stuff to sweat so you'd better prioritise. Well, I was prioritising.

Neither of us said anything. I sat and he stood and we were obviously waiting but I wasn't sure what for. Then I heard the tok tok tok of the blades and sand blew up around the courtyard, the two women who'd been laying out the food now rushing forward to cover it with linen napkins – too late. When the dust settled Ismaelevich was on the phone again and it was getting properly dark, the heat dropping dramatically and giving me goose bumps.

When he shut the phone he tossed it onto the table.

'Got to start a new one now. Ten calls only,' he explained. Hmm. Well, that's not eco-friendly. He must have a great big yeti of a carbon footprint.

'*Nu*, Faith Zanetti. They've made the connection. Your face is all over the news – Alex's girlfriend wanted for question about the death of his first wife. Nowhere to be found.'

He seemed basically amused by this and led me inside to a little cool room lit with five candles inside ornate brass bowls that made patterns on the walls. There was a very familiar painting of a ballerina above one of the lamps. Pretty incredible since this wasn't even one of the man's official homes.

'Is that . . .?'

'Yes.'

And, incongruously, a GINORMOUS television taking up most of the room, a little upholstered mahogany sofa in front of it. Abram flicked the TV on and sat down, patting the space next to him with a bit more intimacy than I might ideally have liked.

He found the news but he didn't have to go to an Egyptian channel as I had done back at the hotel, in the bit of my life that was now becoming categorised as 'before'. Al-Jazeera International was running it as the lead item. Ugh. And I hate that picture of me. It's my bi-line picture and they won't let me change it because they like the idea of having babes on the paper. They kind of poufed my hair out and persuaded me to put some lipstick on and I look like some sort of 1970s disco diva. Not, obviously, that this was a key issue right at the moment.

'British journalist Faith Zanetti, a reporter for the *London Chronicle* [they always say this in order to distinguish the paper from the internationally far better known and intergalactically better respected *New York Chronicle*] is wanted for questioning today in relation to the apparent murder in Cairo yesterday of Eman Sorokina, the estranged wife of Alexander Sorokin.' Here they showed the ghastly shots of her body but not the close-ups. 'Sorokin, a former FSB captain, defected to Britain from Russia three years ago and is known for his harsh criticisms of the Russian's presidency. He is thought to have met journalist Zanetti in Cairo.' Oh is he, indeed. 'Egyptian police are keen to interview both Mr Sorokin and Ms Zanetti in relation to what officials are now calling a brutal killing.' Cut to interview with moustachioed police chief translated into weird English by the nearest Arab to the mike in London. Bloody hell, it was Sabrina anchoring as well. That somehow made it all the more ghastly.

'What do you think?' Ismaelevich asked me, turning off the television and plunging us into conspiratorial silence. This was not good. In my view the further away you can get from any of the Russian oligarchs the better. This, for example – not far enough.

'I think I'd better phone the desk,' I said.

Abram laughed. 'Did he do it?'

I wanted to shout 'No!' but I just wasn't quite sure any more. It seemed unlikely. I mean, why would he want to do that? He said he loved her. On the other hand . . .

I shrugged. 'But I know it wasn't me though. I'd better go and turn myself in, tell them what I know, which is diddly squat.'

'Diddly squat?'

'Nothing. I just want to go home and see my son.'

'You want to get on Alex's flight? We could make it. I've got documents.'

Christ. I could as well. Just go home and tell the English police I'm innocent. Some nice chap with a skinhead and a hangover who'd believe me because I'm white. And, more saliently, because I really never met the woman. And never come back to Cairo again. But something just wouldn't let me do it. I didn't want to run away. And I kind of did want to run Alex's explosion story, which I was sure was true. If I could prove he'd been framed for his wife's murder and prove that the FSB had poisoned him, then it would be an incredible piece. Huge. Now I'm not saying that wasn't a pretty tall order . . .

But it was about to get a lot taller.

Chapter Thirteen

'This is absurd,' I said, some time the next day, pulling the headscarf thing on. I looked in the little Islamic arch-shaped mirror and laughed. 'My hair does not fit under it. There is no way I am ever going to look remotely Egyptian.'

Ismaelevich doesn't do defeat. 'Cut your hair off. There are lots of fair Egyptians. Blue-eyed with freckles from Alexandria. Plenty.'

He sent one of the girls for scissors and I stood in a vast, cool, low-ceilinged lounge cutting off my hair in the flickering candlelight. They were kitchen scissors, maybe even bone-cutting ones for the stubborn necks of geese, and I hacked it off close to my head in huge frizzy clumps. Seeing as how I don't go in for jewellery or skirts I have always thought of myself as not being vain. However, there are degrees of everything and it was strange to let my only elaborate decoration fall to the ground golden like this. What does shaving your head mean? Humiliation. Conformity. Abdication of your own will. That was it. Abdication of your own will. Hmm. And whose will would you be bowing to now that you've shaved it? Always a man's. A lizard skittered across the floor in front of me.

The skirt had an elasticated waist and was made of thick nylon. The girl who had provided it (fortunately she seemed to have a spare) laughed when I put it on, and the sweet cotton blouse was a bit too short in the arm, but the head-dress fitted now and, frankly, I probably wouldn't arrest me if I saw me walking down the street near a crime scene. Even if I'd seen me at the bloody crime scene only this morning.

I wanted to go back to the hotel for my computer and wash-stuff but Ismaelevich easily convinced me that that would be suicidal. What did he have riding on Sorokin's innocence? Didn't he have anything better to do than organise disguises for mad murderers? Apparently not. This, I thought, betrayed his interest in all this as serious. I wondered who it was he wanted to put into power in Russia when our little crack team had effortlessly toppled the current regime. Himself like Don said? Probably. Or just someone who'd give him back his aluminium plant.

'See what you can see. Come back tonight,' he said, toss-ing me a phone which he expected me to catch and I did. It wasn't a test. Failure surprised him time after time.

When the car drove round from behind the house, a big black Mercedes, the sun was coming up and from here I could see those there pyramids in the desert through the morning mist. I could imagine feeling the breathtaking beauty of it in another life. But not in this one. The car was air-conditioned to inner-fridge temperature and the windows were blacked out. I was also separated from the driver by what was, I was pretty sure, a bullet-proof screen. In fact, obviously, the whole car was armoured. There is a big market for this in the Former Soviet Union. I expect Ismaelevich has cornered it.

'Tams! It's me!' I hissed into the phone. I was whispering loudly for no reason at all. And I wasn't really sure it was me. It certainly didn't look like me. Except for the cowboy boots. Nobody could find any shoes to fit me so here I was, all covered up like a devout-ish woman but wearing cowboy boots. They didn't show under the skirt if I walked slowly.

'HOLY FUCK, ZANETTI, WHAT'S GOING ON?!' she shouted, and I was sure the whole of Canary Wharf had run into her cubicle to hear the conversation. I could also hear her leap out of her chair and slam her door shut. 'YOU ARE SO FIRED. I'VE GOT YOU ALL OVER THE FUCKING FRONT PAGE! WHERE HAVE YOU BEEN, YOU MAD COW?'

I lit a cigarette and laughed. Deep pockets these skirts have got.

'Calm down. I'm here. In Cairo, in a bloody burka. I'm sleeping with Alex and it's all just—'

'WHO THE HELL'S ALEX?'

'Sorokin. Alexander Sorokin. Anyway, I'm . . . I was sleeping with him and all this shit started happening. He's got an amazing story. I mean, conspiracy stuff that we've heard before but he was actually involved, you know? When he defected he only said he knew about it. But it turns out he actually did it and then grassed. They're all out to prove he's mad and he's deeply in with Ismaelevich, who's sort of cute actually and . . .'

'Yuh. Yuh, Faith,' She had been puffing on her NicoPipe but it was all too much. 'SOMEBODY BRING ME A FUCKING CIGARETTE IN HERE!' she yelled out of her glass-office door. 'Just got to disable this smoke alarm,' she muttered, and I knew she was climbing onto her desk to knock the batteries out. 'Yuh, Faith. I've no fucking idea what you're on about. Don sends me these pictures of some mutilated girl and a half-baked interview with a sorority chick whose mother just died that I obviously can't use. I had to get Martina to write the democracy story using Don's shots of that girl the police tortured. Seriously, you are really hurting me, Faith. And now you're murdering people.'

Nobody has ever, in the whole history of time, sucked as hard on a cigarette as Tamsin was sucking on hers. 'Ta,' she said to someone, to her saviour, her hand over the receiver.

I looked out of the window at the rosy edges of the city waking up, strange to be in this freezing cold pod, untouchable.

'Look, Tamsin. Listen to me,' I said, knowing there was little chance of getting any concentration out of her panicked brain. 'The police didn't torture her, I don't think. That is quite a good story too. Abram Ismaelevich is manipulating – well, paying – the El-Baz family, trying to get El-Baz elected so Ismaelevich's hotels don't get nationalised. You know, he runs this whole Sharm Al Sheikh empire? Anyway, Jamila, the tortured girl, is all part of this thing but she doesn't seem to understand that. I'll write it before the elections. What date are they?'

'Eleventh.'

'Right. But first I need to find out who killed this woman and what Alex's deal is,' I told her.

'Oh, perfect. Well, in your own time, Zanetti. No rush. I'll just sit here paying your hotel bill and making excuses for you in morning conference, shall I?'

'That would be great, thanks.'

I was about to hang up when she thought of something. 'Oh. Zanetti. You do know about Sorokin, right? He's in UCH with some kind of severe poisoning, they're not sure what. Could be ecoli. Could be, like, hemlock. Who knows. On the news every ten seconds. Accusing the President of

145

killing him personally, AND his wife. Scotland Yard all over the shop, sending a Counter Terror command out to Cairo. The works. Someone's taking him seriously, at any rate.'

'Oh Christ. No way!'

'Yes way. He's a British citizen. Don't mess with 'em.'

'Shit. I've been holed up with this bloody oligarch on the run from the police. Alex only left here a few hours ago. I didn't think he'd start going for publicity. I wonder how much Ismaelevich's paying him.'

'Well, I'm telling you. He arrived at UCH last night some time, chucking his guts up.' She laughed. 'You haven't fucked him recently, have you?'

I banged on the screen behind the driver's head and he swerved into the side of the road where I got out and threw up next to the decaying carcass of a dog.

'Zanetti? Zanetti?' my phone wailed from its beige leather air-conditioned seat.

I suppose it was telling that I called Tamsin first.

'Come and say hi to Mummy,' Kristy cooed, stepping softly across the floor of my flat, so ordinary to her, another universe now to me.

'Mama!' Ben croaked. I tried very hard not to cry. Why toss my emotional crap at him? I didn't have to be here, wearing a ridiculous disguise, suffering from sodding arsenic poisoning, possibly under suspicion of murder. Aiding and abetting, at least. Do they have that charge in Egypt? I could have got a job in a bookshop and been home every night for tea. And right now, quite frankly . . .

'Hey, darling. Hello! Guess what? I've got a scarf on my head!'

He laughed and I clenched my eyes shut so that I could almost feel his fat hands clutching the phone, squashing it

146

into his cheek, his nappy falling off and his feet planted solidly, tiny pink toes, on the floorboards.

I told Kristy she'd have to stay a bit longer than I'd thought. I'd contracted something and I didn't want Ben to get it, but not to worry.

'Hey! You're in all the papers!' Kristy told me. 'We cut the photos out!'

Superb. Excellent. Little boy cutting pictures of his murder-suspect mummy out of the papers. Might as well just book him right on in at the Anna Freud centre now.

And then my third call – just as we were driving into Cairo proper, a man piling the apples up on his stall under the grumbling overpass – me close to tears, shivering in the back of the car.

'Eden! Eden! Oh, thank Christ! Where are you?'

'Me? Where am I? I think the whole world is more interested in where are YOU, darling!'

'I'm in Cairo. Oh God, it's so good to hear your voice. Listen, whatever Sorokin's got I think I might have too. In any case, I can't go home yet. Do you *read* the papers? Please can you go and get Bennie and take him to Brandeglio or something?'

'Faith. Trust me. I got on a flight as soon as I heard.' Well, of course he'd heard. Silly me. 'I'm on the Gatwick Express right now. Be with him in an hour.'

I wiped the tears off my face with the side of the headdress. Handy. Keep in control, Faith.

'Oh. Right. Well, can you tell Kristy cos I just asked her to stay on.'

'Faithy, listen. I'll worry about all that. You just do what you have to do there. Sorokin's a notorious nutter. You've probably got amoebas. Drink lots of vodka! You're good at that.'

Well, thank God for Eden Jones. Perhaps Alex had got poisoned by a mouldy old falafel at Bottega, after all. Perhaps I'd got over-dramatic about the whole thing. Hell, I hoped so. But that was only one aspect of this nightmare and Eman Sorokina, on the other hand, was still dead.

I went to Alex's flat first. I was beginning to adapt to my new personality and found that I was walking differently, more meekly, my head slightly bowed. There is no way of striding confidently along dressed like this. It strips you of any personality that is not, basically, subservient. Hey, maybe not everybody finds this but it was certainly my immediate feeling.

The car had dumped me at the crossroads by the colossal McDonald's and I thought about the piece of trivia that there had never been a war between two countries that both have a McDonald's. I love this. Surely it can't be true? Anyway, beacon of peace and prosperity such as it is (or of moral and physical degradation?), there I was outside it, identity-less and come to think of it, looking in at the plump people munching burgers and piling in fries, slightly peckish.

Alex's street had no pavements and a lot of traffic, like most streets in Cairo that aren't in the old city (medieval, eerie and beautiful as it is), and I had to shuffle along the edge of the parked cars like all the other women, though I had it easier than most of them who were carrying bags of shopping and dragging children. I waited outside his grey building – the type where the lift never works and cats piss in the foyer – until a woman went in and I pushed alongside her as though we were friends and greeted the boab with a nod when he greeted her. He was, in any case, busy with his cigarette rolling.

When I got up to flat K I was frightened to go inside,

almost prepared to be confronted with a rotting corpse or a plutonium factory, but it was just the same. Apart, perhaps, for the piano. I went into the bedroom: some clothes in the wardrobe, shoes on the floor, a comb on the tacky dressing table, the kind of thing a male designer had thought a woman might like.

Cables for a computer but no computer. I wasn't the first to come and check it out since it all happened. Had he known what was going on and grabbed the important stuff, I wondered. Hmm. I opened the fridge, smiling at how similar I was to Don though I wouldn't admit it to him, and I took a swig out of the open vodka bottle inside and then immediately panicked. Could it have been the vodka that was poisoned? Everyone's always on about how pure vodka is. I caught a glimpse of myself in the hall mirror – Islamic headscarf, all-engulfing blouse and skirt, swigging vodka out of the bottle – and I stepped back. But I noticed that also by the mirror were a few letters, in a neat pile, untouched. Perhaps whoever else had been in here had come before the boab brought the post in.

Okay, so it was unconnected to anything Alex and I had been discussing. Unconnected to Abram Ismaelevich, Egyptian politics, internal FSB wranglings. But it was jolly peculiar all the same. There were two things that looked like bills, some restaurant fliers and then six other letters. All from within the country, all personal, all with handwritten envelopes in English. I opened one (I have fewer than zero qualms about opening other people's mail) and the first thing I pulled out was a photograph of a naked bloke with a hard-on sitting on his sofa at home with some plants and stuff behind him, holding his willy and smiling at the camera.

Right then.

'Dear Alex,' the note said, written on a Post-it. 'I loved

your pix! You are some hunk. Here's mine – I was thinking about you. Let's meet! I'm renting in Ma'adi but I guess we'd better hook up in town first if we're going to play by the rules.

How about the Bottega on Friday night. Shall we say seven? As you can see I'm already hard for you, sexy!

Greg.'

Today was Friday. Did he mean this Friday? The letters could be old. I sat down on a conveniently placed chair. These flats are always chock-full of chairs for some reason. Cheap dining chairs like you might buy at a warehouse off the North Circular. Well, bugger me. Or rather . . . well, you know.

I went back to the fridge. In for a penny, I thought. I do, of course, think exclusively in proverbs, sayings and clichés. I lit a cigarette and took the rest of the letters over to the sofa with me and put my feet up on the coffee table, aware again of how I must look. I pulled the bloody headscarf off and ruffled what was left of my hair, cropped short and uneven. Greg, Billy, Tarzan (please), Johann, Lyle and, the odd one out, Khaled. A lot of big willies. A lot of suggestive notes. Do big willies turn gay men on? I know men often expect women to be turned on by them, are immensely pleased by them. I've never ever met a woman who is so much as half-interested. I mean, we can enjoy incredible sex before the willy aspect of things ever even comes into it. Odd.

I had no idea what to do with this information. I had no idea what it might mean, if anything. But I was absolutely stunned. Look, I'm not saying that his being a bisexual bloke who cruises strangers means that he's a murderer. Or even means that he's a fantasist. It means something though, a niggling something. I suppose this: that he was hiding himself. That, whatever the truth, he wasn't quite who he said he was. Converted in Chechnya? But what does Islam have to say about practising homosexuality? Nothing good I'll wager. Wanted the disguise of a new name but chose the amazingly flamboyant Alex Karamzin! Hated the corruption and lies of the FSB, people making themselves rich by deceit? But he allied himself to a man who may share the target of his venom but who is certainly no angel. Hunted by his former colleagues, fellow *osobysty*? But he was adamant that the closest of them, Danilenko, couldn't possibly have harmed him. And what about this mysterious Sasha? Wouldn't a man who was afraid for his life check out at least the name of the person he was lunching with? And Pyetya? Why didn't he suspect him, whoever the fuck he was? And now here were these guys with their dicks out suggesting that he had more on his mind even that I'd imagined. Oops, I finished the vodka.

The thing about vodka is that it makes you high and alert before it makes you drunk and weepy, before it makes you get out your guitar, before it makes you reminisce about the army, before it makes you go to bed with your wife's sister, before it makes you punch someone, before it makes you fall asleep on the metro with blood pouring out of your face. I was still at, and planned to remain at, stage one. I called the big five hotels and got put through to Danilenko's room on my fourth try, the Rameses Hilton. He picked the phone up.

'*Slushayu*,' he said.

'Hi. Can we talk?' I asked him. He hung up and called me back from a mobile.

'Who are you? Scotland Yard?' he asked.

God, he was on the ball. I mean, he was hardly going to be fingered for the Eman murder (was he?) and the Brits hadn't actually confirmed Alex's attempted murder by poisoning. Did this mean he, Danilenko, had poisoned him or just that he watched BBC World News? Who knew.

151

'No. No! I'm not Scotland Yard. I'm a friend of Alex's. Of Alexander Sorokin's. Meet me. It's important,' I said.

Now clearly I had entertained the idea that this might not work as a gambit, but it struck me as being worth a try. My general approach in life is that it is always, pretty much, worth a try. And in this case I'd got lucky. It was always possible that Danilenko had as little a clue as to what was going on as I did.

'Café at the El Hussein Hotel in half an hour,' he said, audibly exhaling smoke.

I would have objected if he hadn't hung up so quickly. The El Hussein Hotel is right by, well, kind of in Khan Al-Khalili market and opposite the Al-Azhar mosque. I put my disguise back on, wearily. Luckily, it wasn't Ramadan but even so this had to be the most crowded place in the whole of very crowded Cairo. I suppose that was the point. Not only that, but it is a really disgusting filth-pit, though very nearly charming in its old colonial way. Nearly, but not quite.

I couldn't face another cab, the fumes and the frustration and I wasn't feeling superb, so I walked. Call me crazy. Anyway, nobody could claim I didn't have plenty to think about on the way. Could Alex and I have been poisoned by the hotel nuts? He HAD eaten more of them . . .

In the end, hoping that my sense of direction wasn't too skewed, I cut through the market to get to the hotel. Coloured light bulbs are strung across the narrow, dark alleys and more swinging bulbs light up the stuff at each stall. Towards the outer edges of the market a lot of these are kind of normal shops selling spices in hessian sacks by the scoopful (cumin seeds, turmeric, cardamom pods, chillies), piles and piles of pink and white coconut sweets, Turkish delight in cardboard boxes and slabs of pistachio halva. There was a coffee stall with bags of flavoured beans for you to smell in a handful and then an actual fez stall with all the old brass fez shapes on a kind of barrow with a brass gas stove over which to shape the felt onto the required size of mould. The old guy seemed to be doing a roaring trade, and inside his shop there were all these wax heads wearing his fezs. Mostly though it was clothes, gelabayas on rails to be reached with a long hooked pole, baby stuff laid out on tables blocking the alley and millions of scarves – silk ones – shawls and pashminas. Then all the tourist stuff, of course – papyruses, coffee sets, lampshades, shishas, leather camels, busts of the pharaohs, interlocking pyramids, gold jewellery, jet cats and perfume stalls with banks of old glass-lidded bottles where they promise to make up your perfume to the exact specification. They stand there shouting, 'Chanel No. 5!' and 'Rive Gauche!' Apparently they do it brilliantly – you can't tell the difference except for the lower price and prettier bottle.

Now normally I get hassled out of my mind in Khan Al-Khalili, chased by crowds of young blokes, some wanting a shag and some wanting me to buy their beautiful glass lampshade which I would very much want if they'd only shut up about it. But now, in my new outfit, nobody even held out a baklava for me. Amazing! And odd from the anonymity point of view. There aren't many places in the world where I've felt anonymous, but all you had to do was put a headscarf on. And this does not mean buy a scarf and wrap it round your head with all the blonde poking out the edges in the way that some travellers and all TV correspondents do in a nod to local custom. This is the real thing, solid-ish with cardboard in it and not a visible strand. Hell, I hardly had a strand left anyway.

The air in these cobbled alleys is the only sweet air in Cairo, I think. None of the cat piss and rotting garbage, tanneries, pollution and cigarette smoke. It smells of coffee and cinammon here, of honeyed shisha smoke and baking bread. And past that café, the Fishawy, which is always packed with Cairenes and foreigners spilling into the alley from low wooden tables and chairs, everyone smoking pipes and drinking tea, I was almost tempted by that hot sweet yoghurty stuff with nuts in that the women seem to drink. An American girl was having her arms hennaed by an ancient Sudanese woman whose brush-holding hand was dyed completely black by her work.

Two young Cairene guys in tight jeans were trying to chat her up. The American, not the henna artist. I assume they were asking her if she liked fucking – usually the approach. I wonder what their wives, mothers, sisters think of the way they behave around Western women? Do they too believe these women are whores who are basically asking to be raped? Surely not.

At El-Hussein Square I skipped totally unmolested, head bowed, up the stairs to the café at the top of the hotel, with views over the square, mosque and market. There was a couple sharing a shisha, a toddler on the woman's lap with a dummy in, she was in headscarf just like me. Otherwise a few backpackers drinking mint tea and some very bored-looking waiters idling around and smoking. Oh, and a Russian guy in a suit sitting in the corner with a beer.

'Faith Zanetti,' I said, holding out my hand and sitting down.

Danilenko looked up at me, baffled. He was typical FSB material. Pockmarked skin almost grey with the cloud of smoke it had always lived in: no sun, no fruit or vegetables and a lot of vodka. His eyes were grey and blank too, giving nothing away. He had a big head and big hands and those shoulders that seem to be standard-issue in the Russian military.

'Grigory Danilenko. I didn't expect an Egyptian. You

154

sounded English on the phone,' he said, gesturing me to sit down in the seat I'd just sat down in. Well, my disguise was working then.

'No. No, I am English. I was involved with Sorokin and I don't want to get taken in for questioning about his wife's death. I wasn't there, didn't know her and am not about to start getting interrogated now. I'm a journalist. I really just want to get home to my son,' I explained, thinking there was no harm in being honest with this bloke.

'Understood,' he said in Russian, very nearly smiling.

'So. You were at Bottega with Alex yesterday before he got ill. He thinks he was poisoned, as you know. He doesn't think you did it. Who is this Sasha who was with you?'

Danilenko raised his eyebrows. He looked as though he'd expected me to be bringing him information, not trying to get some.

'Sorokin is a madman. Our president has already dismissed his allegations as the nonsense that they are.' Had he? I must watch more telly. Well, responding at all is a big deal in itself, a sign that this was being taken seriously. I had yet to see the footage, of course, of a shifty-eyed President trying to look innocent. 'I am astonished that the British media is taking the slightest notice. No, I didn't poison him. I brought him a business proposition from a very reputable British oil firm. Sasha is the middle man, if you like.'

Funny how often people say that. If you like. What has what I like got to do with it? I like gin martinis.

'What's his name?'

Danilenko laughed, raising a hand to bring the waiter over. 'What will you have, Miss Zanetti?'

'A beer, please.' I smiled at the waiter. I have rarely seen anyone look so shocked. He pursed his lips and walked away.

'I could tell you his name, but what good would it do? Sasha didn't poison him. Nobody poisoned him. Or maybe Ismaelevich has poisoned him. Or he poisoned himself to make the president look guilty. I wouldn't put anything past him.'

'Then why did you want him to come into business with you? If I was choosing a business partner, a "madman" wouldn't be my first choice.'

Danilenko laughed again. 'That would depend on the business! Sorokin is good at obeying orders. Brutal when he needs to be. But he will go over the top. On the other hand, sometimes you need a man who will go over the top.'

The waiter plonked my beer down in front of me with a glass. I said '*shukran*' and swigged it out of the bottle just for shock effect. Well, honestly.

'He didn't obey orders to keep quiet about Dagestan. He didn't obey FSB orders to kill Ismaelevich. I still don't understand why you wanted to do any kind of business with him if this is what you believed. He believed you were good friends, allies, colleagues,' I tried, prodding, poking, trying to grasp.

The call to prayer was singing out from the tower of the mosque and there was a general movement towards it down on the street.

Danilenko tapped the side of his glass with one finger. 'Maybe he WAS obeying orders. Maybe he was never ordered to kill Ismaelevich. Maybe he was ordered to tell Ismaelevich a lie. To become close to him. To spy on him. Maybe his shouting about explosions was so that the FSB could dismiss him, make his friendship with Ismaelevich more convincing. Did this occur to you?'

Hell, you know what? It was so fucking complicated that it hadn't occurred to me, I must admit. But now he mentioned it. I mean, nobody leaves the FSB, right? Wasn't that what Don said? What everyone says? In a way, wasn't Danilenko's mad theory less mad than an agency guy suddenly saying he doesn't like what he has to do and please can he have a few years off while the service cleans itself up from the inside?

'Umm. Not exactly . . .'

I tell you the crap thing about these headdresses, though. Your head doesn't half itch under them and you can't get in to scratch it.

'All right, but say you're right. I still don't understand what you and . . . "Sasha" want with him.' I ploughed on.

'And I don't mean to be rude but it's none of your business. And now that he's done this again, well, obviously . . . we don't want him any more. So . . .' He swigged his second beer back and pushed his chair out to get up.

'If there's nothing else.'

I, however, was drowning in my beer. In the end I had to spit my mouthful somewhat unattractively into my empty glass. Not that attractiveness was really the crux of this particular moment.

'Done what again?' I asked, when I'd finished spluttering. He was standing behind his chair. I held my breath, hoping that he wasn't going to say what I thought he was going to say.

'Killed his wife.'

'Again?' I raised my eyebrows.

'No? Well. He wouldn't have mentioned it. St Petersburg. On leave after . . . Well. After that. Nice girl. Good violinist. We all played together once.'

He smiled in a 'those were the days' kind of way, apparently not at all fussed about coming all the way to Cairo to put a business proposition to a murderer. Or, I realised, a murderer may have been precisely what he was looking for.

'Christ.'

I was leaning my elbows on the table but Danilenko was desperate to leave. This wasn't the type of meeting he'd been anticipating.

'Happened a lot back then. When men weren't getting paid. Morale was very low. Took our troubles home with us. Always a bachelor, me.'

Hmm. Shocker.

He put some money down on the table and walked out. I finished my beer alone, glared at by the waiters. The heat was dropping outside, the stonework seeming visibly to relax. So this should teach me. Do not get into bed with butch Russian men who have already demonstrated serious instability by unexpectedly trying, and failing, to jump over you. Rule Number One.

The toddler came up to my table and tried to give me her dummy. I made a face at her, she laughed and ran back to her mum who smiled over in apology and acknowledgment of the pleasant burden of little children. I smiled and realised that this woman had taken me for a friend, because of the headscarf. Strange and sweet. She must not have noticed the beer.

I rapped my fingertips on the formica tabletop and crumpled up a napkin. Then I uncrumpled it again and smoothed it out under my palm. I just couldn't make these versions of Alex fit into one possibly-poisoned man. The bloke who'd seduced me so easily that night, the tied up guy in his flat, the friend of Ismaelevich, the friendly uncle, the wonderful pianist, the paranoid accuser, naively vehement idealist, the bisexual predator, the murderer. Who the hell was he after all?

Well, I couldn't resist. Plus I'd drunk a lot of vodka and now a beer, eaten nothing much and been sick a few times.

158

I probably shouldn't have been making decisions. But I made one.

'Good evening?' the Bottega maître d' asked me officiously. Oh my God! He was thinking of not letting me in! Normally he would be guiding me in with a hand in the small of my back, knowing that the place would be making a killing from my table.

'Oh for fuck's sake. It's a disguise!' I said much too loudly. 'I'm English and I'm looking for a friend.'

He leapt back, confused. Ah, and here was my friend.

'Greg!' I beamed. He looked different with clothes on. It was hard not to laugh, recognising him from that picture of his glistening erection.

Greg was absolutely terrified. He blanched and leant down for his briefcase, ready to run. I seriously think he was afraid I'd kill him. I was Alex's jealous wife, devastated by what she'd found out. Perhaps this had happened to him before.

'No! No. Greg, I'm English, I'm not . . . I'm not his wife or anything.' Thank the Lord, I said under my breath, or maybe I just thought it. 'I just came to tell you he's very ill. Gone back to London. I'm sorry.'

Greg loosened his tie, very much relieved. 'Jesus, you gave me a shock.' He grinned. 'Whoah.' He held both hands up in a mock-scared surrender.

'Yeh. I know. Sorry. I've been getting shock after shock myself lately. I know how you feel. Drink?'

'Sure.' He smiled, surprised I was drinking. I really really really wanted to take this thing off. I mean, the short hair should be disguise enough. I could always wear, say, a red T-shirt or something.

Greg was by far the nicest person I had met for days. He

was working for an investment company, attracting business to Egypt, and he'd been here three years. He lived in Zamalek and was from San Francisco and found the dating scene in Cairo extremely difficult.

'You sleep with a lot of Egyptian guys who talk about how they're looking for the right girl to marry, to fall in love with. And when I'm like, "I'm kind of looking for a relationship" they're all like, "Eeeiu! Are you gay or something?" And that just leaves the foreign dudes but, to be honest, it's more of a family posting. So . . .'

'So this is a website you got Alex from, is it?' I wondered, sipping a gin martini. The first person in a veil to do that in here, I bet.

'That's right. Truly, to be honest though, I know a couple of the guys he's already slept with and I heard he was cute. I usually only answer the ads when I've already heard good things about the guy. Otherwise it can be scary.'

'I bet.' I nodded. And how. 'He had a wife, you know?'

'*Had* a wife?'

'Yes. She was killed yesterday.'

'Dude.'

'Exactly.'

'Did he kill her or what?'

'I don't know. I was sleeping with him too,' I said, looking him right in the face. He looked as if he managed to get down to the beaches a lot. There is good diving in Egypt.

Greg laughed. Nice white teeth. Well, Americans do. 'What are you trying to suggest?' he said loudly and mouthing emphatically. 'That he might have been . . . BISEXUAL?!'

Okay. I realised how ridiculous I'd sounded. And, of course, that was the least of his foibles.

'Sorry. Yes, I suppose he must have been. Must be! I wonder if his wife knew.'

Greg took a long slug of his beer. 'They usually don't. I dated a married guy for a year once. He kept saying to me, you know, face mail, that he was going to leave her but . . . well, you know what they're like.'

'What, men? I do! Bastards!'

He laughed. I liked that – face mail. 'No! Straight guys!'

'What are they like?'

'Bastards!'

Okay. Well, this was fun, but it wasn't getting me anywhere and I was feeling rough again. I got ready to go.

'Look. Take this number. I don't think he did kill her, but if any of your friends who knew him can think of anything, please call,' I said, and gave him Don's mobile number and my email address.

'Sure. Will do.' Greg agreed. 'So, I'm kind of glad I never met him now.'

'Yes. You should be.' I nodded and went outside to text the big black car man, the back of whose head I would look at all the way home to Ismaelevich's house.

Chapter Fourteen

There were two cars parked at the front of the house: a hire car and a blacked-out embassy thing. Far from being an inaccessible safe house, it seemed like everyone and his boab was coming to the party. I hopped out, desperate to get back into a half-normal outfit, and went through the courtyard into the big lounge which was where the voices were coming from.

I tore my headscarf off and somebody said, 'Oh fuck me!'

When my eyes adjusted to the gloom they confirmed what my ears had already suspected. Don was here. Was he in cahoots with Ismaelevich too, for God's sake? Oh shit. I remembered I'd stupidly given him the bloody address.

I peered around and saw that he was sitting at a table by himself, lit by the glow of his laptop and smoking with a deep wheeze. Ismaelevich was on a sofa, leaning forwards, elbows on knees, talking to the two besuited British Embassy types who faced him on the opposite sofa. Ah, no. Not embassy. These were the Scotland Yard boys. Wow, that was quick.

They both got up.

'Faith Zanetti,' I said, striding forward and holding my hand out. Neither of them took it.

'Oh. Okay.' I nodded, retracting it. 'I'm not having my period or anything, you know.'

Neither of them smiled.

'I am Assistant Commissioner Cameron and this is Deputy Assistant Commissioner Summerfield. Scotland Yard Counter Terrorism Command SO15,' the white one said. Summerfield was black but, oddly, almost identical to Cameron anyway.

'Cool,' I said. They sat back down and Ismaelevich glowered at me, presumably trying to convey a variety of messages. The main one was, I deduced, 'You psychotic bitch, you gave my address to the fat photographer. You could have got me killed.' And the other ones, I imagined, related to any information I might have uncovered today and how I shouldn't tell these policemen any of it, no, none at all. I tried to look sheepish.

'As you have probably guessed, Miss Zanetti, we are here investigating the suspected poisoning of Alexander Sorokin in Cairo on Wednesday and Mr Ismaelevich is helping us with our inquiries. We would also like to speak to you as we understand you spent time with Mr Sorokin on the suspected day of the suspected poisoning. With your permission,' Summerfield tortuously explained.

'Yuh. Or without it. Sure,' I said. 'You're not going to be telling the Egyptian police where I am, are you?'

Summerfield and Cameron raised their eyebrows in unison and looked at each other.

Cameron answered. 'We are working with the Egyptian police at the current time, Miss Zanetti,' he said.

'Fuck.' I sighed. I just so didn't want to get trapped in a

hot, fly-infested interview room with a violent moustachioed sex-starved twenty-five-year-old. Let alone two of them.

I tried to make some sort of conspiratorial face at Don when I noticed he was crying, quietly.

'Excuse me.' I smiled at the Yardies. 'McCaughrean?' I said, going over to him. 'What's your deal?'

He wiped the back of his hand across his eyes and put his cigarette out in an inlaid mother-of-pearl ashtray. Or if it hadn't been an ashtray a few moments ago, it was now.

'I've been such a tit, Eff Zed. I've just been a complete and utter mammary gland. And this is a punishment. I know it!'

'What is?'

Cameron interrupted. 'We have just received confirmation that Mr Sorokin was, unfortunately, poisoned as he suspected himself. With radioactive thallium. His urine contained a huge amount of gamma radiation. We're lucky that he knew what had happened, because the usual tests don't run to nuclear material and he might have died before anyone found out why. He ingested a huge amount, though we don't yet know exactly what it was that he ate or drank or when he ate or drank it. We do know that there were more than four billion becquerels in the source material and the idiots, excuse me, but it's true, had it leaking all over the place. The trail is ridiculously easy to follow. It will mean, I am sorry to say, that anyone who came into contact with him after his having been poisoned will be, to a greater or lesser extent, contaminated. Unfortunately, you will have to be tested, obviously, Miss Zanetti.'

Was I supposed to understand what any of this meant?

Ismaelevich seemed actually to growl.

'That IS unfortunate,' I said, still not quite registering the full import of this information.

'I'm being framed. No way he's been poisoned,' Ismaelevich muttered in Russian, turning his growl into a smile and a cough for the Scotland Yarders. Weird. I mean, if absofuckinglutely everyone thought they'd been framed then who was doing the sodding framing? Eh?

'Call me Faith.' I sighed and collapsed into a pretty chair, feeling immediately sick.

'We're gonners, Zanetti,' Don moaned.

'Oh shut up, Donald. You didn't even see him. Get a grip on yourself. Anyway, you're always a tit. She'll forgive you. Ira always does.'

Ben. I couldn't die of anything. I wasn't leaving Ben.

And I'd known really. It wasn't like normal being sick.

Ismaelevich was signing a heap of documents on his lap one by one and Summerfield was supervising. He used the biggest, blackest, shiniest Mont Blanc fountain pen with gold trim. Very new rich. A real posh person, which was what Ismaelevich longed to be but never would be, would have used a biro. And kept a lot of dogs. It was the second generation Ismaeleviches, currently at Eton, who would perhaps claim that territory.

'Is that why you came out here?'

'Yeh,' Don snivelled.

Somehow it was his snivel that made my, far more justifiable, snivels come on in earnest. I was, hard though it is to admit, terrified. Since my son was born, you see, I have developed that awful courage-quashing thing that is Something To Lose.

I grabbed the mobile phone I'd been provided with out of my ludicrous skirt pocket and scuttled, cockroach-like, into the corner of the room, turning my back on everyone in some effort to affect privacy. I should have gone outside but it was too urgent. I called Eden.

'Jones! I've been nuclearly terrorised. I'm fucking—'
Come to think of it, I was about to burst into tears in an oligarch's monastery.

'Shhh. Shhh. Yes, I saw him on the news a second ago. He looks like the most incredible shit. Do they know what it is yet?'

'Yes, it's bloody radiation.'

'No, I know. But exactly?'

'How much more exact does it need to be for Christ's sake, Eden?'

I could hear Ben laughing at something in the background and my whole body physically hurt with longing.

'A lot, Faithy. An awful lot. Some things have antidotes.'

'Man alive.' I sighed, lighting a cigarette to Summerfield and Cameron's apparent horror. Does nobody smoke any more? 'It's called thallium, apparently.'

I could hear Eden's computer keys clicking, efficiently. 'Look. He ate it,' Eden said, firmly. 'You didn't. If you had done you'd look like him. Remember the *likvidatory*?'

I did. We'd both been doing Chernobyl tenth-anniversary things back then, interviewing all the firemen who were first on the scene. They'd had no special protection and a lot of them had got seriously ill with radiation sickness, but recovered. Most of them, those that didn't get incinerated on the spot, are still going strong. It was a good and reassuring point.

'Hmm,' I said.

'You're going to be fine. I mean, presumably you didn't do anything more than.'

'No. Just that. Oh God, Jones . . .' Why did I hate telling him if I'd slept with someone? Pathetic. Especially since Eden has always been known for being Shag Central.

Okay. So, I was a bit calmer about a green, glowing, bald death. I chewed the inside of my mouth and tried to keep it shut on the gripping subject of what Danilenko had said about Alex killing his first wife, but I realised that this was not the time or place to be bringing it up.

Where did I meet Mr Sorokin? The Nile Hilton. Did he say he feared for his life? Yes, he was running away from someone when I first met him. Who did he meet that day? Danilenko, 'Sasha', Pyetya who works for the Egyptian Government, and me, but in London. Did he mention any specific enemies? Pretty much everyone, but mostly Russia herself and the senior FSB people, including the commander of his former unit, who had organised the apartment bombing and apparently pretty much got away with covering it up. And murdered a suspect once with a pair of shears.

It was surreal to be interviewed by these two extremely Scotland Yard Scotland-Yard-types, in the low, dark, candle-flickering lounge of Abram Ismaelevich's house in the Cairo desert. Especially in a skirt and blouse and with a shaggy cropped head of hair.

Ismaelevich was livid, simmering, boiling, blistering with rage under his 'I am just more British than the British' veneer that he had put on for the bobbies. I imagine he thought of them as bobbies.

Don, of course, was just very very drunk. I realised this when he stood up to 'go for a slash' and staggered in the gloom, knocking a stool over and swearing. He had hired a car and bombed down here, smashed out of his brain, to commiserate with me over our imminent death, seemingly forgetting that he was only supposed to come if he didn't hear from me for a FEW DAYS.

'Couldn't believe it when fucking Khordokovsky came out yelling at me with about four fuckers with sub-machine guns behind him.'

'It's Ismaelevich, Don. Khordokovsky's in prison.'

'Whatever,' he said. 'Pinned me to the fucking ground. It took me fifteen minutes to convince him that nobody followed me and that I'm just a pissed snapper looking for Little Bo Peep.'

Yuh. Well. Congratulations to Ismaelevich for so much as beginning to understand him, that's all I can say. I didn't dare ask what had happened with Dahlia. I assumed she'd dumped him or something. I can't imagine remorse kicking in unnecessarily in Don McCaughrean.

So, eventually the suits left, promising to send a CBRN (chemical, biological, radiological and nuclear) squad down to take blood and urine, and advise on treatment. They didn't tell me I was going to be taken in for questioning about Eman's death, but they didn't need to. I'd known since I saw the poor woman on television in my hotel room less than forty-eight hours and a thousand years ago. Ismaelevich and I were not to leave the country.

The three of us, unlikely a group as we were, physically relaxed with their departure: shoulders slumping, jaws unclenching, spines curving, stomachs let out. And Don seemed to sober up immediately. Had he been pretending? The bloke was unreal. Ismaelevich, smiling, straight away had a couple of bottles of vodka brought in and one of the girls poured us Russian-sized shots into delicate pink-and-gold tea glasses. She'd brought gherkins out too.

'*Ty ogurets!*' I said to Don, holding one up. It means 'you are a cucumber' but it's a kind of funny way of saying 'well done'.

I had now, at last, changed back into my jeans and a T-shirt in the loo (marble sink with a bowl of floating lilies by it) and I walked over to Don's computer with my betrousered swagger back when he beckoned for me, slightly somber-faced.

'Look at this,' he said. We were almost starting to feel at home. God knows what Abram's other houses are like.

I was looking at a grainy photo, an old photo, a horrible photo.

'Christ, Don,' I complained, leaning over him to peer closer. 'Why are you showing me this?'

It was of a dead girl at the bottom of a staircase in a sea of blood. She was blonde and she was lying near a Soviet-looking lift with blue metal letter boxes swinging open above her. She was in such a similar position and location to Alex's Egyptian wife that, despite myself, I understood immediately. And I realised, as I understood, that I had believed Danilenko from the moment he'd said it, in the horrible black snake-pit of my heart.

'What the fuck is this, Don? Where did it come from?'

Don shrugged in his damp short-sleeved checked shirt. 'You tell me. Anonymous. What do you think it is?'

'It's Alex's first wife. I met a guy today who said he'd done this before. He was like, "And now he's done this again." All exasperated with him like he was in trouble at school "again" or something. It's got to be from Danilenko. But why to you? How would he know to send it to you? Why not to me if he's so desperate for me to know?'

Don looked into his vodka glass as though hoping that there was some hiding there that he hadn't noticed on his first swig. There wasn't.

Ismaelevich came to look at the screen. Don burped.

'He killed his first wife? When?' Ismaelevich wanted to know. 'Pretty girl.'

I shook my head. 'No idea. But I'd like to find out.'

Now that I knew what it was, I could taste something in my mouth that went with the nausea and vomiting. A

169

kind of metallic taste, something bitter that made me wince.

I ruffled my head and wondered what Ben would think of my haircut. Would the rest of my hair fall out? Ben loved pulling at my curls. What if he didn't recognise me? I wanted to scream and cry and go home. At least now I'd got a home to long for. I turned away from the computer and paced about behind the men, smoking and then hating myself for having started again.

'Abram? You've been so kind to me. And to Alex.'

'What do you want?' Ismaelevich asked. God, he was good.

'Is there any way you could get me and Don into Russia? I want to go to Petersburg and have a nose into this murder here. See what happened. I know it seems insane, but I think it might help us . . . you know . . . to find out what's going on now.'

Well, it was true. Had his first wife been murdered? And if she'd been murdered by Alex then why hadn't he been packed off to Siberia with all the other wife-killers and tax dodgers? And if she hadn't then, well, maybe we were looking at two terrible accidents and a Putin-approved poisoning. But if, after all, Alex was someone who did go around killing his wives willy-nilly, then the likelihood of the whole explosions story being true was probably slimmer. Gnarly but right, I think.

'He is bisexual, you know? Met blokes via some kind of contacts Internet thing,' I said quietly, watching the air move in the patterns on the walls from the brass candle bowls. I sat down.

'You what?!' Don perked up, staring at me, his blue eyes blood-shot, rheumy. 'He's an arse bandit? A raider of the midnight chocolate cupboard?'

170

I sighed. How did I end up being friends with this guy?

'No, Don. He is bisexual.'

I enjoyed being the calm one after playing the other role in Bottega with Grigory.

'So Eman found out and he killed her?' Ismaelevich suggested, lighting the biggest cigar I have ever seen. Big cigar: small willy? Very possibly.

'You know what? I would believe anything at the moment. So, maybe, yeh.' But he wouldn't have killed someone for that, whatever his old KGB gang-member honour had told him to do.

'But he seemed so into you, Eff Zed. And all the time he was giving boys a back door . . .'

'DON!' I shouted, not wanting to hear another bloody word of this crap. 'Do you not understand the word bisexual? He liked BOTH.'

Don snorted so hard that snot actually came out of his nose and he had to wipe it away with his hand. 'Yuh. That's what they all say,' he howled. This was his all-time hands-down favourite subject on the planet. 'You don't get many aged bisexuals though, do you? It's just what they say when they don't want to shut the closet door behind them. Too scared.'

'Don, are you trying to tell me something?'

And then, to my utter amazement, Don blustered and blushed a kind of deep deep purple, like the colour you might imagine someone goes when they're having a heart attack.

Well, it explained a lot, that's for sure.

'No problem,' Ismaelevich said, rolling up his shirt-sleeves in that down-to-business way men have. Sexuality wasn't interesting to him. Just power and money. 'But I can't come with you, I'm afraid. I abhor salt mines.' He waited for the required laugh. 'My plane's at the airport. I'll see what documents I've got for a woman. You can presumably exit and enter on your own passport, Mr McCaughrean?' Well, he wasn't wanted for murder, was he?

Don got to his feet. 'Yes, sir. Absolutely, sir,' he said, in awe of the oligarch and clueless as to how to behave in front of him.

Chapter Fifteen

We got into Leningrad late at night. Oh, all right, then. St Petersburg. It is amazing what money can do. Not a secret, of course, but genuinely amazing. The helicopter that had taken Alex to the airport and was, therefore, probably radioactive and would need be tested, took me and Don out into the starry sky and over to the same airport in about twenty minutes. Don is not a big fan of the helicopter.

'If those blades stop whirring, we're toast,' he said, gripping the sides of his seat and shutting his eyes.

'Yes, Don,' I said.

'We'll drop like a stone.'

'We would, Don, yes.' I nodded.

'Just some twisted metal and burning corpses in the desert sand.'

'That's right.'

This conversation lasted us all the way there and we were taken through the VIP procedure for the TransAero Moscow flight. This involved walking from the helicopter with a nice TransAero lady called Agafya, through some empty airport corridors where a lot of the bulbs didn't work and out onto the tarmac where we got onto the nice TransAero plane. An Egyptian airport authority woman met us at the bottom of the stairs and glanced at our passports. Mine was Russian and alleged that I was Nadezhda Davydovna Razumikhina who is, or was, ten years younger than me and from Novosibirsk. I can't imagine anyone half-zealous thinking I looked much like her, though she was blonde and not dramatically fatter or thinner than I am. Anyway, on we got, First Class thank you very much and I'll have another glass of that, please.

Don wedged himself into his seat and scratched at his neck. 'Why are we going to Russia again?' he asked, tipping his champagne glass up as high as he could, to get the last drop.

'To see if Alex killed his first wife. Ekaterina she was called, apparently.'

'Well, we don't know if he killed his bloody second wife, so who cares?'

'Yeah, but somebody else is looking into that. And killing his first wife would be a pretty major clue if you ask me. Though it might not be allowable evidence in Egypt. Fuck knows.'

I didn't even have hand luggage. I didn't have anything. Just the clothes I'd got to Ismaelevich's in before Alex had been swept to London.

And what I really needed was a bath. I took the little wash kit bag thing into the loo after take off and undressed completely. I filled the sink up with water and had as near to a shower as I could manage without flooding the whole plane, even washing the scrub that was left of my hair in the tiny weeny metal sink (as a courtesy to fellow passengers please wipe the sink down with a paper towel after use). I threw my underwear away, cleaned my teeth, splashed my face with cold water, put my clothes back on and returned to my seat

174

(with my tray table in the upright position) to get drunk with Don. In the end though he passed out quite quickly, so I watched one of those Chinese films where they throw knives and fly and stuff. It seemed to go on all the way to Moscow and I never quite managed to grasp what, exactly, the plot was. Hell, perhaps there wasn't one.

A car was waiting to take us to the station where we got on the Red Arrow to St Petersburg, leaving at midnight. Ismaelevich's generosity did, apparently, know some bounds. He hadn't booked us a compartment each.

'After you, Donski,' I said, standing out in the corridor with a big group of elderly American tourists, all of whom were fatter than Don but none as smelly. I had opened the car window on the way to the station to let the Moscow summer air into my lungs. Well, they couldn't get much more damaged than they already were, surely. It was balmy and breezy, a wind coming in from the river and people out on the streets drinking beer and flirting. The trees in all the courtyards were still green and you could feel the good mood of a whole city just delighted that it's not winter. Women everywhere in short skirts and shorts, happy and free to choose to be a lesbian plumber if they want to be. Nice to observe after Cairo. The neon signs were flashing and the traffic was serious, but there is a carelessness to Moscow in the summer as everyone crowds outside to make the most of it. A lot of drunken drownings, of course.

Don slumped on to his bed, depressed. 'What am I going to tell Ira?' he asked, his hands over his eyes. The carriage lady came in with glasses of tea and a sandwich. Her grey uniform was tight and looked old. She'd been doing this since they woke the whole train up at six in the morning with the Soviet national anthem. Anyone could see that. She'd turned the heating up to full so that some poor gasping

sweating passenger would have to bribe her to turn it down –
the controls were in her compartment. I would leave it ten
minutes before resigning myself to the fact that I was that
poor passenger.

We handed over our passports and the money for the bed
linen (I ask you) and she shuffled out to rip someone else off.

'What did you tell her about Cairo?'

'Told her I was doing a story about belly dancers.'

'What did she say?'

'She said, "You've just done one."'

'And what did you say?'

'I said, "I'm doing another one."'

Right. Well. True enough so far.

'Don, call her up, say you're just doing this thing here
with me and you'll be home to Peredelkino tomorrow or the
next day.'

'What if she can tell?'

'If she can tell she'll kick you out and then have you back
when you've suffered enough. If she can't tell, you're fine.'

'And what about Dahlia?'

'What about Dahlia?'

'I love her.'

'Oh, Don. Get a grip on yourself.'

I drank the tea sitting on the edge of my bed and I
watched the forests go by in the night. When I called Eden
he said that he and Ben were in bed watching *Braveheart*.

'What?'

'Well, I think Bennie's nodded off,' he admitted.

They were still in London, staying at my flat. I wasn't crazy
about this as it was a bit close to moving in and might confuse
Ben but, given that I was contaminated with deadly radiation
and was a possible murder suspect, I thought I wouldn't sweat
the small stuff.

'Edes, can you do something for me? Can you break into Alex's flat and check out his stuff?'

'Lemme think . . . NO!'

'Pleeeease,' I wheedled. 'Earls Court Square. Number twenty-two. Flat 2. Go on. bet nobody's been round yet.'

'No. Probably just special branch, the FSB, CIA and Mossad.'

'He won't have let them yet. Does he have a choice? Oh, God. I don't know. Please have a glance. Come on! Help me out here.'

'If I do will you and Ben come and live in Italy with me?'

'Okay,' I said.

'You know you won't.'

'True, but I really want you to do this so I lied.'

'Hmph. How are you anyway?'

'Not that bad, actually. I'm getting less scared. It was a good point about the *likvidatory*. Still a bit sick.'

'Good. Well, love you.'

'You too.'

I know I should have said it in full but it's just so bloody hard to choke out unless you're sure. Funny how it seems such a big deal your whole life until you have children and then you find yourself saying and meaning it forty times a day, qualmless.

I think we were basically already there by the time I finally went to sleep. I didn't eat the sandwich. I may have radiation poisoning but I'm not suicidal.

The station in St Petersburg is at one end of the Nevsky Prospect which, at dawn, is devastatingly beautiful. Lots of puffy-eyed people crawling off the train into the very pale pink light and out into the morning-after city. Street sweepers, drunks, police cars and ambulances but, otherwise, relative silence. You could even hear the birds in the spindly trees. The trams are only just hauling themselves into action when the Moscow train gets in and, since Don insisted on dumping his bags at his friend Boris's house, we duly hauled ourselves up the Nevsky Prospect alongside one, dwarfed by the buildings, numbed by the journey.

This is the Venice of the North. It is nothing like Venice. There are canals and the buildings are grand and elaborate. It is, I admit, lovely. But, entirely unlike Venice, you can feel the brutality and the bleakness. There is a reason why Gogol set all his going mad stories here, where nothing makes sense. And so did Pushkin, come to think of it. This is the city where Anna Akhmatova queued outside the Crosses prison for days on end to see her son, along with thousands of others. This is where Peter the Great kept, well, everything, but his everything included his collection of aborted foetuses, freaks of nature, body parts. The whole grandiose fantasy was imposed on a hostile swamp by a power-crazed autocrat, and thousands of people died building it. It's damp, unutterably cold in winter, eerie and unsettling. But it is beautiful.

So in what ought to be predictable Don style, but I was surprised as usual, it turns out that his friend Boris is the megastar Boris Grebinshikov who lives in a big old communal apartment off the Prospect, up some stairs graffitied by fans over the now many decades of his career. He used to fill the Lenin Stadium no problem. He used to be a big problem for the Communist government and he has recorded with Annie Lennox and all sorts of other people. He is a Buddhist.

'Oh, hi, Don,' he said when he opened the door in glasses and vaguely Hare Krishna-ish robes. He didn't comment on the time and he must already have been up because the apartment smelt of coffee and incense and there was Eastern spiritual music on. I wandered into the warm fragrant dark behind Don. Oh, no, I tell a lie. The music was not 'on'. It was actually being played live by a group of four monks who sat, cross-legged, on the floor in one of the rooms off the hall.

'Hi, Borka. Can I leave some shit here? We're on a job.' He didn't introduce me and, without my hair, Boris didn't ask him to. I had never realised how much people's reactions to me were dependent on it.

'Sure,' Boris said vaguely. He spoke with an American accent.

I was on the verge of saying what a huge Akvarium fan I am (the band of which he's the lead singer) and how much I love the *Snow Lion* album. But being a fan doesn't come easily to me. I am almost genuinely in love with Mika (who, if you honestly don't know, is a twenty-four-year-old boy singer) but it is so embarrassing – unrequited, unrequitable love – that I can hardly admit it even to myself.

'You want tea? Green tea with orange, mint or verbena? Or coffee – fairtrade?'

Don said yes but I kicked him and instead we landed ourselves back in the street looking for a taxi.

'That was Boris Grebinshikov, Don.'

'What was? Oh. Yeah.'

We got a cab outside the Grand Hotel Evropa (all top-hatted doormen and business centres) and within ten minutes all the glamour had entirely evaporated from our trip. I'd got Lyuda from the paper's Moscow bureau to find out which police station had been responsible for the investigation. It was six years ago, she told me after a couple of mouse clicks. She is a genius at this kind of thing. Probably KGB herself, but I never asked. Contacts everywhere though, admittedly, the current correspondent would probably have all kinds of big footing issues with my using Lyuda without her consent. Well, she can fuck off with her five kids and her Goldman Sachs husband. (Petra Pears – no, I swear. It's her name. Had five kids before she was 30 and then went to journalism college. Well, she could afford to because Mr Pears was bankrolling her very lovely life.)

You see, the beautiful old St Petersburg, the Peter and Paul fortress, the Russian Museum (which houses my favourite painting of all time – Repin's Ivan the Terrible Killing his Son), the Hermitage, the Marinsky Theatre and all the crumbling old buildings, big old communal apartments where these actors, writers and dancers live in Bohemian paradise, the Literary Café and the places where *Crime and Punishment* gets filmed about twice a year in one language or another – this is a tiny part of the city. Where most people live, well, it's the same old story. Most people live in hideous, soulless, cheaply and quickly built and badly maintained tower blocks in endless sprawling estates that surround what foreigners think of as St Petersburg. A bus, tram and metro ride from the centre and a whole other world away.

This, apparently, was where Ekaterina, Alexander and their son, Lev, had lived. On the third floor of House 29, Korpus 7 of Engels Street. So the obviously drunk policeman on the desk of station number forty-six had told me. After a fair bit of money had changed hands and a fair number of files had been wrenched out of their musty cabinets.

'Why d'you want to know? We couldn't get anyone for it. She just fell and bled. I remember,' he said. His bloated face lit up a bit at the memory of being fresh to the job, hungry, optimistic. The decline so hideous and so swift. Didn't get anyone for it. Hmm.

Don sniffed and hugged his camera bag tighter.

'We're looking for the son. We want to adopt him. Distant relations,' I said, putting my arm warmly round Don's middle and then pinching him hard.

'That's right!' he squealed.

The duty officer was counting his money and obviously didn't give the faintest toss why we were interested. It was impressive, in his state, that he'd found the file at all, or, indeed, that it still existed.

Don and I pored over it together. I passed him one of the more gruesome pictures and he screwed his face up. The inquest verdict was as close a translation as you can get to 'accidental death' and she was buried at the Lenin Cemetery just behind the estate where she'd lived. Nobody had even bothered to change the name of the place. Another half-hour's conversation about precisely what it was worth and why it was definitely worth more than that and he didn't have to tell us anything anyway – ten thousand roubles – bought us the name and home telephone number of the police pathologist who was having a day off for her daughter's birthday.

However, agreeing that she could make her daughter's birthday a whole lot more special with our money, she said she'd meet us at the cemetery in two hours. She'd bring her equipment and have a proper look at the body if we could get it out of the ground by then. She wouldn't be involved in an illegal exhumation but neither would she report it. Don and I, in the meantime, went to Katya and Alexander's block of flats. There was, in fact, a bit of grass growing up around some of the buildings now and the saplings that had been optimistically planted had a leaf or two to show for themselves. The shop that served the Engels Street blocks was typically shabby, selling mostly spirits and beer but with a glass-fronted fridge of sausages, salamis, cheese, eggs, kefir (yoghurt stuff) and milk. Don bought a carton of kefir, drinking the whole thing and wiping his milk moustaches happily away on his sleeve. The bored girl in a white uniform with hat and dry, bleached hair took the carton back without making any kind of facial expression and tossed it in the recycling bin.

Outside the shop some swarthy types squatted in front of upturned boxes on which they displayed tomatoes, cucumbers, bunches of dill and some apples. It was getting hot now and they had moved into the shade near a burnt-out car. Clearly there was gang stuff going on here as well as domestic murders.

Nobody answered from Alexander's old flat, but the neighbour remembered them well, even fondly. She wiped her greasy hands on her apron and sucked at her gums.

'Played music. Piano. Violin. Sweet little boy. I used to give him chicken bones to chew. Shame what happened. She must have had a weak heart.' She sighed. 'That lot, now. Fighting. Swearing. He'll kill her in the end.' She threw glance at the opposite door and snorted. I knocked on a couple more doors while Don tried to get some moody shots of the estate from outside. Those who remembered her just said the banal positive stuff that people always say when something awful happens to their neighbours. Nobody said they thought he'd been involved though, and nobody seemed that shocked. Well, it was a while ago, I suppose, and things had been worse then. 'Maybe,' said the man on the floor above who was actually called Vladimir Ilych (Lenin's name and patronymic), 'she threw herself downstairs in despair.' I could see it wasn't impossible. 'Still. She died with dignity,' he mumbled. 'And honour.' Hmm. Well. Okay. Not sure if I'd entirely agree.

*

The kindergarten that their son attended was at the back of their block: a climbing frame painted blue, a swing and some markings on the square of tarmac for games. Detskiy Sad 128. One of the teachers, a kind-looking woman with a comforting bust and gold teeth, remembered Lev and Katya. She shushed the toddlers who clung to her apron and told them to go and get the jigsaws out. My heart ached for Ben.

'Nice girl. Too young to have a child, I thought, but we all are aren't we? I've got a mother now who's fifteen. Can you imagine? Fifteen? Toma's mum. She must have had him when she was thirteen. Well,' she said. She had cried when social services (that's not what they call it, obviously, but that's what it is) came for Lev that day. His dad just didn't turn up for him. He'd been drinking a lot and everyone knew he was in the forces. She'd taken him home herself and waited up all night. Then she took him back to nursery in the morning and that's when they decided to take him in, just until his dad came to his senses. But he never did. Never came.

'Well. You have to cry. That was his life over with. In this godforgotten country.'

'Yes.' I nodded, shifting my weight from boot to boot and looking at the collages the children had made of a jungle. I think it was supposed to be a jungle. Don was crying, of course.

'Come on, Donski. The cemetery calls,' I said, trying to sound perky, but we were both depressed, deadened by the routine horribleness of the things that happen to people. And this isn't the screaming torture, death and horror that gets the big reactions. Just the bleak crap that goes on on a sunny Petersburg afternoon with the white dandelion seeds flying through the warm summer air.

There was a burial going on at the cemetery. A gangster of some kind, it looked like. There were a lot of boy-racer cars parked outside and a few thuggish types drinking beer and leaning on them, guarding them presumably. They weren't trying to hide the guns they had shoved into the pockets of their jeans. Through the gates some young women in short skirts and high heels stood around, one of them crying. Most people were carrying red carnations in small cellophane packets.

The caretaker, or whoever he was, sat on a foldaway chair outside his hut, smoking happily in the sun. He had his sleeves rolled up and a gold chain round his neck with a cross on it.

'Good day,' he said, smiling when we greeted him. But when we explained ourselves his face fell. He stood up and pulled his sleeves back down, buttoning them up and leading us into his hut. There was a kettle and some cups, a picture of Jesus and Mary drawing-pinned to the wall and a plastic Tupperware box with money in it. 'This is serious. This is a very serious matter,' he said quite a lot of times.

Don took a picture of him that I didn't think would come out, but what do I know. Don always hides behind his camera when I am doing tricky negotiations.

He refused, Stanislav did, to take roubles and would only even consider foreign currency.

'A thousand dollars,' he said. 'No less. I would be breaking the law and that is something I have never done. Would never do. It is a very serious matter.'

Liar, I thought though, in the end, it wasn't the negotiating line I took.

'I understand that, Stanislav . . .?'

'Vladimirovich.'

'I understand that, Stanislav Vladimirovich, and in order to give full monetary value to the service that I am so rudely asking you to perform, I am willing to offer you a hundred dollars in cash, which, I'm sure you will agree, is very generous.'

'Madam,' he scoffed, 'you must understand that this is a very serious matter.'

Okay. So this went on for some time and in the end he took $250. Now, obviously, no newspaper sanctions bribe-giving and you can't get it back on expenses. But, equally obviously, everybody does it and the editors know about it and you can get it back on expenses. You call it a tip. 'Tip to grave diggers at the Lenin Cemetery, St Petersburg – $250.' Ludicrous, sure. True, also.

So, in typical Russian fashion, our Stanislav goes piling over to where this bloke is being buried and takes the two grave diggers off that job to dig Katya Sorokina up. Admittedly, the coffin (large and black with brass handles) had already been interred and the diggers were waiting for the mourners (such as they were) to leave so that they could fill in the hole, so it wasn't a big deal. But it did seem a bit, well, disrespectful, I suppose. Still, this wasn't the time to start having reservations and Don and I watched with a grim interest while these two blokes started digging, me with my bare eyes, Don through his lens.

Now, when someone says 'exhumation' you kind of imagine a plot of grass and some soft earth. It wasn't like that at all. I hadn't realised that most Russians get cremated, so it was pretty incredible that there was anything left of her anywhere. Anyway, hers was a small plot crammed into a long row, each plot with a low grey plaque at its head, names and dates only, no money for a picture or statue. These were the paupers' plots, I supposed. Over where the body lay was a large piece of granite, basically like an enormous and deep tray with lots of gravel in it. This first had to be removed, hacked through with the pick-axes that your grave digger apparently has handy at all times.

One of them was an old bloke, too old to be doing this physical stuff really, obviously having difficulty, his checked shirt drenched with sweat, muddy boots sliding around as he worked. The other one was a shirtless teenager, a tan from doing this all summer, a bird tattooed on to his left arm, a woman on his back, scrubby blonde hair and low-slung jeans. He smoked as he lifted the big pieces of broken stone onto the path, raining gravel.

Finally – and it didn't look like six feet to me, more like three, maybe someone had been lazy – he leapt into the pit they'd dug and single handedly hauled the coffin out of the grave, raising it above his head and pretty much slinging it forward. He was covered in mud.

'Christ,' Don muttered, leaping backwards, afraid Katya's ghost might jump out at him. Or, more probably, as scared as I was that the coffin would disintegrate on impact and we'd be staring at a corpse.

'Let's wait for the pathologist,' I said, standing back and leaning against a tree to smoke. I hadn't been sick for more than twelve hours now and was wondering slightly if I'd even been contaminated at all. A blackbird stood on top of one of the little plaques and looked at me, his head cocked. 'Hello,' I said, and the grave diggers turned to look at me, both slouched on their spades now, smoking too.

Well, she was already an hour and a half late and it was baking hot and humid by the time she arrived, all of us batting little clouds of mosquitoes away, though by the time you see them they've had you, I'm told.

'*Zdravstvuitye*.' She nodded to Don and me, calm and confident, carrying a huge black pilot's bag over one shoulder and a tiny red patent leather handbag over the over. 'So, this is the girl,' she said, looking down at the muddy coffin, so clearly robbed from that big hole in the ground with the smashed-up gravestone around it. 'Open please,' she said, rightly identifying the man capable of the job. Tattoo. Her grey bob bounced around her little gold earrings.

While he winched the lid off with his pickaxe, she took a mask, gloves and white coat out of the bag she'd snapped open like a tool kit. Well, it was a tool kit.

As the lid came away, partly crumbling to dust and partly splintering into big shards, there was a loud crash from behind me. It was Don, fainting. How he holds his job down I have no idea.

'I'll get him some tea,' Stanislav offered, all nice now he'd been paid enough to put a new roof on his dacha.

'Could you?' I smiled, sitting Don up with an arm round his shoulders.

'Come on, mate. Get a couple of shots, eh?' I said, comfortingly.

'Mmm? Oh. Yeah. Right. 'Course. Just got a bit hot.'

'Sure. Bill Gates over there has gone to get you some sweet tea. Okay?'

'Great,' Don agreed, lying back down again in the patch of grass under a not very healthy-looking apple tree.

Svetlana was getting to work, fishing glinting instruments out of her case as she knelt by the box, breathing heavily in the heat through her surgical mask.

'Completely decomposed, I'm afraid.' She shook her head. I put my cigarette out and went over for a look, quickly wishing I hadn't.

God, but the long-dead don't look good. The skull still had an almost full head of curly blonde hair on it, flattened and dirty, but absolutely there. There were a few bits of dark flesh

(I assumed) on her face and some scrags hanging onto her wristbones and hands. Her earrings lay by her skull, fallen off when the ears rotted, but her silver necklace with a little heart pendant was still around her neck. I had expected that appalling smell but there wasn't one, I suppose because the flesh was all gone.

All the other exhumations I've seen have been of the very recently dead: mass graves in Bosnia and Rwanda. This is worse because of the smell and the horrific wounds, but it is less fundamentally terrifying, existentially terrifying, because it's somehow the decay – the acknowledgment of what we'll all be – that really bores into your soul.

'Fractures to three ribs, the right arm in . . . one . . . two . . . seven places, fractured hip, clean break to the lower femur, two fractured toes on the left foot.'

'What about the skull?' Don asked, suddenly standing with a plastic cup of tea in one hand and a fag in the other. He looked fine.

Svetlana turned to him. 'Yes. It's interesting. She does have skull fractures, but if you're asking me to say she's been murdered I can't do that. They are more coherent with a fall than with someone taking a blunt instrument to the head, or any other part of the body. This is not a person who has been beaten to death or, in my view, been fighting another person. We would have more hand injury, more facial damage, a broken nose or cheekbone.' She spoke that very educated kind of Russian that is going out of style as pop culture consumes the vast expanses of the whole entire country.

I paced up and down a bit, getting too hot. 'What about poisons? Can you tell anything about that?'

I felt a bit stupid. My autopsy skills are somewhat limited. Like, I've basically no idea what they do or how they do it. Only that they can test for stuff.

188

'Well. Nothing that attacks bone. I can take a flesh biopsy and run tests for the more common poisons in the lab. Get the results to you for tomorrow.'

I liked this woman. I could imagine being proud to work on her team in her Petersburg lab, putting my white coat on in the morning, taking the body out of the fridge . . . well, you know.

'Thank you. Let me give you my number.'

While I was writing down the Ismaelevich mobile number on a piece of cardboard I'd ripped off my cigarette packet, with a biro I'd borrowed from the tattoo man, Don started fiddling about in his camera bag. He got out a big grey thing like an old fashioned mobile phone and started waving it over the body, his reservations about staring at corpses apparently completely overcome. It clicked. And then it clicked some more. A light on top of it flashed blue.

I handed the number to Svetlana and went over to Don. 'No way!'

'Sure. Why not? They were flogging them off at Izmailovo a few years ago. It's a Geiger-Müller tube. Ira likes me to wave it over fruit at the market before I buy it.'

'And?'

'Pretty fucking highly radioactive, baby,' he said, squinting sweatily at the Geiger counter read-out. 'Seriously, it's going crazy. She must have got 5,000 rems.'

Svetlana whistled. 'You would have to have a reaction go off inside you to get that much. Or be standing on top of reactor number two at Chernobyl. Let me see that thing.' She grabbed it off Don. All of us had stood back.

'What if she ate it?' I asked.

Svetlana was staring, stunned, at the read-out.

She looked at me in that never-seen-anything-like-it-before-in-my-life sort of way (that people quite often look at me in, though not always for the same reason).

'Well. This really isn't something I know very much about,' she said. 'But yes, I suppose, if somehow it could be taken orally. I don't know. At this level, this many years later, this would be a huge and immediate exposure. I don't know . . . coma, massive haemorrhage, quick death. This is incredible. Do you mind?'

She took a clipboard out of her bag on the floor and copied down the reading. Then she transferred a bit of flesh from Katya's nose into one of those urine sample bottles (though I guess we knew now what she'd find), sealed it, labelled it, popped it away with her other stuff, including mask, gloves and coat (which, I imagined, would need to be burnt now) and stood in front of me. Waiting.

It was thirty seconds before I realised what she was doing. Tip to Police Pathologist Svetlana Bruikhina: 15,000 roubles.

That night, back at Boris's on the Nevsky, Don and I drank vodka and listened to Boris Grebinshikov play the guitar in a dark kitchen with all the big old windows open to the courtyard, his voice sweet and clear and sad, his songs seeming to breathe life into Katya's irradiated corpse with the suggestion that all life is a dream and that the dance continues elsewhere. Hey, I was drunk, what can I tell you?

I called Eden and Ben, ready to cry and tell them that they were all that was important to me, but Eden was in efficiency mode and Ben, for the second call in twenty-four hours, was asleep.

'Hi. Listen, I'm looking up this radiation stuff now. If it's second-hand, like you've been hanging around someone or something that is hugely contaminated, then you're basically okay. Nausea, headaches, should wear off. Dicey, because you get a fortnight's latency period when you think you're better and then your hair falls out and your insides start melting. But that's not going to happen. As long as it's not inside you,' he said, enjoying being the lecturer, the doctor with good news, the – oh dear, yup – the parent.

I nearly said, 'Thank God we used a condom.' But I restrained myself with a bit of gherkin.

'Sorokin's looking bad. His skin has blistered. He seems to have news cameras trained on him twenty-four hours a day while he shits his organs out,' Eden said, sipping something. I imagined it was my bottle of Sancerre out of the fridge.

Hmph.

'Don't they just give them potassium? I'm sure there's something.'

'Depends how much he got,' Eden told me. 'You any closer to knowing who gave it to him? Scotland Yard are fingering these risk control blokes who used to be in the KGB.'

'FSB.'

'Whatever.'

'The ones he met in Cairo?'

'Yeah. I saw it on the news. They showed pictures of the place they went and stuff. All sealed off now. Nuclear material on the wine glasses. The works.'

'God. Well, it's a horrible place. Anyway, it looks like someone nuked his ex-wife too. The first one. The Russian.'

'Noooo!'

'Yup.'

'So, I went to the flat . . .'

I jumped up and down with glee and Grebinshikov stopped playing briefly. 'Sorry,' I whispered, wandering into the hall: dusty parquet, coats, slippers, wellies. 'Oh, you are a total ANGEL!' I squealed.

Eden laughed. 'I was in and out in ten minutes because Kristy could only do two hours. Anyway, I basically just sat there and watched DVDs and tapes.'

'Did you climb in?'

'No. I'm forty-five years old, Faith. I got the key off the old geezer downstairs.'

'Oh,' I said. Eden could charm anything out of anyone.

'So, I watched these tapes. Mostly very surreal gay porn. And a bit of normal porn.'

You don't have to tell me about very surreal, I thought. 'Normal?'

'You know what I mean, Faith! God. Anyway, I found three interesting ones.'

'Porn films?'

'No. Other crap. I mean, I didn't watch everything. He's got hundreds of them. But there was a separate pile, a kind of no-genitalia section that was in the kitchen so I concentrated on those.'

'And nicked them, I hope.'

'And nicked them, obviously. Took a few of the others too just for—'

'I know what porn is for, Jones.'

'Yuh.'

'So?'

'So what? Oh, yes. So. One of a bloke in uniform beating the shit out of a bloke in no uniform tied to a chair with a bag over his head.'

'Sorokin?'

'No. A kind of swarthy type . . .'

'The beater, I mean. Not the beatee.'

'Oh. Well, yeah. Very hard to tell. Grainy. But definitely possible. I mean, I've only seen Sorokin on TV. When he defected with the big blonde beard and now with his skin going black . . . But, yes. Could be.'

'Okay. And?'

'Well, there's a great one of the Egyptian Interior

192

Minister, who I vaguely know and it's definitely him: Yosri El-Baz he's called.'

'Yes, I know,' I said, crossly. I mean, give me a radiation lesson, sure, but seriously.

'So, on the tape he's having sex with these two fat belly-dancer women. They do a whole routine for him, and it's shot from the wardrobe or a hole in the wall or something, and then they're just going at it like crazy. I didn't have time to watch the whole thing.'

Okay. So, that was absolutely fascinating, though I couldn't begin to work out what it meant. When I did, I would have the answers, I thought. I got butterflies in my stomach and went back into the kitchen for my vodka. It was just like the Russian prosecutor who was trying to nail Ismaelevich that time years ago and was then exposed by a tape just like this and had to resign.

'Wow,' I said. 'Holy shit. That's huge.'

'Is it?' Eden asked. 'Presumably they're all at it.'

'Yes, but . . .'

'Anyway. Then the worst one. The one I wished I hadn't watched.'

'Was—'

'Yeah. It was another police torture deal but someone kind of senior-looking, wearing his hat and what have you, and they're in this grey tent, not a cell, and anyway, the prisoner is another southern-looking bloke, Chechen, Dagestani, hard to tell. He's tied to the wall, or bits of him are, and the commander or whatever is actually hacking him up with a pair of shears. Like these huge garden shears, and he's shouting and . . .'

'Shumayev,' I whispered. 'It's Shumayev.'

'Who?'

'Oh, you know. Warlord. Remember when we got trapped in that flat outside Grozny with the—'

'Yeah.'

'It was his people doing the rebelling that day. You must remember.'

'Oh God. Yes. Yes, of course.'

'Okay, listen. Don't lose them. And take Ben away please. But not, clearly, to wherever you take the tapes to. Okay?'

'One of them is a disc.'

'Eden.'

'Right.'

That night I slept on a sofa at Grebinshikov's, under a vast Lucien Freud painting of his wife splayed out post-coitally on a rumpled bed. I dreamt that I was dead and talking to Eden about what I wanted him to tell Ben about me, how I hoped they would cook brownies together one day and talk about me and how much I'd love to have been there. How I hoped he would take him ice skating at the Rockafella Centre, olive picking outside Jerusalem, swimming in the Dead Sea. How he should tell him that I'm watching from behind the glass all the time, my arms outstretched and holding him though he can't know it. I woke up with my face wet with tears.

Chapter Sixteen

It was strange to be watching it on television. Strange that this wasted man – surrounded, as perhaps he had longed to be from the outset, by cameras, notepads, the world's messengers – was the same man who'd played 'Name that Tune' on my back not very long ago at all. He had been so desperate to be taken seriously, to be listened to and understood, desperate for the media to take notice of what he had to say and to take revenge on those people he considered to have betrayed him. But he died calm. In a calm kind of agony, feeling, knowing, perhaps, that he had not lived in vain. Thinking, as his insides burnt, that at last justice might be done.

I was back in Cairo when I heard about it, back at home – well, at Ismaelevich's place, God help me. I'd seen Don off in Moscow (we'd flown this time – I couldn't face another train journey with this pissed and alternately remorseful, randy, tearful, belligerent friend) and had watched him trudge away to the Metro, ready to go and face the music, such music as there was to be faced.

'I dunno, Eff Zed,' he'd said when I kissed him goodbye. 'I just don't know.'

'None of us do, Don, you idiot,' I explained to him. 'None of us do.'

This seemed to console him.

On the plane back to Cairo, where I can't say I was in any clamour to go, I thought about the tapes. I would have thought about them a whole lot more if the English woman across the aisle hadn't chosen me to tell about her affair with some old man and how she would have fallen for him whatever age he was because they were just such soul mates. 'You know how some things are just predestined?' She worked in PR which, if you asked me, said it all.

I tried to work out a way that Alex could have had those tapes without knowing he had them. I still wanted him to be the victim. You know, that they were planted in his flat or he'd been given them but hadn't ever watched them because he'd thought they were porn too and had put them in a special 'films I haven't wanked over yet' section. But no. They were his and either they were being used against him or he was going to use them, was using them or had used them against someone else. All three were without doubt blackmail tapes.

And after all, my brain tapped at the inside of my eyes, he abandoned his son. Oh shut up, I told it, but it wouldn't. Not even with seven vodka miniatures swilling around in it. And a packet of salted broad beans. What is with that?

I used my fake passport (so exciting, the first one I've ever had) to get back into Egypt, though I was VIP'd again so I barely needed one. I wasn't sure what my status was here, whether they'd even tried to come and run the CBRN tests on me yet and whether the Egyptian police knew about my whereabouts from Scotland Yard. Or even if they still cared where I was. The black Mercedes was purring right where it should be, if, I noticed now, a bit scuffed on one side, and the interior was icy cold just how I knew it would be. I smiled to the driver when he opened the door for me, but I didn't have a clue if it was same guy as last time because of the divider and, anyway, the obvious protocol (ignore the staff). I can see how you can really get used to this life.

I shut my eyes in the car and registered that I was almost looking forward to seeing Abram bounding out of his monastery like a big happy dog, asking me what had happened, all glitter and hyper-intimacy, focused attention from his orange eyes. The drive to his house was getting shorter and less arresting too. You know how drives you know well go by quickly, and even the most spectacular scenery becomes just, well, just part of the scenery? I mean, pyramid schmyramid. It was AGES ago. No need to keep on making a fuss about them two thousand years after the fact. Oh, not really!

I may have nodded off, but when we pulled up I could tell immediately that things were different. For one thing, the wisteria was dead now: shrivelled brown clumps instead of the fat grape-like bunches. And a lot of the shutters were closed, the gravel outside looked – what? – untrodden, I suppose. And untyred. Ismaelevich wasn't here.

I was so annoyed to be disappointed that I slammed the car door a bit too hard and stomped up to the closed gates to the courtyard with more vigour than I otherwise might have done. I'd bought a little carry-on bag in Petersburg: shampoo, soap, toothbruth, toothpaste, some new underwear, T-shirts and even a new pair of jeans. I dropped it on the floor and climbed onto the gates but climbed off again when I heard them buzzing. One of the girls came out to meet me as they swung, electronically, open. It was Lamia, who'd lent me the skirt.

'*Ahlan wa sahlan.*' She smiled.

'*Ahlan biki.*' I smiled back.

'Mr Ismaelevich is in London. He instructed me to make you at home for as long as you desire.'

Desire. It only really gets used in advertising and servant-speak. In French it just means want, basically.

'Oh. Thanks,' I said, following her through into a low wing I hadn't been in before and, finally, into a massive, domed-ceilinged bedroom with its bathroom through an archway but very much part of the room. If you were sharing the room you would have to go and poo elsewhere. I do not like en suite bathrooms. The further away from your bed, the better. I would prefer someone traipse outside to the end of the garden than defecate near my head. The room had cold stone floors and white walls and a deep echo.

'The chapel,' Lamia told me. Yes, I could see it now she said it. 'I'll get you some tea.'

When she'd gone I flicked on the television and perched on the edge of the bed to watch it. Sorokin was the big story on all the news channels. It took me a moment to realise that the story was his death. '*Alexander Sorokin finally succumbed today to the huge dose of thallium that has been racking his body and mind for . . .*'

Hmm. Wasn't that what they got that journalist Schekoshikin with? Yes, it definitely was.

They showed those awful pictures of him in hospital and then went to the steps outside where – oh my God – Ismaelevich stood next to a lawyer who was making a statement. No! Reading a statement that Alex had written before he died. The flashes were going off all around him and a whole bouquet of microphones was held up to his face but he was, well, of course he was, completely unflinching.

It was the expected stuff about how he'd been persecuted by the FSB since he tried to blow the whistle. How they'd killed his beloved wife to discredit him and how the President himself was the murderer of, basically, all the above.

At some point the ranting tone stopped and Ismaelevich stepped forward, appeared to falter, to look tearful, as he read out a passage, a quote from one of Nikolai Karamzin's poems. A police siren wailed in the background.

'What is our life? – a novel. Who is the author? – anon. We read it only falteringly, we laugh, we cry, we sleep.'

He read it in Russian first, before translating it. It's better in Russian.

I smiled sadly. That about sums it up, I thought. Was that why he'd chosen the name Karamzin? Had he planned this all, moment for moment? Was his death the life's work of a madman?

I flicked around the channels to hear Ismaelevich's reading again. And again. And again. Then there was all the dissection. I imagined the producers of every news show in the world frantically calling all their Russia and espionage contacts, trying to get someone, anyone, into the studio. I'm sure my phone was ringing off the hook at the bottom of the Nile somewhere. Or trying to.

An ex-spy who runs one of the risk assessment firms, many of which Alex had done work for, was saying that he'd always had it coming to him, it was amazing he'd survived this long, that the FSB didn't ever put up with subordination in its ranks, that the President was probably none too upset about it but wouldn't have had to order it directly. There were ex-pat Russians commenting all over the place and CNN actually had Danilenko himself in their Moscow bureau saying Sorokin had probably been murdered by Ismaelevich, but that he was pleased to see his friend go quietly, 'with dignity and honour,' he said. Hmm. Now where had I heard that lately? Dignity and honour. I should drink less.

Against my better judgment I ended up glancing at Al Jazeera English in an effort not to miss any commentator on any channel talking about Sorokin. No mean feat with the television control, this. Lamia came in with mint tea and sahlab, that yoghurt drink, on a tray. I wondered if she lived here full-time and, if so, where her family was. I considered getting chatting, but, in the end, I just couldn't be arsed.

And by the time I'd *shukran*'d her out of the room, Al Jazeera had moved on from Alex's death to Eman's. '*Recently suspected of murdering his ex-wife, Sorokin insisted he was being framed. New evidence may support his claims as the Cairo inquest into the death of Eman Sorokina has just returned a verdict of accidental death.*' Woo hoo! Well, 'woo hoo' for me at any rate.

I raised my eyebrows. Yeah, I thought. They haven't run a fucking Geiger counter over her, I bet. I knew what had caused all the dramatic haemorrhaging. At least, I thought I did. But what I didn't know was how he'd got her to eat it and why he'd taken a much smaller dose himself. To give himself time to be seen by the world? Very possibly. Both his wives had died fairly instantaneously. Neither was ill beforehand. He must have stood them at the top of the stairs and, what? Kissed them and spat a capsule into their mouths? Offered them a sweet or a shot of vodka? Preposterously James Bond, I know. But it really is like that in this world.

I once met the old SIS duffer on whom the character of James Bond was based. A friend of Ian Fleming's who was out doing dirty work while Fleming was sat behind a desk. Unfortunately, the only thing he wanted to talk about was sex, and he was a bit deaf (hey, he was ninety-one), so I completely cleared the restaurant (Itsu in Piccadilly) by screaming my head off about sodomy.

But thinking this through, how he'd managed to get the thallium into these women, I realised I had accused him once and for all in my mind. Well, not just accused, but tried and sentenced.

While the rest of the world was running documentaries about the evils of today's Russia and the resurgence of the KGB, having bought Sorokin's story hook, line and sinker, I felt that I knew the truth. If I could persuade Tamsin to run it, this was going to be huge. Highly controversial, but huge. I lit a cigarette and tried to force all the information mushing about in my mind into the format of a piece. But what to do about the Ismaelevich/El-Baz angle? Obviously Sorokin, as I was now beginning to think of him as I distanced myself, was involved somehow but it seemed separate from his KGB stuff, just something else he'd got mixed up in, something else to feed his bizarre fantasies of self-importance and rebellion.

It's like all those people who are addicted to making money. They hardly spend any and never feel they've made enough to stop, to retire. They're in the office sixteen hours a day, putting yet another billion in the bank at the end of the year. It seemed that Sorokin, like Ismaelevich, needed to feel involved at the top level, in the know, above the law.

I paced about, cooling my feet on the floor and fishing the pistachios out of the yoghurt drink to crunch as I walked. Why, I wondered, was Ismaelevich so interested in Sorokin and his fate anyway? He had seemed irritated by him at the end and they certainly weren't friends. I suppose he needed him, undiscredited, to prove to the world what Russia was capable of, to open the door for him somehow to go back and hatch another power plot with or against a different president.

I made a tiny box out of my cigarette packet, a skill taught to me in Lyons when I was fourteen. I sat down and stood up again. I approached the picture of the harbour that hung on the far wall. It was by Dufy. God, to spend that kind of money on art and then stick it in the guest room of your sixth home. Not even a home. It didn't look like anywhere that his wife and kids had ever been. I tried to call Jamila but her phone was dead, the number unobtainable.

I did worry that talking to her honestly, explaining to her how she was being politically manipulated, would shatter her very endearing idealism, but someone was going to have to point out to her what she'd got herself into before someone else ended up persuading her to eat cyanide in a police cell. I probably shouldn't do it over the phone though. Face mail is always better for anything vaguely intense (ha!). And I wondered about the 'El-Baz with the prostitutes' tape. Had Ismaelevich seen it yet? Maybe he wouldn't need to now. Maybe it was all over: Sorokin finally dead and gone. Or maybe he had seen it and had Sorokin killed for sending it? Grrrr. WHAT was going on?

I fell asleep on the huge bed under the sweeping mosquito net in my clothes, with the television on. I haven't done that for years. And I hadn't phoned Ben, but I did dream about him. One of those vivid dreams about the very place you're in – I dreamt he was asleep in this bed in the crook of my arm and I could feel his warmth and his breathing against me, could smell his hair and was holding one of his tiny hands.

I woke up, dry-mouthed and more tired than when I'd gone to sleep, to watch yet another twist in my story unfold on the plasma screen against the wall where the altar had once been. Some kind of installation art irony here that I refused to so much as address. I do loathe that kind of stuff. I once went to an exhibition full of crap that looked as if a thirteen-year-old boy had made it all – sex dolls in weird positions and stuff – but it was all supposed to be fantastically ironic and full of important messages because, in fact, the models were made of bronze and marble and stuff. Puh.

'*Serving FSB Captain, Grigory Danilenko, was killed in a traffic accident in central Moscow just hours ago while on his way home from a television interview. Danilenko was named by Scotland Yard last week as the main suspect in their investigation into the bizarre murder of his former colleague, Alexander Sorokin, the defector who ingested more than . . .*' Blah blah blah.

Not only this but the woman (oh well, okay – it was, it was her, it was Sabrina) went on to say that another FSB bloke from some special unit, Petrya Radishchev, had died of a sudden heart attack aged only thirty-eight, at his home in Pskov. '*By what may or may not be an astonishing coincidence he also met Alexander Sorokin in Cairo on the presumed day of his poisoning.*' I didn't think there was any coincidence involved. So, I thought, hardly even awake, that leaves Sasha. Nobody, not even the Brits, had managed to work out who the fuck Sasha was (despite Sorokin's pre-expiration description of him, insistence on his presence and Christ knows what), though the trail of radiation that he'd had leaking out of his pockets showed anyone who was interested what planes he'd been on. So Russian, that: a strangely sophisticated murder so rubbishly carried out. A completely bizarre mixture of absolute brilliance and utter incompetence. And I knew, at this point, that nobody would ever work out who he was. It wasn't so much a question of whether or not he'd done it, but under whose orders. Sorokin's himself? Ismaelevich? The FSB?

It was like that bloke in Dorset who got shot in the head on his doorstep and the only possible reason anyone could come up with was that he shared a surname, Scott-Linden, with a judge who'd sent some Russian gangster down. The judge lived, and lives on, in the next village, though he has an awful lot of police protection now. Anyway, there wasn't even a clue, not an anything – a car, a plane passenger – NOTHING to identify the killer. Although odds are on that he was called Sasha.

And I decided, while I was drinking cold mint tea and searching under the bed for another cigarette, that I must never introduce any men to Ben ever again. He had been in my bloody home, this irradiated madman. He played trains with my son, made love to me in my bed, cooked a potato, egg, butter and cheese stir-fry that I couldn't eat, in my kitchen. I had liked him. He had looked like the sky over Siberia. I had tasted his blood from the cut on his lip. If I weren't me, if I didn't try so bloody hard never to feel anything, I might even have loved him. He didn't let me fall into the Nile. I noticed that I was crying but didn't bother to wipe the tears away. My shrink told me it was healthy to mourn. It didn't feel very sodding healthy and I seemed to find myself doing an awful lot of it.

That was it! The thing that had been prodding my skull from the inside. He'd told me about the Kamera himself, the chemical weapons facility in Moscow that makes up bizarre poisons for traceless hits. He'd said they had something that just 'melts you on the inside'. Was this it? Ingestible thallium? Had he eaten it on purpose right in front of Danilenko? Had Danilenko known what he was doing?

The sky over Siberia. He was from the Urals. His father was a nuclear physicist. Okay. He did military training (when the hell did he have time to learn the piano?) and was transferred to the service. He was in the FSB. It was beginning to occur to me that he might have worked at the Kamera himself. That he was trying to tell me that in an oblique way.

And this is when the phone rang. I was surprised by this a) because I had turned it off after each call because I haven't got the charger and b) because I wasn't aware that anyone had the number. But it was Jamila and I had left the phone on by mistake.

'Faith? Faith Zanetti?'

'Yes. How did you get the number?'

She paused. In retrospect (ah, well, of course) I might have been suspicious. But so far she was one of the few people I'd met since I came to Cairo to cover the pro-democracy rioting who seemed half-normal. Or, at any rate, not a power-broker of the shadiest kind. It was just a story then. Interview the rioters, get some access to Karima and go home. Oh, well, with a riverboat belly-dance picture special on the side.

Now I was looking at the world from the smoke-and-mirrors perspective that was, is, actually the truth. I realised that the democracy riots were actually all part of Yosri El-Baz's campaign, not an organic rebellion, and even perhaps entirely orchestrated by Ismaelevich himself. El-Baz must have the backing of someone else too – the British or the Americans – in order to have the confidence to start demonstrating. You wouldn't do that just for an oligarch with some hotels. Or would you? It would depend on your cut, I suppose. But what had he promised to do that this government doesn't? Clamp down harder on Islamic fundamentalists? Oppose Iran? Persuade a neighbour to accept Israel?

'Can you come to Karima's now? It's urgent. There's something I need to show you,' she said.

'Um. Well. Sure,' I said. I was assuming the Merc was at my disposal. And I was right.

Chapter Seventeen

Outside, my boots crunching on the gravel, it was raining. It never rains here. The driver brought out an umbrella to help me into the car without getting wet. I suppose he is used to dealing with women who don't like getting their hair wet, or something. Ruins the blow-dry, does it? Or just ruins the chic look in general. It makes my hair frizz out even more than it does all by itself. Did, rather.

Cairenes have no idea what to do with rain. They behave as though it is sulphuric acid pouring out of the sky: everyone running wildly for shelter, trampling over each other, pulling any available material over their heads. I saw a boy by the side of the motorway crawling under his wooden cart while his donkey had to bow its head and bear it, waiting out the storm on the hard shoulder. In the city a group of girls stood in a shop doorway, squealing with excitement, jumping up and down, besieged by the weather. Cinemas and cafés would be packed. There was no question of going anywhere until it was finished, like that advert set in a hurricane in New Orleans where they have to party and drink some repulsive sweet alcoholic drink all night while the wind whips up outside. It was shot before the whole city was, in fact, obliterated by a hurricane, of course.

Zamalek looked strange in the rain, the red earth of all the gardens dark and dense, the palm fronds dripping fatly and the river pockmarked and swollen. At the Le Bon building the boab was hunched on the porch, hugging his knees and wondering what the world was coming to. I told him where I was going and he leapt up enthusiastically to take me up to the door, keen to have something indoors-based to do. The car waited on the kerb, the driver smoking inside with all the windows shut.

A lot of bedraggled stray cats, who normally roam the bins and rubbish tips with which Cairo abounds (no really), were skulking under the bushes at the sides of the lawn.

Now, I did know that this was likely to be interesting. But I hadn't really figured on quite how interesting. Just the fact that Jamila was summoning me to this flat was intensely strange. The last time I'd seen her here she had obviously not felt that she had even the right to a glass of water and now she was having friends round. Well, an acquaintance. Anyway, she opened the door herself and not in a maid's uniform, either.

I can't remember now whether it's my job that makes me able to see the horror in someone's face or whether it's blindingly obvious to anyone. But Jamila had a look about her that I'd seen a million times before. It is terror and elation. A liberation that comes from overstepping all boundaries and a blind fearlessness of the inevitable consequences.

She was veiled, as usual, but all awry. A lock of gingerish hair was peeking out from under her headscarf and she looked, somehow, as though she'd been in a fight. Her clothes, baggy in any case, were pulled and tugged, she had spilt something down her blouse and she was breathing hard.

In a different world I would have thought I'd caught her with her boyfriend. Her eyes were wild, her face flushed.

'Hi,' I said, standing on the threshold.

'Come in,' she told me, glancing out into the corridor as the boab skipped down the strairs. She seemed to be checking for something, someone. This was not a gracious invitation to come in. She grabbed the sleeve of my leather jacket and dragged me in, slamming the door behind me and staring into my face, daring me to guess. Fresh roses stood in a complicated glass vase on the hall stand and the windows were open – the curtains blowing in and the marble floor wet where the rain had fallen. This, if nothing else, was sign enough that the snail was not in his shell. These must be the only open windows in Cairo this morning.

And that was quite apart from the smell. You can smell it, even when it's fresh. Everybody knows that. Dead people do not smell good. There is the bitter sweat of their fear, then they often vomit before the end, the emptying of the bladder and the bowels when it's all over and, in this particular case and so many others, the warm, sweet smell of blood. Absolutely everywhere. I quickly realised that it was on the bottom of Jamila's plimsolls and she had trodden big foot-shaped splodges of it all over the black and white slabs of the hall. These plimsolls would surely be Exhibit 1, handed round the members of the jury in a plastic bag to be inspected while the forensics person explained their significance. Do they have juries here? Well, whatever. I was jumping the gun. So to speak.

'Jamila, what happened?' I asked her, addressing her as a joint victim, though I could see from her face that she had, in fact, been on a killing spree. I'd seen the same look on the faces of some of those boys in Rwanda, riding the back of Toyota pick-ups and screaming blood lust. One of my death-row blokes described his murders (he was one of the few people on death row who really had committed his murders and wasn't mentally subnormal) as being 'the ultimate high'. And there is a level on which this is definitely true. You can see it in their eyes.

'They set me up,' she said, grabbing hold of my T-shirt with both fists, leaving smears of blood on it. I did have enough space in my brain for one little part of it to think, 'Oh, here we go. They'll be after me for this now too. The blood on the T-shirt angle.'

She was appealing to me in some way. I really hoped she wasn't going to ask me to help her escape. Actually, this was the first time I'd properly considered what it was she might want, so consumed was I by my ex-lover's death, international intrigue and what have you – I had a lot on my plate.

'Yes,' I said, still standing there.

'They explained what they had done, how they had had me tortured at the police station, said how grateful they were, how much I had helped. They said they hadn't let him do what he would normally do . . .'

Well spotted, Don, I thought.

'Was I supposed to be pleased? To thank them?' she asked me.

Now don't get me wrong. She'd had all my sympathy until about two minutes ago. A terrible thing to have gone through, ghastly to have been a pawn in someone else's game. But it did strike me that her counter-attack might have gone a touch over the top. And I hadn't actually seen it yet.

She pulled me into the front room where Don and I had drunk champagne and where Karima had tossed her lovely hair at us and bared her lovely fangs and showed her lovely claws. One of the chaises was overturned, a vase was smashed and the flowers scattered on the floor, every piece of furniture had been shoved against and there was nothing in here, but nothing, that didn't have blood on it. She must have been going at this for some time. Both her victims were naked and both her victims had been tortured by an amateur (well, her) before being shot in the . . . everything. But head, certainly. There were bits of brain on one of the curtains. I wanted very badly to throw up but couldn't quite create the opportunity.

'Oh, fuck, Jamila. Jesus. What have you done?'

Karima was identifiable by her blood-soaked hair, pretty nails and vast enormous ring. El-Baz, her father, by his imposing moustache, the age of his body and just the general likelihood that this must be him. Well, this would put Ismaelevich's plans on the back burner.

Both had had their hands tied behind their backs and, judging by the stuff scattered around, she had been cutting at them with a pair of nail scissors and burning them with cigarettes that she hadn't smoked (a lot of fags were lying about on the floor, lit and stubbed out, presumably on skin). This was very very seriously grim. I purposely didn't look at the genitalia on either corpse.

'Did you do this on your own?' I asked her. I could see that she'd had father and daughter sitting naked on chairs, because there were two of those delicate French dining chairs upturned on the parquet. One with a snapped leg.

'Yes. This was my helper.' She nodded, picking up a semi-automatic handgun from the green marble mantelpiece. It was, I was fairly sure, a Walther P99.

'Where did you get that?' I wondered, thinking that it would be difficult for an ordinary girl to get hold of a weapon in Cairo. At any rate, hoping it was.

She shook her head wildly, her eyes golden, half-laughing,

half-crying but clearly not about to tell me where she'd got it from. I wondered where their clothes were. But I really was going to be sick.

'I'm gonna throw up,' I said, running out of the room and into the nearest door that might have been a bathroom. It was – pedestal bath and a bowl of pot pourri – and I had flushed the loo and splashed my face with water before I saw the Sudanese maid, crouched as small as she could make herself in the corner, shielding her face, shaking.

'Oh God,' I whispered, going over to her. She flinched away from me touching her but looked into my face, begging for rescue. I glanced over to make sure the door was definitely locked, fished out my phone and dialled the Nile Hilton. It was the only thing I could think of. Nothing happened. Oh God. Ten calls only. He actually had them cut off after ten calls. Amazing. Okay. Plan B. Ummm. 'Stay here,' I told Samira. 'I'm going to get some help. You'll be fine. Just stay here. It's all over,' I told her. I should have been so lucky.

Because it really didn't occur to me that THIS, of all things, was what she might want. I came out of the bathroom shutting the door behind me and faced the barrel of Jamila's gun.

'You knew,' she said. 'So you would have worked this out quickly enough.'

Oh Christ. She wasn't seriously going to kill me too, was she? Well, certainly not if I had anything to do with it. I did, however, have her absolute insanity on my side, I thought. This wasn't a well thought-out plan with a glorious conclusion in mind. This was wild revenge, an orgy of anger and pain. I felt sure that there must be a way to get her on my side or, rather, to get me on hers. The trouble was, she was thinking a lot faster than I was.

'You write a piece. Write for your newspaper. You will write that Karima told you about her mother's suicide, that they were planning a violent coup. That the security services must have killed them. That a plot was uncovered and . . .'

The rain outside was getting heavier. I stood in the hall trying to look into Jamila's eyes behind her gun.

'Okay. I'll talk to the desk about it when I get back to London,' I offered, not imagining for a moment that that might be what she meant. I was trying to sound casual, you know. Throw her off guard. Well, nothing was coming to me here.

She even managed a smile.

'Now. Write it now. I have your computer here. In there,' she told me, nodding towards another room off the hall that, from here, looked like a library or a study.

'My computer?'

'Yes. I went to get it from your hotel room.'

This stunned me. It was this, rather than the psycho murders and the current gun-waving, that surprised me the most. That really made me nervous. More planning than I'd imagined. And, again, making me the key player, an integral part of her genuinely frightening plan.

I kept finding that rather than being a cog in some larger wheel or, more to the point, someone who was observing and noting down the behaviour of the cogs and the wheel, I was the whole bloody wheel itself, the cart driver, the wheelwright. How does this happen? I tell you what, I planned to go back to London, resign and go and work in this sodding risk assessment world that takes ex-hacks and ex-spies and any adrenalin junkies down on their luck.

Okay, well I didn't have a lot of choice just at the minute so I took directions from her mad gun-pointing (I wished I'd known what the likelihood of her having a bullet left was) and went into the study. It would have been an idyllic room in other circumstances. El-Baz was obviously a big collector of books and they were packed into floor-to-ceiling shelves with brass ladders hanging off a rail to reach the high-up ones. The desk, a big European boss-type thing, walnut with leather, was piled high with papers, pamphlets and three different laptops, a Tiffany lamp perched on the edge. There was a huge fan not whirring in the centre of the ceiling.

Part of me was waiting for the police to come. Had nobody heard the shots? Was it the rain? Had everyone thought it was thunder? Surely not. And another part of me didn't expect them at all. I ruffled my head and this made me think of Ben. There we go. That was the kick up the arse I'd been waiting for. Survival instinct kicking in like crazy. You are NOT taking my baby's mum away from him, mad girl. Absolutely no fucking way.

My computer, a white iBook with a sticker of a hippo over the Apple, was right in the centre of the desk, open and switched on. The flat's wireless connection was working just fine. I always find that strange when death is in the air – that most things haven't noticed, the rest of the world is doing its thing, bouncing signals off satellites and generally getting on with shit. I flicked my mail button. The inbox had 304 messages in it. Many of them were offering me cut-price Viagra. But most were requests for me to appear on Sorokin-related coverage. Jamila poked me in the back. 'Write!' she said. Yeah. Sure.

'Just opening the page,' I chirped, sweating, needing a cigarette, acutely aware of my total lack of an escape plan. The only thing I could think of was the most crazed: wrestle the gun off her. Dicey in the extreme. And it wasn't as though this was one of those 'she might not have it in her to kill a person' scenarios.

Who the hell was 'GWoozle'?

Ignoring the barrel-shaped pressure in my back while I knew she still needed me, I flicked the email open.

Greg! I had completely forgotten about Greg.

Faith, hey! It was good to meet u at Bottega that night. I didn't say thanks for coming to tell me I was getting stood up. I guess I was kind of interested in the guy after what you said and guess what? I put out my tentacles and found a guy who had sex with him one time and then – warning: this is the weird part – Alex paid him, PAID him, a lot of money he said, but not how much to come over and tie him up, cut him in the face and then leave by the fire escape. He told him never to contact him again, but this guy was basically quite freaked out. Know where I found him – www.getoutofmyface.com! It's kind of a chatroom about bad contact experiences. I put out a message did anyone know Alex.

Anyway, FYI and all. You will be pleased to know that last night I met a nice gay guy (never even been to bed with a woman) who works at a think tank. So – no more!

Lovenstuff,

Greg. Xxxxx

To read this in my present situation very nearly made me smile. But not quite. The happy-go-lucky tone, and he was talking to me. Me who might well not live out the hour! And what about the content?! Holy shit. Well, that pretty much wrapped it up, I supposed. But I still believed Sorokin about the flats he'd blown up. It was his conscience, perhaps, that had sent him mad. I thought it but I didn't really believe it.

214

I think mad people might use some event as the excuse, the catalyst, for letting their madness loose but, if you look back at their life, you always but always find that they were already nutters in the first place. Jamila would be no exception.

'What do I write, Jamila?' I asked her. 'I'm happy to do it for you. I know they used you and that was wrong. The police will be lenient, you know. Especially because they were used too, right? Whoever they bribed to do that to you, he hasn't made the force look good. They might thank you for exposing the corruption and bringing the organisers to justice.'

Was she that stupid? There are many that are. I know a lot of them.

'I doubt this,' she said, a smile in her voice. Not that stupid then. No, well. Fair enough.

I replied to Tamsin's 'WHERE THE FUCK ARE YOU ZANETTI?' messages from when I'd disappeared with my radiation sickness and murder suspectness. *Hi Tamsin. I'm about to file a short piece which we would like you to run. Tks. FZ.*

So far, so good. Jamila didn't say anything and the message swooped off the screen onto a screen in lovely safe gorgeous rainy homely near-my-boy Canary Wharf. Tamsin would be worried by this. I've never filed an unsolicited piece before and she would notice the 'we' and be scared for me. Unless, of course, she was at home with flu, say. In which case I would just die here.

Jamila piped up at this point. She smelt terrible. After a nicer scent of lemons there was adrenaline. Sour. And so damp in here with the strange rain, pounding down outside, the forever blue skies dark grey. 'Write what they did to me. Write my story. Write they killed themselves.'

Righty-ho then.

'Not the police killed them?'

She had forgotten this and it stalled her. She thought about it. 'No. Killed themselves. I will go and arrange the bodies. You move, I will kill you too, Faith. You write.'

It struck me that she would be extremely hard-pushed to make that look like a suicide. Let's strip naked and torture each other for a bit and tie ourselves up and then I'll shoot you and then I'll shoot myself – whaddya say? Actually, thinking about it like that I bet it has happened. These two wouldn't do it, though. Even if . . . even if he was being blackmailed and his career and family life were over? Hmm.

No! His own daughter. Please.

'When Jamila Ashwari was released from police custody last Thursday, friends and family were shocked by the evidence of torture her body so clearly displayed.'

The *Chronicle* loves a dropped intro. Bit of colour and THEN the who-what-why-where-and-when sentence that newspaper articles famously lead with.

It took twenty minutes. I tried to treat Jamila like a colleague, telling her that we already had the art – Don had wired his pictures of her over – trying to get a congratulatory tone into my voice so that I could kind of high-five her and then run the fuck to a police station. But each time I looked over my shoulder she looked more insane than the last time. Her eyes were beginning to look milky like a blind person's and she was shaking, her body, I suppose, starting to go into shock.

And then, just as I'd hit send, she started stroking my hair with her left hand. Okey dokey. Right. Well, this is probably good, I thought. I reached up very slowly so that she had plenty of time to decide how to react and I held her small and freezing cold hand in mine. I didn't dare look round now, but I knew she was crying.

216

Very very gently I moved my chair out, scraping it across the varnished floor, the whole room full of the smell of rain and the river. I pulled her down onto my lap and held her, as much like a child as I could manage, rocking her slightly and letting her cry. She wrapped both arms around me, still holding the gun, and buried her head in my neck, mumbling something, as fragile as a bird with a broken wing. I pulled her right arm forwards and took the gun out of her hand. She released it like a sleeping child releases its doll and I put it gently on the desk. So far, so good.

Unfortunately, it was this moment that Samira had chosen to make her bid for freedom. She clattered noisily out of the bathroom and screaming loudly, wailing for help, she ran across the hall towards the front door. I knew what was happening but Jamila had perhaps never known that Samira was here. Terrified, she leapt up and ran out of the room shouting in Arabic, her vigour restored, her murderous hatred reanimated. Well, now or never. I picked up the gun and legged it past Jamila towards the door that Samira had so kindly left open on her hurtle down the stairs and into the bewildered arms of the boab. As I reached the top of the staircase I saw him on the phone (a stupid pretentious black Bakelite thing that took three quarters of an hour to dial any number) to the police, Samira shaking in his embrace.

Jamila, who had followed me enthusiastically, now stabbed me in the back of the neck with the pair of nail scissors she'd been using to such repulsive effect earlier and then jumped on my back, clinging to me with both hands. Twisting and jumping and desperately trying to shake her off, I hit her on the head with the butt of the gun and ran her into the banisters. She fell and lay there, her face disfigured with rage, and I don't know what came over me. I turned back and aimed the gun at her head, gently squeezing the trigger as I knew how.

It clicked like a Geiger counter but she was out of bullets. I would have killed her. Chucking the thing back into the flat, my prints all over it, I ran down the stairs, out the front door, across the lawn and I hurled myself, gasping and shivering, into the smoky, steamed-up car. I banged on the glass until the driver pulled off, and we'd turned the corner by the time he asked me where I wanted to go.

'Nile Hilton, *min fadlak*,' I told him, shouting through the glass, clutching my neck with my hand. I wasn't under suspicion for the Eman murder any more and they hadn't found out about me being here for these ones just yet. I wanted to bandage myself up, make some calls, pick up my stuff and lie in the bath for half an hour before all hell broke lose, as it would surely do.

Chapter Eighteen

I would have liked to run up to my room and double-lock the door, but I didn't have a key. It was an embarrassing ten minutes at reception, with me looking as though I'd been set upon by a herd of hungry camels, while they verified my identity and issued me a new keycard. I couldn't take my hand away from my neck and the blood was pouring through my fingers. Apparently ignoring this, they told me my maid had been in to pick some things up and that I had a large number of messages. Well, I would have.

'She was not my maid. Please do not ever admit anyone to my room for any reason. You must have a policy in place! Do I LOOK like a person with a maid?'

Absorbing my outward appearance and appreciating my point, the assistant manager said he hadn't been on the desk when she came and he would look into the reasons for her admission. Yeah. Okay. Okay. Whatever.

I had my key in my hand and had almost made it to the lifts when I got a tap on the shoulder. So I over-reacted, flattening myself to the wall and holding my free hand up. I'd had a bad day.

'Faith! Allah! I have sent message and message to your room. I even knock on this door! You look so different. Hair.'

Yeah. Hair and dramatically bleeding wound to neck.

It was Dahlia. And not just Dahlia, but Dahlia plus her working outfit: jangling discs, belly-button jewel and a large number of diaphanous green scarves wrapped around her in an erotic manner. She noticed my reaction to her get-up but seemed to have no comment as to the state of me.

'Wedding upstairs,' she said. Well, when wasn't there at the Hilton? Every time I glanced into the banqueting hall there was some poor woman sitting up on the dias unable to move for netting and beading, and an awkward guy standing next to her in a tux and a moustache that he wasn't quite old enough for. Often they were both smoking fags. Very Cairo.

'Dahlia. Hi. I've just . . . I'm having . . . things are . . .'

She looked at my bloodied T-shirt, neck difficulty and general unkemptness (though I am never knowingly kempt) and raised her finger to her lips.

'I say nothing!'

I smiled. She was nice. Say what you like about Don McCaughrean but he actually does have good taste in women. Especially given that all he does is take whatever he can get.

'Don is trying and trying to be in touch with you. Important news. He calls me. He calls me a lot.'

'Yes, well, that's another matter entirely. Okay. Listen, I've been a bit . . . out of circulation but I'll give him a buzz right now.'

'Good! So . . .' she said, walking away with a wiggle to indicate that she was off upstairs to get dancing.

'Okay. Have fun!' I waved, and got into the lift.

I was annoyed not to have grabbed my computer from the

slaughter scene, but I let myself off given the circumstances. The call to Don could wait until after a shower. I went into the bathroom and dabbed at my neck with a wet face cloth. Actually, it was no particularly big deal and, once clean, looked almost disappointingly minor. By the time room service had brought up a giant elastoplast it had stopped bleeding and was more like some kind of shaving cut. Not that I often shave my neck but you know what I mean.

It was glorious to be back in my room with my raggy clothes folded up on a chair by the chamber maid, lovely clean sheets, little pots and potions in the bathroom and a chocolate on the pillow. Not that I even like chocolate (I know, I know) but it speaks to me of home. The light on the phone was bleeping like crazy and there was a heap of messages from reception on the desk.

I was clean and wrapped in a fluffy white robe against the freezing air conditioning by the time I hit the phone.

Don sounded drunk. 'Zanetti! Hey! Have you seen . . . you know who . . . how is she?'

This was McCaughrean trying to be subtle because his wife was in the house. Honestly, the woman should hit him over the head with a marrow.

'I just bumped into her at the lift. You know Jamila?'

'Yup. Yup. Beautiful girl. Tortures herself. Yup.'

'Does NOT torture herself. Is tortured by a paid policeman or someone pretending to be a policeman as part of the El-Baz campaign. She finds this out and horrifically murders Karima AND Yosri El-Baz and tries to murder Faith Zanetti but Zanetti bravely escapes with the Sudanese maid and flees the scene to make urgent call to Don McCaughrean from Nile Hilton hotel room 1220.'

'You what?'

'Nothing. I'll tell you later. What's the message?'

'What message?'

'Your message. For me. Urgent.'

'The message! Yeah. Yeah. Well, not urgent but kind of weird. So Ira knows a girl from Semforov 90, was a friend of the Sorokins and all that. I was talking to whatsisdeadnuclearface about it in that shit-hole with the green slime that night.'

'Were you? I tuned out.'

'So Ira's talking to her about the whole shit and it turns out his mum, Sorokin's mum, died when he was six in a big nuclear accident at the plant. Massive massive exposure, instant death with haemorrhaging. I'm not saying it's, you know, it's not a clue, but it could have helped make him the fucking nutjob that he is.'

'Was.'

'Was.'

'Hmm. Yeah. Thanks. I'm finding a lot of stuff that seems to show him up as pure loony. But if it's just him being psycho, then who killed Danilenko and the other guy?'

Don burped loudly and I could hear him lighting a fag. 'Yeah, I saw that. Weird. I dunno. But you know what those Dignity-and-Honour cunts are like. Knock off anyone just for a laugh.'

All the physical and mental haze that had been consuming me since I got back here from Russia completely evaporated when he said that. I was lightening sharp and every muscle rigid. Glancing up at the balcony doors I saw the blue sky pushing back the grey and the blistering sun start to bake the rain off the city.

'What cunts exactly are those, Donski?'

Dignity and Honour. It was a phrase I'd heard a lot lately. Since I met Alex. So, when someone was described as having died with these two attributes to their name, was it some kind of code? Had they in fact been killed by the cunts mentioned by Mr McCaughrean?

'You know, the FSB boys who suddenly had toss-all to do except uphold the twatty honour of their organisation. And you know what that means, right?'

I did. Upholding honour always means doing the lowest, slimiest, most dishonourable thing ever, like stoning teenage girls to death or kicking them to death or throwing women onto stoves, dousing them with petrol, and all the woman-hating shit that men do the world over. I assumed that Don was talking basically about a hit squad.

'Yeah. Jesus. Who are they?'

'Who the fuck knows. It's like the Masons. You only know if you are one. They're just fucked off because Communism's over and they look a bit silly.'

'Right. Do me a favour, Don. Can you get that pathologist from Leningrad to go round to the Sorokins' old flat, upstairs to the guy on the floor above. Ask him to call me. Or the police. Don't care who goes.'

'Sure,' Don promised, and I knew he would. He could get the results of the biopsy while he was at it. Though I didn't expect any surprises there.

'I CAN'T SAVE YOUR SORRY ARSE ANY MORE, ZANETTI, YOU SKELETAL SLAG. SAM IS CHAMPING AT THE BIT TO SACK YOU. WHAT IS GOING ON?' Tamsin screamed at the top of her voice when I got put through. 'What was that shit you filed earlier? Are you fucking dyslexic? Are you fucking thick? That wasn't a piece. What was that? It sounded like something you'd only agree to write if you had a fucking gun to your head. It's a fucking insult to the business. It's an insult to me. It's an insult to the editor, it's a fucking—'

I interrupted at this juncture.

'I did have a gun to my head. I was hoping you would realise this and call the police to have my laptop traced and then rescue me. Thanks a lot, Tams.'

'What?'

'This nutty girl who had just done a huge Valentine's Day Massacre of the interior minister and his daughter held a gun to my head and made me write that piece. Then I tried to kill her but there were no bullets left and I ran away back to the hotel.'

'Yes, Faith. I see. Well, that's clear then. And now that we have paid for your empty hotel room for days on end, do you think perhaps you might actually grace us with a story? It would be so lovely if you could possibly manage it.'

She was being sarcastic. She is good at it.

'Yeah. I'll do you a big splash on the murder just so nobody else gets in first with a spoiler, but I need to follow it up because Abram Ismaelevich is knee-deep in this but I'm short on proof that he had anything to do with the murder. It's Jamila Ashwari who killed them. The tortured girl from the democracy demos. And you know what? Sorokin's involved too.'

'Sorokin is dead. Remember? You were contaminated, no? What happened to that?'

'I wasn't very contaminated. I do remember and I'm quite close to a BIG story on that too. Give me a couple of days.'

Tamsin sighed as though she was expiring years and years of aggravation and exhaustion. 'El-Baz murders within the hour. Forty-eight hours for Sorokin. And then get your bony arse back here because you have a lot of explaining to do and I can't afford to keep your mini-bar open all hours.'

'I won't touch it.' I smiled and put the phone down.

I emailed Ben at Eden's address, a big photo of a lion cub

and 'I LOVE YOU' in as big a font as I could manage. I would have called but I found myself pulling my clothes on in a frenzy, collecting up my stuff. I was having a hunch. Don would have laughed at me; 'The Zanetti hunch' usually resulted in him lying under a car in a huge firefight. Eden would have laughed at me; 'The Zanetti hunch' had landed him in a provincial Iraqi jail cell before. But what can you do? Ignore them? Well, I can't.

Jamila had smelt of lemons. Jamila's hair was slightly gingery. Jamila's eyes were bronze-coloured, though khol had made them seem black.

I put a call through to the police, though it was the main operator and it took them five minutes to find someone who spoke English – my pathetic Arabic just not up to the job. I told them who had killed the El-Bazs and where to find her and then I set off there myself.

Thank God the car was still waiting. I was beginning to love this guy, even though he'd tried to kill me outside the City of the Dead. Hey, I'm not stupid. It was all becoming clear to me now. And he was only following orders, after all. Isn't that what everyone's doing when they do something vile? Though, admittedly, sometimes they are, like, God's orders or Satan's orders or the Mother Ship's orders. Well, you know what I mean. I wished I could remember who was walking on the outside because, if I was right, he shouldn't have been trying to kill Jamila.

The desert was visibly steaming dry and all the trees were dripping. The motorway and the smaller roads were covered in mud.

This time the whole Ismaelevich residence was surrounded by men with cocked machine guns. There were four of them up on the road and another six round the house,

225

all local hire by the look of it, but nonetheless sinister for that. They waved us through with a glance at the registration, but I wouldn't have wanted to be someone they didn't fancy waving through.

None of your '*dobro pozhalovat*' and hearty handshake this time. There was someone on the gate (which had been open so wide the first time I'd come that I hadn't even noticed it was there) with a walkie talkie and he had a long conversation that he seemed to imagine I wouldn't understand, before the gates swang back.

'Short-haired girl dressed like a bloke here,' he'd said, in Russian. Then he ran a metal detector up and down me (one of those ones on sticks, like at the airport) and reported that I was unarmed. Which I was.

I peered around wondering which way to go when Lamia came out, eyes down and not smiling. If I'd ever wanted to chat I had definitely missed my opportunity. She managed to bring herself to show me in though.

'Ah, Faith Zanetti. Yes. I thought you might show up. What do they say? Like a bad penny?' He kind of, well, giggled.

'Do they?' I asked.

He was sitting in the lounge looking a bit haggard, legs crossed, arms folded. There was a suitcase by the coffee table. No candles, no flowers, a bit dark and dank since the rain. It looked like an abandoned hotel more than a home now. He was getting ready to leave. He saw me notice.

'Back to London again. I need a holiday from Egypt for a while. El-Baz betrayed me. He couldn't help it. A man can't help it. Some men. But it was stupid and I had invested a lot of money in him. A LOT of money, Faith. Do you know how much is a lot of money?'

'Probably not,' I admitted, standing still with my hands clasped in front of me, wanting a cigarette but I didn't have any.

'No. Well, I do,' he said and clapped loudly. Lamia, who had scuttled out, scuttled back in again. 'Fetch a packet of cigarettes for Miss Zanetti please. And some matches.'

'*Da-s*,' she said, nodding. This was a very bizarre thing to say, incidentally. Not only was she speaking Russian, but she put a 's' on the end of 'Da' which is a very old-fashioned way of denoting respect, talking to your superiors, not used since long before the revolution. Delusions of grandeur on Ismaelevich's part to train them this way. But really.

'So you killed him? Them?' I didn't have a lot to lose in asking, I decided.

Ismaelevich laughed. '*Ya*? Me? No! I don't kill. I am a businessman, Faith. Not a common bandit.'

Right. Sure. This was just like the President's thing. He wasn't going to be signing death warrants for the FSB to just go on revenge sprees, but they know what he wants and what they can get away with, be rewarded for. It is not as direct as going round with a pickaxe, or even asking someone else to go round with a pickaxe. But it's just a culture in which someone will think, 'I'll just nip round with a pickaxe, it will put me in good odour with those on high.'

'So, was it the keeping his dick in his pants side of things that let him down?' I wondered, knowing full well but wanting to see what Ismaelevich would say.

'It's one thing to do it. Another to do it in such a stupid way that you can be filmed, can be blackmailed. To sleep with whores,' he hissed, looking twenty years older all of a sudden, sitting there in the damp gloom. He had that Bill Clinton thing of only being handsome when he turned the glitter on.

While I took issue with his course of action, I agreed that it was stupendously stupid for politicians to have sex with prostitutes. Surreal. I mean, the one thing we know about these people, before we call the number on the card in the phone box, is that they will do pretty much anything for money. I mean, shalo?

'Yes,' I said.

Lamia handed me an unopened packed of Marlboro and a box of Egyptian matches. I unwrapped the cigarettes, stuffed the cellophane into my jeans pocket, took a fag out and lit it, sucking in greedily. Ah, that's better.

Ooh. But he was carrying on, talking to himself more than to me. But talking. 'They were blackmailing me. Blackmailing El-Baz. It was all over. He fucked up really badly. The things I did for him. For them.'

'For yourself,' I added, throwing caution completely to the wind.

'Ultimately we all put ourselves first,' he agreed, unfolding his arms, sinking back.

'Who was doing the blackmailing?'

I didn't really think he'd actually go as far as telling me. But we'd come this far. And anyway, he was on a roll apparently.

'The tapes were sent to a lot of people. Various people made use of the tape. Some of them wanted money. Some of them wanted power. Most of them wanted both. To keep the secret. Maybe I could have paid them all, won El-Baz the election, kept my hotels. But I don't like it when someone has power over me, Faith. I don't like it.'

No, well. That was clear at any rate.

'Who made the tape?' I asked in a whisper. Something about the stillness of the room and the smell of the storm burning up in the afternoon sun was allowing us to speak. I felt that if I moved from where I was standing he would up and leave, and me none the wiser.

'Sorokin,' he said, disappointment on his breath.

Oh, him again, I thought.

Betrayed by his own.

It was arrogant and stupid of me to suppose that I had him talking by some wile of mine, some cunning journalistic ploy that makes people tell me everything though there's nothing in it for them. Absurd now I think about it. He was talking to me like this because he didn't give a shit what I did or didn't know. Couldn't give a shit because, as far as he was concerned, I wouldn't be around much longer anyway.

But I trudged on: wanting, needing confirmation for some of my wilder theories. To the questions I'd asked so far I already knew the answers. But there were surprises to com, the Lord knows.

'How did you buy . . . how did you persuade Jamila? She's so, she seemed so, idealistic.' I said, looking around for an ashtray. This had almost become an interview. I think there is something in people – a desire to confess. It has to be the right moment in the right atmosphere, in fact, in the right lighting (always a bit dark). I've often found on night flights you get the person sitting next to you just confessing. And once they start, there's no stopping them. A desire to be understood? Forgiven? I don't know and I don't suffer from it myself.

I expected one of his super-sincere answers. He clearly felt himself to be absolutely in the right. All his actions justified by clear reason.

But he laughed. His eyes flashing.

I walked over to one of the brass bowls and ashed in it, partly rebellious, partly better than ashing on the floor. He made no comment, seemed not to have noticed.

He clapped for Lamia again and I sat down now, aware that whatever the moment had been it was now broken.

'Ask Sarochka if she's ready, please. Tell her I'm waiting,' he said, and looked at me. 'Tea?'

'Sure.'

Lamia scuttled away again.

I wasn't one hundred per cent sure quite how to phrase this question and ran through a few possibilities in my head. A pale brown snake slithered into the room, raised its head and slithered out again back to the courtyard where it must have been basking.

'Abram, what do you think happened to Sorokin? Really?' I was pleased with 'happened to'. As though he'd possibly just slipped and fallen into a rogue pile of thallium.

Now he laughed even harder, again not a real laugh but a dismissive sort of bark. He twisted the signet ring on his little finger.

'The guy was a lunatic,' he said. An undeniably popular view, I had discovered. 'I wouldn't be surprised if the FSB was still paying him. He made that tape for them, disseminated it for them. And before, when I still trusted him, he showed me a tape: his commander, some Jew- and Chechen-hating tough guy, cutting Shumayev up into pieces. Told me he'd sent it to them, promised them he'd send it to the BBC if they didn't let me back into Russia, if they didn't stop threatening him. But nothing ever happened.' He shrugged. 'Maybe he never sent it. Maybe they paid him off. I don't know. But I will tell you this. We all wanted to see him dead. Everyone.'

I was beginning to realise this.

But as everyone round here seemed to know, it's not hard to kill a man. Why didn't they just bloody do it?

'But you didn't kill him. You took him to London.' Death for some, of course. But a pleasure for most.

Ismaelevich put his talking to half-wits voice on, thinning

230

his lips and enunciating too clearly. 'I sent him to London because I didn't want him dying in my house. What kind of message would that send out? And why did I pretend to be friends with him, even though every idiot's dog knew I'd stopped paying him? I'll tell you, Faith Zanetti. I spoke to the media outside the hospital because—'

'Because?' I was wondering where the dog was going to come in. And how I, supposedly an investigative reporter, wasn't privy to the information that this hound enjoyed.

'Because it was clear he had won a PR battle. By dying like that. And I wanted the world to see that it was my battle. Not his. But mine.'

'Right,' I said, nodding and trying to stop my face demonstrating the fact that I thought he was FUCKING INSANE.

'And you know what!?' he said, standing up now in a somewhat scary manner.

'No.'

'You know who else could have killed him?'

More Sorokin haters? Wow. How did the guy manage it? Personally I had quite liked him, may he rest in peace.

'The Georgians. He was involved in an oil thing where he was double-crossing everyone, double-agenting like he always did. I only trusted him. Stupid, stupid!'

He wasn't really angry. He was smiling and very obviously didn't think he'd ever been stupid in his life. He just knew that normal people sometimes say that sort of thing.

'I am so naive. I trusted him. He showed me a film, he showed me a film that they'd used, the FSB, to try him, to kick him out and shame him. He beat someone or something. I don't even remember. I just remember that I believed him. It probably wasn't even him on the tape! They probably just put him on trial so I would trust him. So he could come to me

231

and be trusted, so he could spy on me. The President hates me, obsessively.'

Now, I am no big fan of Russia's president, but on this one, I could see where he was coming from. There wasn't much to like here.

I lit another cigarette and Lamia put a tray of tea on the table. Those little coloured glasses, the brass tea pot and the baklava that had so charmed me the first time, now looked like the crap they serve you in Casbah-themed restaurants in London where teenage girls go to smoke shisha and be chatted up by men who think they are whores who might suck their dicks if they compliment their eyes enough. However, I couldn't remember when I'd last eaten and so I popped a little pistachio pastry into my mouth and watched Lamia pour the mint tea. And then, no, but really, I was staggered to watch Lamia, such a gentle-looking girl, follow her orders. These were to tip a few drops of something from a vial, or whatever it was she had in her fist, into the pink glass. The Faith glass. Now who would have thought that she was a bloody murderess? But, hell, who wasn't around here? I nearly killed someone myself earlier. She popped the container back into the pocket of her long skirt, very possibly the one I'd worn myself, bowed her be-scarfed head and handed me the glass.

I tried to catch her eye, to give her a 'How could you?! We're friends!' type of look but she wasn't about to meet my gaze.

'Mmm. Yum yum. Thanks,' I said as loudly and as insincerely as I could, but she was already on her way out. I held the cup though the tea was so hot that my hand was burning. Then I put the tip of my little finger into the tea and my skin sizzled. I bit my lip instead of saying ouch and looked at the fingertip which was blistering and fizzing and going black.

Okey dokey then. Some kind of acid which you ideally wouldn't want searing down your oesophagus.

Ismaelevich wasn't even looking. Was this one of those orders he hadn't even needed to give? I put the glass down and was strongly considering trying to take my leave. Perhaps I should pretend to take a sip and then leave so that they would assume I'd die in the car and they could dump me – my driver friend could dump me – at the roadside to be eaten by the donkeys. Or whatever. And why was poisoning suddenly all the rage? I can't remember the last time I was aware of it as a murder weapon. Grigory Markov and the poisoned umbrella in London twenty, thirty years ago. Cleopatra, of course. But now it seemed there were laboratories in every country in the world coming up with ingenious ways to do it. This attempt on me, however, was perhaps the more old-fashioned approach. They might as well have just come on in with an asp. What is an asp? I had still not concocted a plan.

And before I'd managed to make any vital decisions, Jamila walked in. She looked a tad different though. That is, a lot different.

Her long ginger hair was brushed and loose, cascading over her naked shoulders. She was wearing a red boob tube and I could actually see all the bruising still: a mark of honour perhaps? Ah, there we go, honour again. She had tight white knee-length trousers on and red patent-leather wedge high heels. Her finger- and toenails were painted red and she wore heavy black eye make-up and glossy red lipstick. She was slim and delicate and I could now see that her breasts were a) disproportionately large and b) fake. I was surprised Don hadn't paid them more attention when he was photographing her.

It was an utterly staggering transformation. Extreme

makeover city. But it completely confirmed what I had discovered for myself – that the headscarf and stuff is a transfiguring disguise, something that makes most people completely ignore you and others judge you in a very particular way. There is no way you can really spot someone under there and it reminded me of John Simpson and his burka thing in Afghanistan and then those male bomb plotters who tried to escape wearing them. Abram smiled at her, genuinely. The first time, I realised, that I had seen him smile for real. Amazing that he still knew how.

'My sister, Sara,' he said, holding his arms out for a hug. She fell into them and then faced me. Oh my God! A team! I had never read or seen anything about his having a sister. I suppose because she was always the undercover side of the operation. Though she'd been playing a twenty-year-old, I could see now that she was thirty or more.

Right. I get it. Or do I?

'Sorry about earlier,' she said in Russian. 'I went a bit crazy. Got a bit too far into character. All very Stanislavsky, I'm afraid. I've been undercover too fucking long!' She was genuinely sane-seeming, genuinely apologetic, gritty and hard talking. Nothing like Jamila. 'I get very method!'

Yyyyyyyyyuh! Mmmmm. Hmmmm.

I just had no response to this. She seemed to be suggesting that her mass murder was a bit of an aberration but what's a blood bath between friends (and I could see that it didn't count – she was only acting – she really was that mad) and it was soon going to be back to Moscow, back to drama school or whatever, and best forgotten. But she'd tried to kill me. And now they had just tried to kill me again.

'Um. Jamila . . . Sara? They'll find you, you know. You can't just, I mean . . .'

I have no idea what I was trying to say.

234

'They'll find Jamila!' she said, brightly. Very brightly. She looked like a paint bomb had gone off and her eyes darted about, laughing. 'She went straight home from the scene and committed suicide in her apartment. Plan B, that was, I'm afraid. You were Plan A, but you ran off like a frightened rabbit!' she explained.

'But— She won't be identified.'

'Her parents will identify her.'

Oh God. I see. Someone called Jamila really had at some point lived there with her parents. And she was now . . . Okay. Got it. You'd need to be trained by the fucking FSB to grasp this stuff, if you asked me.

It was obvious that they set no store by human life, particularly not mine. Should I pretend to die? Would they leave and I could crawl off for help? Or might they put a bullet in my head before they left just in case? The latter, I thought.

'I must just, er . . .'

'First on the right,' Sara told me, delighted with life, an actress on a high from a standing ovation, the performance of a career. Brava! Bouquets! Thank you, daaahlings!

I left them to their love-in and went straight down the open corridor to my old bedroom. Pretty weird that I had ever felt comfortable here. But I had. Nobody saw me, nobody bothered me. I was, of course, as good as dead already.

Jamila's clothes were on the bed and Lamia, the murdering bitch, was gathering them up, presumably to be burnt.

I smiled broadly. 'Just wanted to use the bathroom,' I told her and she fled. Well, you would.

I had chosen this bathroom because I knew it had a window. I climbed out of the window, little latticed thing, feeling jolly clever and pleased with myself. However, I was

235

now in the garden. Crouching down below window-level in the blazing heat, I crept round to the front of the house where the gunmen were. Right. Run for it or brazen it out. No choice really. I waved at my driver who was reading a porn mag and smoking a fag with his arm out of the window. He leapt out of the car, put his cigarette out obsequiously and held the passenger door open to me. Clearly the message 'Merc not at Faith Zanetti's disposal any longer. Faith Zanetti dead' had not yet gone out.

I hopped in, trying to look carefree. I wished I'd had a half of Sara's training. The woman was incredible – her Arabic must be perfect. And I wondered if you start believing in your fake personality when you do those deep cover jobs. I bet you do.

'Nile Hilton,' I sang, breezy and blithe. 'Ever so quickly if you wouldn't mind.'

He pulled off, the thugs moved away from their posts to let us out on to the drive.

Oh hurry up hurry up hurry up hurry up hurry up, I begged him silently, rocking to make the car move faster, get me the fuck away from here. Miraculously we made it out onto the pyramid road and we were following the stream out to the motorway. Was it all over? I started, stupidly, to relax. But, nuh uh.

I was just getting myself a cigarette when two things happened at the same time: my driver's phone rang behind the glass and he picked it up.

'*Marhaba?*'

And also, ten police cars came screaming down the road towards us, heading for Ismaelevich's house, throwing up dust like there was no tomorrow. It did not take a genius to realise that it was now or never. The driver had got his message to get rid of me and he'd do it before the police realised what was going on. Not that I had time to actually have that thought. It's retrospective. I just swang into self-preservation mode for the third time that day. I was getting good at it.

I opened the car door and jumped out, rolling down into the stream and assessing my injuries as I went. Nothing broken, I didn't think. I was in shallow water and had twisted my foot. I was very muddy and a ragged horse was walking towards me on its own, in the shade of a hundred palms, the pyramids silent on the golden horizon.

Up on the road, the Mercedes had been stopped and there was a lot of shouting and screeching of brakes. I waited where I was, trying to digest the information that had been thrown at me, feeling very very happy to be alive, even if I was standing in a river with a horse in a desert.

'Hello,' I said to it as it approached. It stopped for a second and looked at me. Then it carried on, eventually pushing its muzzle into my chest. I reached up and scratched it – hang on a sec – her behind the ears. 'Hello, sweetheart.' I stroked the soft fur on her nose. 'It's nice and cool in here, isn't it. Cool those hoofs down.'

She agreed with a little snort. The noise from the road had receded. The cars had all gone. Driver arrested? Almost certainly. There was no way Ismaelevich would be arrested for anything. Nor Sara, of course. They'd covered themselves and he'd be back in London by evening. She would be wherever she would be, but her Jamila days (years?) were over. She must have enrolled in university, she must speak undetectably fluent Arabic. She was probably in the FSB. Let's face it, most people seemed to be.

'What are you doing in here, anyway?' I asked my horse.

She looked behind her and I saw a boy walking down the middle of the stream with a rope in his hands, white baggy trousers rolled up to the thigh, half-naked, baked dark brown by the sun.

'*Assalaamu alaikum*,' I said, sociable, normal, just standing in this here stream chatting to the horse and you.

'*Ualaikum asalaam*,' he said, smiling, bright white teeth.

Chapter Nineteen

I dreamt that Ben was in my arms and I was in my bed. I wrapped myself around him and he wrapped himself around Mallowy bear and the pale buttery sunlight slipped round the side of the curtains making us stir under our crisp white duvet. I opened my eyes, squinting, and looked around me for a second before smiling to myself in absolute ecstasy. I kissed Ben on the cheek and could have just eaten him whole.

'Boy!' I said to him without waking him up, climbing out of bed and reaching for the travel clock. Ten-fifteen! Bloody hell. That was quite a sleep.

Well, I'd been at UCH until about midnight. Test after test after test. I knew I'd only been exposed in a minor way but, obviously, I didn't want to put Ben at any kind of risk. The boys had flown in from Italy at the same time as I'd got in from Cairo and I'd made Eden wait with him all day while I got myself well-and-truly tested. I called them about every ten seconds from the phone I'd bought myself at the airport in Cairo and they got totally sick of me. 'We've just come into the zoo.' 'We're at the gorillas.' 'We're looking at the flamingos.' 'We're just in the caf.' 'We're in the giraffe house.'

Somehow, being close but not being with him was far worse than being thousands of miles away. 'Faith! Get lost! We'll see you when you've finished!'

My nurse had worked on Sorokin's analysis so she knew what she was doing.

'I can hardly detect anything, Faith,' she said. 'Just what you'd get from an average X-ray, or a long-haul flight. You certainly won't pass anything on to anybody else!'

She had a long blonde plait that went all the way down her back and was somehow comforting. I hoped Sorokin had felt comforted. I walked away towards the exit down a long Victorian corridor: fluorescent lights hanging from the ceiling; thick-painted walls; signs to radiology, neurology, nuclear medicine swinging on hinges; machines bleeping; phones ringing; beepers going off on belts; a smell of institutional food and disinfectant, and I was free. Free from the whole terrible thing.

In the end it was in a little café on Marylebone High Street that I squashed my son against me so hard I thought I might bruise him. They were sitting on high chairs at a kind of bar, looking out of the window at the church across the road. Ben was eating a lemon meringue tart with both hands and Eden was reading the paper, an espresso cup in front of him. I couldn't believe that he took Ben's presence so much for granted that he could sit and read the paper. What luxury! I put my face up to the glass and squashed my nose against it. Ben laughed and reached out for me and Eden looked over the top of his paper. Then I ran in and grabbed him with a vow never to let go again. Which would probably piss him off at university, Eden pointed out.

And now, back home, hoping that some of that taking for

granted would come my way soon, I put coffee on and leant against my table, looking out of the window at Hampstead High Street on an English sunny day. The heap of letters looked menacing and I took the top few off the pile. Phone bill, water bill, electricity bill, gas bill, final warning, inland revenue. Christ. I sorted them into 'hell letters not to be faced' and anything at all that looked as though it might be nice. There was only one letter in the second pile: a hand-written envelope, something inside folded fatly, obviously personal.

Dear Faith . . .

Wait. I ruffled my hair in preparation. Who knew? Perhaps I looked gamine like this. I needed my coffee. I went and poured it into a mug, blowing across the top of it.

Dear Faith,

I know now that I am dying and the world knows too. I am sorry for involving you in this history and I hope you will not judge me too harshly. I want you to know that, although I used you, I did also like you and I enjoyed our time together, particularly as I knew my own time was running out.

I chose you because you are famous and because you are famous for these big investigations, foreign stories, famous for getting things right. I know you won even an award.

Yuh. Big shit. Who hasn't won one? God, foreigners are naive about the British press. Well, anyway . . .

I came to Cairo to target you. I refused to go on that TV show unless you were the other guest. You remember? Can you believe I even had to have sex with that presenter

241

for this plan?! Well. Nobody was chasing me on to the shisha terrace and nobody had attacked me in my apartment. I just needed to know that you would not be afraid. And I needed to ensure that you believed me. Because my story is true. And now the world knows that.

I lied and I want to say I am sorry. But here, now, is the truth. The only thing that matters is the truth.

The system got me in the end, Faith. So I apologise and I wish you a good and happy life.

This was something I had to do. I used not too much, so it could be slow. Time to talk. Time to make sure they knew he was guilty.

Give my love to Ben.

Alexander.

This last line sent me into the bedroom to check on Ben. Fine. Asleep. Good. I wasn't sure that the only thing that matters is the truth. In the long run.

Ugh. But, I mean, what was I supposed to think? I knew now that anybloodybody might have written this. And 'they', all of them, were good enough to forge his handwriting beyond detection. Though I'd probably have it tested anyway, in the end. It could be true. It might not be true. He was saying he'd killed himself. Obviously. A confession. Well, that would suit a lot of people who had Scotland Yard on their backs. Not least the FSB who were still being hounded for the identity and whereabouts of this Sasha. I mean, please. What were the chances?

And all I really cared about now was being safe and being with Ben. I wasn't going to try and stitch Ismaelevich up. I wrote the piece on the plane: the El-Baz follow-up with my scoop about their coup attempt and the belly dancer blackmail, a female murderer and her description. I

242

couldn't bring myself to say that the murderess, Jamila, was already dead – just out of respect and pity for the real Jamila's presumably baffled parents. Though I did try to suggest that whoever the police picked up wasn't the culprit. A cop-out. I know. But I had my priorities straight now. Sorokin, who didn't, was dead. Sometimes the truth is not worth dying for. Not as a mother.

So, I wrote the Sorokin piece too – how he was a suicidal madman, a fantasist and serial blackmailer and how he'd been involved in the El-Baz murders (as the person who sent out the tapes). All the cloak-and-dagger conspiracy nuttiness. How he was probably still FSB in the end – they never leave. It turns out that those blackmail tapes had been around for a while, had hit the covers of the Egyptian tabloids while I was there. Shows how much I'd known. Pathetic really. I collapsed down onto the sofa now, bewildered by the letter, all my doubts swarming around again, though I'd tried to swat them one by one.

The doorbell rang. Shit. I had planned to be dressed and all croissant, bagel and smoked salmon central by the time Don got here. But I'd been, well, I'd been distracted by my letter from the grave. So, I was going to be entertaining with only boxer shorts, a T-shirt, coffee and a pint of milk to assist me. I buzzed him in and kicked some stuff under the table, including some pieces of wooden train track. God, that felt like a long time ago.

He took the stairs slowly and heavily and burst through the door gasping for breath.

'I feel like one of those fucking firemen walking up the twin fucking towers, Zanetti.'

'It's the first floor, Don,' I said, kissing him on both cheeks.

'Fucking disastrous haircut, Eff Zed. You look like a dyke.'

I was about to shut the door at this point when Dahlia came in behind him.

'Oh! Hi! Hi! What a surprise!' I said.

She grinned and took my whole head in her hands to kiss me hello. She smelt of Chanel No. 5, very strongly indeed.

'Hello, darling. Nice place,' she said, looking around and not meaning it. It is kind of a bedsit. I'm sure she's never been in a residence this small in her life.

Ben, woken by the commotion, wandered in past the curtain and Dahlia scooped him up in her arms and kissed him all over, pinching his flesh and sighing with pleasure. Ben laughed his head off as though he was being tickled.

'Lady!' he squealed.

I laughed too at his delight and we were all feeling jolly friendly.

Dahlia sat down on the sofa and waited to be brought delicacies. That's what it looked like at any rate. Like the poem where the boy's friends bring him tea and cakes and jam and slices of delicious ham, bicycles to ride and chocolates with pink inside. I thought she'd quite go for the latter.

'So,' I said, looking from Don to Dahlia and back again.

'Yeah, well. When you find the right girl,' he said.

'And umm . . .'

'Ira? Well, I think we've all agreed to, well, to share.'

I raised my eyebrows. Blokes. Honestly.

I made some more coffee, enjoying the feeling of my bare feet back on my own floorboards on a sunny London day.

'So did you get anything from that pathologist?' I wondered, though I'd pretty much put the story to bed in my mind.

'Mmm. Well. She went back to the flats and the one you mentioned was empty. Hasn't been occupied for ten years. No old bloke. Vladimir Ilych – I mean, please! Who the toss is called that? Nada. It must have been the radiation getting to you, Eff Zed.'

God, but they were good these people. Dignity and Honour. All these little clues. Like they fucking WANTED to be found out. If only the old man had been there with a normal explanation I might have stuck by my suicide story. But they put their little clues into everything because they know you'll never but EVER bloody find them. And I think it was now. I think it was in this moment, with Eden's boxer shorts on and my son nuzzling the bosom of Egypt's most famous belly dancer, it was then that I first considered seriously that Sorokin had been killed by his ex-colleagues, by this Dignity and Honour. Or, as Don had so sweetly put it, those Dignity and Honour cunts. Not suicide. Not Ismaelevich. It was them who had set him up, set me up, even to a large extent, set Ismaelevich up. Fucking incredible.

'And the wife?'

'Thallium. Yeah. Massive dose. Ingested. Nothing else. Not even a trace of booze.'

I sighed. Don sighed. Dahlia looked baffled.

'Poor old Sorokin,' I said, shaking my head, picturing Alex sat there, all excited about the trains, letting Ben undo the zip, so gentle, so bright.

'Who is this Sorokin?' Dahlia asked.

'The guy who got poisoned in Cairo, you know? Died in London. Ex-FSB defector. You must have heard? It was all over everywhere.'

'Oh. Yes. Yes, I know him.' She nodded.

Don laughed. 'Not like that I hope, gorgeous,' he said, slapping her thigh.

'Sorokin? Sure. Called himself Karamzin. Liked boys. Dangerous guy. One night,' she began.

I went over to her and took Ben. He reached up and rubbed my head, laughing. My new look was just about the funniest thing that had ever happened, according to him.

Don and I stared at Dahlia.

'One night?' I prompted. Oh God, but here we went again.

'Yeah, one night we're doing party at his place, me and Mustaffah, Mustaffah loves the boys, and men come in. Russian men. They are breaking everything, shouting, they beat him very bad. Very bad.' She shook her head and all her jewellery jangled. 'Shouting shouting. They shout they kill his wife again. They shout they kill his son. He shout son already dead and they shouting no, they steal him, put him in children palace in Russia. So Sorokin he weeping and men beating him. Very bad. Then one of them rape Mustaffah. Very bad night.'

I hugged Ben very tight to me and I couldn't stop the tears pouring out of my eyes. So he'd thought his little boy was dead. He hadn't abandoned him at all. This seemed, well, it was just . . . heartbreaking, I suppose. Was it that that had sent him so mad? And knowing he couldn't ever go back to Russia for him?

'He paid me a lot after. And, Karamzin, he was the one,' she said, nodding deeply and staring at Don.

'HIM!? He set that up? You're fucking joking. Why didn't you tell me?'

'You never tell me you interested Sorokin!' she squealed, smiling and wobbling all over like blancmange.

'I think it is safe to say, Dahlia,' I said, wiping my eyes with my hand and looking over the top of Ben's curls, 'that we are both interested Sorokin.'

'It was her in the fucking El-Baz video, you know. Her and a mate from the boat! Can you believe it?' Completely staggeringly, Don looked proud. Actually proud.

'Yuh. This is what I say. Sorokin – Karamzin – he arrange this. He hide in the cupboard. VERY funny,' she said, shaking with laughter. Really. As though it was genuinely funny. Did she not know that he was horrifically murdered because of it?

Well, I guess if it hadn't been her it would have been somebody else.

'Will you sell me your story?' I asked her. As I say, if it wasn't me . . .

'Sure! How much?' she asked.

But of course the *Chronicle* doesn't buy sex scandal stories. Yeah. Right.

That evening, after a long boozy lunch in Villa Bianca during which Ben had tipped a whole plate of fusilli al ragu over Dahlia's very glamorous outfit (didn't I mention? A fuchsia pink low-cut jumpsuit), I told the lovers that there was something I wanted to do.

Ben and I took a taxi to Earl's Court and got out in the lush, early evening, late summer rain on Earl's Court Square. I rang on a few bells to an entrance and skipped up the grim staircase to Alex's flat. It was just a kind of shabby but basically genteel block of rented flats, trying to make dust a feature.

The door was strangely open. I stepped in reverently and saw that everything, but everything that might have been Alex's was gone. Did he have plants, tapes and sofas here too? I wondered if he had a lovely piano. All the huge sash windows had been cleaned to sparkling and the woodwork repainted recently, and they were all open, letting the sorely needed air in. Amazing how you can purge a cigarette and vodka fug – presumably as thick and noxious as the fug in his Cairo flat – with one little refurbishment. The walls were papered in white stuff with a complicated pattern of tiny

247

flowers and the large kitchen had been newly refitted. It was, hell, it was nice in here.

I went back into the hall where a box of stuff, what must have been the last little shreds of Alex, had been dumped. I bent down to look and I could pretty quickly see that this was his stash of porn, the stuff Eden had found on his raid. Had someone kept them on purpose? It seemed almost funny that after such a dramatic and internationally publicised exit from the world, a martyrdom almost, that all that was left to define him by were a few porn videos.

I was lost in my thoughts and Ben was so quiet and still that I was genuinely shocked.

I screamed and Ben burst into tears as a man appeared out of nowhere, towering above me in the dark, coming out of the door of Alex's flat. My mind was swimming with ghosts and assassins and general confusion. But I am me, and I collected myself in two seconds, and felt ridiculous and laughed.

'Shhh, baby. It's okay. Just Mummy being silly,' I said to Ben, and I stood up. I spoke to the silent man. 'I'm so sorry! I didn't notice anyone else was in there!'

He looked at me as though he'd been as scared of us as we were of him and he smiled. He was wearing an expensive blue suit and he was about forty-five with short greying blonde hair and sky blue eyes like, ooops, yup – like the sky above Siberia. He was Russian.

'No problem,' he said. 'I was just leaving.'

I paused for a second. 'I'm Faith,' I told him, holding my hand out.

He shook it firmly, calm, friendly. 'Sasha,' he said. 'I'm Sasha.'

And he picked the box up and carried it downstairs, leaving me and Ben standing there in the gloom.

He had dropped something and I bent down to pick it up, was going to call after him, bring him back.

But I uncurled my fingers and looked into my hand to see that I was holding a small wooden train. A Brio train. I clasped it tight and shut my eyes so that I wouldn't cry. And then I handed it to its rightful owner, to Ben.

'Look, Bennie. A train.'

Ben laughed and grabbed it, clutching it happily and staring at it as though it were the most precious gift imaginable.

'Train!' he said. 'Fun.'

And I thought about the little boy in St Petersburg who hadn't got to play with one of these in the end. Who must be nearly eight now. A little boy who, perhaps, needed a mother, even a hopeless one with a silly job and a long-distance husband. One with a tiny flat but a big heart.

It must have been a fortnight later, while I was in Russia starting the paperwork and staying at Grebinshikov's, that I heard about the hotels. Three of them blown up in Sharm El-Sheikh, apparently by Islamic fundamentalists. All of them belonging to Abram Ismaelevich.

Other bestselling titles available by mail:

☐ Neat Vodka	Anna Blundy	£6.99
☐ Double Shot	Anna Blundy	£7.99
☐ Darkening Echoes	Carol Smith	£6.99
☐ Kensington Court	Carol Smith	£6.99
☐ Double Exposure	Carol Smith	£6.99
☐ Unfinished Business	Carol Smith	£6.99
☐ Grandmother's Footsteps	Carol Smith	£5.99
☐ Home from Home	Carol Smith	£5.99
☐ Hidden Agenda	Carol Smith	£6.99
☐ Vanishing Point	Carol Smith	£6.99
☐ Without Warning	Carol Smith	£6.99
☐ Fatal Attraction	Carol Smith	£6.99

The prices shown above are correct at time of going to press. However, the publishers reserve the right to increase prices on covers from those previously advertised, without further notice.

–––––––––––––––––––––––––– sphere ––––––––––––––––––––––––––

Please allow for postage and packing: **Free UK delivery.**
Europe; add 25% of retail price; Rest of World; 45% of retail price.

To order any of the above or any other Sphere titles, please call our credit card orderline or fill in this coupon and send/fax it to:

Sphere, P.O. Box 121, Kettering, Northants NN14 4ZQ
Fax: 01832 733076   Tel: 01832 737526
Email: aspenhouse@FSBDial.co.uk

☐ I enclose a UK bank cheque made payable to Sphere for £ . . . .
☐ Please charge £ . . . . . . to my Visa, Delta, Maestro.

Expiry Date ☐☐☐☐   Maestro Issue No. ☐☐

NAME (BLOCK LETTERS please) . . . .

ADDRESS . . . .

. . . .

. . . .

Postcode . . . . Telephone . . . .

Signature . . . .

Please allow 28 days for delivery within the UK. Offer subject to price and availability.